I'll Be Gone
for Christmas

T0182372

I'll Be Gone for Christmas

A Novel

GEORGIA K. BOONE

AVON

An Imprint of HarperCollins*Publishers*

I'LL BE GONE FOR CHRISTMAS. Copyright © 2024 by Temple Hill Publishing, LLC. All rights reserved. Printed in the United States of America. No part of this book may be used or reproduced in any manner whatsoever without written permission except in the case of brief quotations embodied in critical articles and reviews. For information, address HarperCollins Publishers, 195 Broadway, New York, NY 10007.

HarperCollins books may be purchased for educational, business, or sales promotional use. For information, please email the Special Markets Department at SPsales@harpercollins.com.

FIRST EDITION

Interior text design by Diahann Sturge-Campbell

Library of Congress Cataloging-in-Publication Data has been applied for.

ISBN 978-0-06-324402-3

24 25 26 27 28 LBC 5 4 3 2 1

To Alex

I'll Be Gone
for Christmas

Chapter One

Bee

Friday evening, December 1, 2023

Bethany is going to fire me."

"She can't fire you—you're her sister. And her business partner."

Bee Tyler took a sip of her Long Island iced tea and shook her head as her best friend and former classmate, Ayana Torres, continued to lay out the tarot cards between them. "Sisterly fidelity is not what holds together our business plan. Trust me," Bee said, glaring at the three cards now spread out neatly on the table in front of her:

The devil. The fool. And death. How divine.

Ayana rolled her eyes and reached for the tiny tarot manual between them. It was meant to explain the deeper meaning behind each image, but Bee figured the cards spoke for themselves. From what she could tell, everything for the last twelve hours—hell, the last two *months*—had been nothing less than trash. Why shouldn't the cards be ominous and depressing too?

"Beth is a little uptight, but she's not *unreasonable*," Ayana said, flipping her long locs over her shoulder before flipping through the pages. "She'll understand."

No, she won't, Bee thought. Her twin might not be unreasonable, but she wasn't stupid either. Bee had messed up. Badly. It would make sense for Beth to act accordingly, with absolutely no response to puppy dog eyes and appeals to their shared bloodline.

Aside from their irritatingly similar names, they had little else in common. Where Beth was a sharp edge, direct and to the point, Bee liked to think of herself as a gentle wave, easygoing and playful. After all, her job in their company, Appetite, was to charm the hearts and minds of their clients' customers. Beth built the app; Bee came up with the pretty designs and flowery words that made it appealing.

The only words that sprung to Bee's mind now, though, were *debt, bankruptcy,* and *failure.*

"Bee, come on," Ayana said, reaching across the table to tap Bee's now nearly empty glass. "It's one client."

"One client that was going to pay us half a million."

Ayana flinched and pulled her hand back. "Okay, yes. That's . . . a lot of money. But you have other clients, and you guys have been doing well for four years. This is your first major hiccup."

"Second. In two months."

Bee ignored Ayana's wide eyes and ordered another drink—a hot toddy this time, since they were sitting near the front door and it was getting cold. Winter in San Francisco was always damp and chilly, and she was annoyed with herself that she hadn't thought to bring a thicker jacket to the bar. Instead, she'd been focusing on trying to look like she might have her shit together, donning designer jeans, a dark green blouse that accentuated her deep brown skin, and a thin leather jacket. She'd even worn sleigh bell earrings, to add a bit of whimsy. She needed to look not just presentable, but like she deserved to share a booth and drinks with the wildly accomplished woman sitting next to her. Ayana might be into hippie-dippie stuff like astrology and tarot cards, but she still ran one of the most successful companies in the country.

She and her wife, Toni, were the founders of Vacate, that super popular app where users swapped houses in presumably desirable locations. Bee had read features about it in *Essence; O, The Oprah Magazine;* and the *Wall Street Journal* in this month alone—and Ayana herself had made *Forbes*'s 30 Under 30 three years ago.

In other words, Ayana was loaded. So loaded, in fact, that she'd just bought Toni a Tesla for Christmas. She'd told Bee about the surprise that morning over the phone, before Bee revealed she'd lost Appetite's latest contract. Ever the classy one, Ayana had shut up about the Tesla and kindly invited Bee out to drinks. She still showed up in a gorgeous white jumpsuit and black Jimmy Choos, though. The waitress assigned to their table had come over three times in the last twenty minutes, ostensibly as a show of good service, but Bee was willing to bet Toni's new Tesla that it was because the girl had yet to see Ayana's ring finger.

Ayana clapped her perfectly manicured hands together. "So, tell me: What happened to that first company?" Ah yes, the first harbinger of financial doom.

Bee sighed, tucking a stray twist behind her ear. "I don't know."

She did know. *That* company—a high-end clothing subscription app for rock-climbing bros—hated her writing. The creative director wanted grittier language, something that appealed to "rough-and-tumble Wall Street dudes" (his words) who wanted to blow off some steam instead of drinking whiskey at their desks after a hard day.

Ayana nodded along as Bee relayed the details, sipping her martini quietly. The tarot cards were still between them, the fool and the devil mocking Bee from the alcohol-soaked table while she studiously avoided looking at death. She really wasn't eager to learn whatever the hell that card meant.

"Okay." Ayana pushed her drink away and crossed her arms. "Well, that's not your fault. Joe's kind of an asshole."

Bee tried not to roll her eyes. Of course, Ayana knew him. She knew everyone. The fact made Bee hesitant. She didn't want Ayana to think less of her. They were friends, but they were also peers—in some circles, they could have even been rivals, the way some people liked to pit successful Black women against each other. Bee glanced around at their fellow bar patrons, some of whom she recognized and others she figured she'd meet eventually at some work function or another. Any one of these people could tear down her reputation if they overheard the wrong thing. Suddenly, her nerves flared, and anxiety bit back the truth from her tongue. Maybe she shouldn't say anything. Maybe she should lie.

But she and Ayana had been close since college, even more so since Bee moved to San Francisco five years ago. And God, Bee needed to talk to someone. It's not like her sister would be keen to listen.

"What happened with Justin?" Ayana prodded, switching out one failed client for the next.

"Honestly?" Bee sucked in a breath and swallowed her pride. ". . . I forgot."

Ayana blinked. "Forgot? Forgot what?"

"The deadline for the proposal I was supposed to send to them, about what the app would look like, what the copy would sound like, the research we'd do, et cetera. It was due a week ago." Bee sighed as she delivered the kicker. "Which was two weeks after the last deadline, before they gave an extension."

"Bee!"

Bee flinched and sank farther into her seat. "I know, I know. I just . . ." She shrugged. She really had no excuse. Deadline reminders were written everywhere in her apartment: the bulletin board next to the kitchen sink, the litany of sticky notes next to her bed, the cork board sitting above her desk. Beth had even texted her multiple times to remind her that her portion of the pitch was due.

But for some reason, she just . . . couldn't bring herself to do it. Every time she opened the document, the technical words her twin had already written mocked her, daring her to attempt something witty or unique. She felt choked by indecision, like every clever concept she'd ever thought of was a fluke and that the next words she typed were a herald of inevitable failure.

"Bee, you're not a failure," Ayana said upon hearing Bee's explanation, but Bee merely snorted and took another sip of her hot toddy. Ayana continued: "It also sounds like you didn't forget so much as you . . . maybe just didn't want to do it." She threw her hands up defensively. "I'm not accusing you of anything, I swear. I'm just saying . . ."

She opened her tarot book again and read through the cards' meanings, then placed her index finger on the last one—death. Great. "Okay, look. This one could mean a lot of things," she said. "But I'm sensing a pattern here with the first two, the fool and the devil. Since death came up last, I'm gonna say it means that something has to change. So"—she raised one hand and began ticking off each finger—"something *was* holding you back, you *are* primed for a new adventure, and something *is going to* or *has to* change."

"That doesn't suck to you?"

"Can I be real?" Ayana reached out and grabbed Bee's hand. The touch was unexpected—an intimate sort of kindness that Bee hadn't experienced in what felt like decades. Save for her ex, Roger, most of her interactions with people were in the form of an email, a text message, or an Instagram post. She straightened, suddenly feeling uncomfortable and overwhelmed. "Honestly, Bee," Ayana continued, "it sounds like you're burned out."

Tears sprang to Bee's eyes uninvited, but she blinked them

back quickly. No way. Absolutely not. She hadn't cried since college—not since that awful Christmas Eve six years ago when her parents demanded she do something "more with herself" than "waste away" writing poetry. Graduating from a liberal arts college with a degree in English was . . . nice, they said, but useless—functionally without value. Not like the great and practical Bethany, whose degree in computer science from Stanford would yield a comfortable lifestyle they could brag to their friends about. Even now, they frequently referred to Beth as the brains behind Appetite. The architect.

Bee was just the one who made it "sound pretty."

And now Christmas was coming up yet again, and soon she'd have to drive home to Albany, their parents' tiny but affluent neighborhood near Berkeley, and hear Beth explain to them how her pretty words—or lack thereof—had cost them two clients in fewer than sixty days.

Something clenched in her chest, but Bee fought it back. She flexed her hand, releasing it from Ayana's gentle grasp, and gritted her teeth in what she hoped looked like a smile as the waitress returned for the fourth time.

"Can I get anything else for you?" She smiled sweetly at Ayana.

"Yes," Bee answered for her. "Another hot toddy. Please."

The waitress glanced at her but didn't leave until Ayana responded with an "I'm good, thank you." Once she walked away, Bee forced out a laugh.

"If she were my type, I'd be heartbroken."

Ayana didn't take the bait. Instead, she pushed their

untouched shot glasses toward the middle of the table. She took one for herself and then gestured for Bee to take the other. Bee didn't have to be told twice; she knocked the tequila back quickly, welcoming the warmth that spread through her body. She shook her head and released a satisfied sigh. When she looked back at Ayana, though, her friend was already pulling out her phone and swiping quickly.

"Okay," Ayana said. "I've decided. You need a vacation."

"Uh, did you not hear the part where I just lost half a million dollars?"

Ayana shoved her phone into Bee's hands. "I did. Which is why I think you should try Vacate."

Her app? Ayana's solution to Bee's multiple crises was to *try her app*? She didn't know whether to be offended or to laugh. Bee's business was in the process of being run into the ground, and her supposed friend was shoving her hot multimillion-dollar company in her face. The gall was truly outrageous.

Bee started to sputter her indignation, mindlessly scrolling down the series of listings that Ayana had pulled up as she tried to collect her words. But as her brain registered the homes, her sputtering slowed. Ayana had input only two filters within the United States: *rural* and, amazingly, *cottage*. The results were all over the country, and they looked . . . inviting. Words like *charming, quiet,* and *countryside* jumped out at her like highway signs, and for a second, the muscles in her chest unclenched. She scrolled down the page, enchanted.

"Cool, right?" Ayana said, and Bee nodded numbly, distracted by the strange feeling swirling at the bottom of her stomach. She felt a little nauseated, and at first she thought it was the lingering indignation, but as she scrolled, she realized it was another feeling entirely.

It felt like . . . excitement.

"I'll leave you to it," Ayana said, putting the three tarot cards back into her deck and then straightening them all out so that they slid neatly into the box she'd brought them in. She placed the box next to the tarot manual on the table, then slid out of the booth. "I have to make a bathroom run."

Bee glanced up from her phone and studied the box and the manual. The fact that Ayana's company was rooted in travel and exploration made sense. Businesswoman or no, she was a wanderer at heart—someone who dreamed big and thought deeply about the world. A person with a big imagination.

Bee used to think of herself that way. Years ago.

She turned her attention back to Ayana's app. Her parents would be so disappointed in her if she skipped their annual Christmas Eve dinner. And for what? To gallivant on a whim to some town she'd never been to? It was frivolous. Wasteful. And Beth? She'd think Bee was being flaky as always. Irresponsible. Flighty.

But then again, they already thought those things, even when she was doing everything right.

Bee took a deep breath. Then she clicked the sign-up button.

Chapter Two

Clover

Saturday night, December 2, 2023

Hark! The herald angels sing, "Glory to the newborn king . . ."
Clover Mills gritted her teeth and resisted the urge
to stomp over to her window and draw the blinds. *Carolers.* December had only just begun, and they were already
outside, disturbing her peace with their good tidings and
cheer.

If it were any other year in their sleepy town of Salem,
Ohio, Clover would have been elated. She would already be
outside, dressed in her fiancé's warm coat and her fuzziest
pajama bottoms, ready to pass out her father's famous hot
cocoa to the town's beloved Christmas choir, while her mom
chatted up the neighbors and smiled slyly when they inevitably asked her for the recipe for her famous mac 'n' cheese.
Clover and her parents and her fiancé would be seated in
cozy lounge chairs in the front yard, beside the signature

Black Santa Claus that her mother had adored, and they'd take care not to wince as their nearest neighbor, Taylor Blankenship, persistently and earnestly sang off-key.

But there would be none of that this year. Clover had neither her mother nor her fiancé, and the sweet sound of coming Christmas outside her window only made her more aware of those two facts.

She considered her next move. If she did draw the shades, they'd see her in the act. In a town as small as theirs, it'd cause a scandal. She could nearly imagine the headline "Clover the Hermit Now Hates Christmas" written across her church's bulletin, then her father getting a text message the next morning asking if they needed to start yet another prayer circle. However, if she didn't move at all, they'd still see her, choosing not to come outside but instead resolutely Scrooge-like in her decision to stay seated at her desk—which was, of course, situated across from the window.

As Taylor Blankenship's voice cracked on *Hail the heav'nly Prince of Peace,* Clover sighed heavily and decided it would be best if she put the carolers out of her mind entirely. They might've been loud, and also not in key, but Clover had gotten *good* at blocking things out over the past few months.

Well, *pretty* good. The email she'd been ignoring for the last twenty-four hours was still taunting her, still marked unread on the open laptop screen she had now returned to scrutinizing.

New request from your chosen Vacate location(s), the subject read.

She chewed the inside of her cheek. She'd managed to

forget that she had signed up on that silly website. She didn't have Facebook, Instagram, TikTok, Snapback, or whatever the hell else was being built by their future robot overlords, and she was stubbornly proud to keep it that way. She didn't even have a smartphone.

But she *had* had a moment of weakness, nearly a year ago. It had been only a few weeks after her mother died and barely a month after she'd ended things with Knox. She had been feeling lonely and overwhelmed, stuck in a house she'd once shared with people she'd loved and lost, and then she overheard someone at church mention something about a cheap and easy way to get out of town.

She'd considered only one location: a city someone else she'd loved and lost disappeared to eons ago. Not that Clover was planning to reconnect with her or anything. Hailey was long gone, probably nothing like Clover remembered from their high school days, skipping classes and sharing dreams. But the memory of those days felt like a comforting fantasy, and she often wondered if San Francisco would be like that too. A distant city she knew nothing about and that didn't know her. At the time it felt as much like a dream as anything else Clover could conjure up. After all, who in their right mind would swap out swanky San Francisco for literally anywhere in Ohio? Apparently one Bee Tyler, age twenty-nine.

But Miss Tyler was ten months too late. Clover had signed up for Vacate before her father's heart attack, and that was the straw that snapped her back into shape. Now she was focused on nursing her dad back to health and on keeping the farm intact. Sure, she wasn't nearly as social as she used to be, but she had the sense to step up and take care of what she did have. And these days she felt fine, mostly. Tired, usually. But fine.

Of course, now that December had snuck up on her, old memories were starting to resurface. What made it worse was that people here were starting to ask about the annual Christmas party her mother used to throw. Earlier that day, while stopped at a red light on her way home from the grocery store, Lester, the man they always bought their Christmas trees from, had rolled down his window and said, "Hoo boy, I can't wait to see what you do with that mac 'n' cheese this year, Clover. I know you learned a thing or two from your mama growing up!" He was a nice man, and he'd meant well, but that didn't mean Clover hadn't had half a mind to sneak over to his tree lot and light all his stock on fire.

Even now she chuckled at the thought.

"Whatchu laughing at?"

The laptop snapped shut. Clover prayed she didn't look guilty as her father ambled in from the foyer. "Taxes," she replied as if her heart wasn't about to explode out of her chest. He looked at her with one eyebrow raised as he held what looked to be a small bundle of feathers. Clover cleared her throat. "How's Bennie?"

As if on cue, the silkie chicken in his hands popped her head up and clucked.

"Oh, fine," he said, patting the little chicken's head lightly until she tucked her head back into her feathers. "Just a little cough. Hannah over at the vet's said she'll get over it soon enough."

Clover gave her dad a small smile. Everyone coped with death in different ways—Jimmy's way was spending a little bit more time with the animals. He'd lately taken to Bennie, who had been shipped to them on accident. She was the farm's only silkie, and apparently Jimmy's favorite child. Clover watched as he whispered soothing words to her, taking long, slow steps over to his favorite love seat, which was positioned directly in front of the fire Clover had lit for him. Then he muttered to himself about whether Bennie would be too warm.

"You know, Daddy, for someone who insists on living on his own, you sure do treat this place like your personal property."

"Because I paid for it!" he said as he dropped into his seat. Then he flicked the switch on the recliner as if it had the final say, and he and Bennie settled in.

Clover rolled her eyes as she watched them. She liked to give him a hard time, but she understood why he chose to visit her every night before retiring to his apartment—the converted cellar that she and Knox used to live in when they were in college. She and her dad were both lonely now.

Even if he did have Bennie.

"Daddy, don't let that chicken do her business inside this house. She's not special just because she's sick."

He responded with an exaggerated snore. Clover sighed and relocated to the kitchen, so she could continue ruminating over the Vacate request in peace. She settled into the breakfast nook, a pillow placed at her lower back for optimum comfort and a blanket draped over her knees. The nook was framed by a large window that overlooked the front yard, and while it was typically one of her favorite spots in the house, she was disappointed to realize that she could see the carolers better from here—which meant they could see her too.

Just as she considered leaving, a sharp giggle pierced her thoughts, followed by the hushed rise of conversation. Against her better judgment, Clover turned. There was Knox, her childhood sweetheart and ex-fiancé, chatting up the carolers as he passed out what looked to be brownies.

Warm, delicious brownies.

Her stomach made a sound of desperation.

She could resist. She *would* resist. Except that . . . well, she hadn't eaten yet that evening. And Knox was a devilishly delightful cook. And while he was still the farm's manager and continued to rent the studio out past the chicken coop, they hadn't talked much beyond business and livestock since she'd unceremoniously ended their engagement weeks before last Christmas.

She understood his need for space. She needed it too. But seeing him out there, continuing some form of the tradition they'd enjoyed together for the better part of their adult lives, made something in her ache. And seeing blond-haired, blue-eyed Taylor Blankenship flirt with him shamelessly in front of her house made Clover want to roll her eyes so hard that, hopefully, she'd never have to see Taylor's stupid cherub grin again.

Ugh. Taylor. She was a fine person, but also, God, she was the worst.

Clover watched as Taylor laid her hand on Knox's muscular forearm, no doubt trying to comment on how strong he looked, despite the fact that he was covered in a massive winter coat like the rest of them. It was a curious thing, to feel left out without feeling jealous, while someone attempted to woo the person you'd once planned to spend your life with.

Clover wondered, not for the first time, if that made her broken in some way. To have had the opportunity to be loved by a man as wonderful and charming as Knox . . . and to not want it.

Knox gently maneuvered away from Taylor's eager hand and turned to face Clover—or rather, the window she sat in front of. She blushed, realizing she was caught. He waved. She waved back.

Then he walked toward her front door.

Frazzled, Clover bolted up, leaving the laptop forgotten on the table. She walked quickly to the foyer and had barely needed to hear a knock before she opened the door. "Knox," she said breathlessly. "Hi!"

He smiled—politely. "Hi, Clover."

They were quiet for a moment, and an awkwardness spread between them that Clover had not yet grown accustomed to. Where was the easy banter they'd always had? The wordless conversation they used to share?

"How are you?" she said, just as he said, "Merry Christmas."

"Oh." She laughed. "Yes. Merry Christmas to you too."

"I baked some brownies for the carolers. I thought you and Jimmy would want some too," he said.

Clover's smile faltered. For a time, he used to say "Father

Mills"—a playful joke between him and her father, the evolution from "Mr. Mills" when they were teenagers to "father-in-law Mills."

Now he was just Jimmy.

"Thank you," she said. She took the half-empty plate of brownies, and with a polite nod, he turned and walked back down the steps and headed toward his studio.

Clover closed the door. She took a deep breath. And then she called to her father.

"Brownies from Knox!" She walked back to the kitchen and placed the brownies on the kitchen island. "And don't you dare feed any to Bennie!" she added.

Then she sat back in her nook, this time fully facing away from the window. She wondered if this would be the rest of her December here: watching a fun-house mirror version of the life she used to live, the family she used to have.

The email in her inbox was still unread. New request from your chosen Vacate location(s).

She clicked it open.

Hi, I'm Bee, the message said. I'm 29 years old and I work in app development in San Francisco. (I know, I'm such a stereotype.) I saw your listing in Salem, and wow, your house looks GORGEOUS. I have to admit, my place is much smaller. It's a condo, but the view is incredible. I'll attach some photos here. I know it's a bit last minute, but would you want to swap houses this month? I'd love to see some snow, and you might enjoy milder weather—plus we have some great events in the city. The Holiday Makers' Market in Union Square is AMAZING.

Anyway, fingers crossed!

xx Bee

Clover looked at the dates Bee requested—they'd swap houses starting next week, and . . . they'd both miss Christmas.

Hm. A few weeks to clear her mind and get away from town, and this house, and all the memories that came with them . . .

It wasn't a bad idea.

Not at all.

Chapter Three

Bee

Monday morning, December 11, 2023

Half a dozen emails and one slightly-more-expensive-than-she-would've-liked flight later, Bee found herself driving from the airport in Akron, light snow falling amid the blankness of night, wondering if she'd just made yet another incredibly stupid decision.

Just thirty more minutes.
Just thirty more minutes.
Just thirty more minutes.

The mantra was the only thing keeping her sane. If she thought about anything else—like how she could barely see the road in front of her, or how that man in the next lane looked awfully curious, or how sixty miles an hour seemed incredibly fast—she was going to veer off the highway. She gripped the wheel of her rental car and snuck furtive glances at the map displayed on her phone. *Just twenty-nine more minutes.*

Thirty-two miles hadn't seemed that bad when she'd tapped the directions into Google Maps. But after getting honked at repeatedly for driving slower than the speed limit, and then honked at again for *just* going the speed limit, and then again, and then again . . . she'd finally started to lose her nerve. She knew how to drive, dammit. She just wasn't used to it. Who needed a car when you had excellent public transportation? But now here she was, sweating and cursing at herself as time seemed to slow. *Twenty-eight minutes.*

Twenty-five . . .

Twenty-two . . .

"Welcome to Salem, Ohio," the Google-automated voice finally announced. It sounded cheery, but Bee felt like she deserved a goddamn parade. She'd done it. She'd survived the highway. Now all that was left was navigating a snow-covered town in total darkness. Cool. At least there were only two lanes. She let out a shaky breath and allowed her grip to loosen on the steering wheel. Slowly, her breathing returned to normal. *Okay,* she thought. *I am not going to die on this trip.* Yet.

And look—the sun was starting to come up. Yay. *Yay!* She sat up straighter. *Yaaaay. I can do this!*

Before the drive, that had been her mantra. She could do this—she could relax and find some peace for the next few weeks. No work, no bossy sister, no demanding clients. No distraction. To mark the occasion, she'd turned her notifications off the minute she'd entered the airport and hadn't turned them on since.

On the plane, she'd ordered herself a glass of prosecco.

She'd turned on a podcast that someone had recommended to her months before about sordid political affairs throughout history, then switched to an audiobook about meditation. Both proved just a tad bit . . . dull. She tried to sleep, but she wasn't used to being wedged between two strangers. Had this been any other last-minute trip, she would've splurged on business class, or at least an Even More Space seat with room to stretch. But she was on a budget. Hence the house swap in the middle of nowhere. Instead, by hour five of the ride, she'd resorted to playing *SkyWords* on the seat-back screen in front of her with the passenger in 6E. He'd beaten her by six points.

He looked to be about thirteen.

Kudos to him, she'd thought then. *He probably has time to read.*

Slowly, as the sky lightened, the sleepy town of Salem began to appear. Bee relaxed into her seat and took in the view. There still wasn't much to see right now, at six a.m., but there were hints of the world that she'd come to visit. She saw now that she was driving past large houses with sprawling land covered in snow and leafless trees. These houses were far apart, and she imagined that you would have to yell at the top of your lungs for a neighbor to hear you. That seemed a bit cold. Lonely, even. But after another ten minutes, she happened upon a tighter cluster of short brick buildings. *Maybe this is the town center,* she thought. Sure enough, with every second, the sun rose higher, and she could make out signs for office supplies, liquor, and food in the growing light.

Though it was entirely dead, the row of shops gave her a

pang of familiarity. If she squinted, it might feel like she was in the Castro, though with *far* fewer rainbow flags and an eerie sort of quiet. Still, the building styles were similar, and the road between was just as small. Small and full of character. Full of life and possibility, even in the darkness.

A flash of light and a screech of tires threw Bee from her thoughts. Disoriented, her spinning head conjured a deer, but those didn't usually come with a set of headlights. Belatedly, she hit her brakes and put the car in park. Moments later, a white man stepped out of the beat-up pickup truck that was now parked in the middle of the road, inches from where her car had passed. She couldn't tell from her side mirror if the man looked angry, but she realized quickly that he had every right to be. In her daze, she'd run a stop sign at the intersection.

This trip wasn't going to kill *her*. It was going to kill *someone else*. *Great*. She sighed and rolled down the window as the man approached, his hands stuck deep inside a large brown jacket and his heavy black boots crunching on the smattering of ice that led to her car. "Sorry," she called, and then, realizing she should probably get out too, she opened the door the tiniest crack, as if to step out. "Sorry," she said again. "I didn't see you."

"You could've killed someone!" the man snapped. He stopped a few feet from her door.

"I am so, *so* sorry," she said again. "Are there any damages to your car? I'm happy to pay for them. And are you okay? Are you hurt?"

The man blinked at her, bright blue eyes giving her a

once-over in assessment. Then he shook his head, his anger gone as quickly as it had come, replaced only with mild irritation. He turned away from her and then back, as if an idea had struck him. "Are you okay?" The question was gruff but sincere.

She nodded quickly. "Yes, I'm fine. Thank you."

As the man walked off, Bee shut her door. She reached for where she'd docked her phone next to the wheel, but it was gone. She looked around, alarm bubbling in her chest. She kind of needed it to find the house.

She took a deep breath; it had probably fallen under the seat. No problem. She opened the door again and bent down, shoving her fingers as far as they would go. She could just feel the edge of her phone, but her fingers couldn't quite get a hold of it.

"Everything all right?" She heard the man's voice behind her.

"Yeah, I just . . ." She grunted as she tried to extend her fingers beneath the seat. "I need my phone."

"Right now?" She could practically hear his eyebrows rising into his hairline.

"Yes, right now." She caught the snap in her voice and cleared her throat. "I need directions. To, uh, my hotel." Better not to give too much detail. Sure, she'd nearly driven the man off the road, but he could be anyone.

"Where you headed?"

"Just a hotel down the . . . road."

"There isn't a hotel down the road."

She raised her head and removed her hand from beneath the seat. The man was in his truck now, but he'd pulled up next to her. "Do you need something?" She hoped he heard the annoyance in her voice.

He looked at her like she was the one holding him up. "I'm expecting a visitor about now. A Beatrice Tyler. Is that you?"

Bee blinked, taking a closer look at the man: white, with dark curls that fell into his eyes—blue eyes. This was a surprisingly handsome man; the picture her swap-mate had posted of her so-called farm manager didn't do him justice. In the photo, he was wearing a hat that covered his hair and eyes, and a nondescript flannel. In person, he was . . . well, he was *fine*.

And she had nearly killed him.

"Oh my gosh." She sat up quickly, nearly hitting her head against the rearview mirror. "Yes, hi. Oh my gosh. I'm just— I'm so sorry. I mean, obviously I was sorry before, but *please* don't think I'm some sort of reckless . . . person. I'm a very safe, uh, very *respectful* guest."

"Not such a safe driver, though."

Bee took a sharp breath, indignation and regret battling each other for words. Then she donned her most dazzling smile. "Can't be great at everything, can we?"

He chuckled, which made Bee feel infinitely more comfortable. "Come on," he said. "You can follow me to the house." He waited as she slipped back into her car. Then he revved the engine and led her deeper into the heart of Salem.

THE HOUSE WAS exactly as advertised, as far as she could tell. Massive, with white siding and a long driveway that led up to the porch. Idly, she wondered what the property value of a house like this was, way out in the backwoods. It'd be rude to ask now, but the answer was only a quick Google search away.

Knox, as he later introduced himself, waited as she exited her rental car, and then he led her up to the porch and through the front door. The photos of the listing were spot-on here too—just as big as she anticipated, though surprisingly devoid of anything that would have suggested the holidays were near. An older gentleman sat snoring in a love seat, a ball of white fluff perched on his lap.

"That's Bennie," Knox said, nodding toward the love seat. "She runs the place."

"The person sleeping?"

"No, the chicken. The old man is Jimmy, Clover's dad." He winked, turning Bee's insides warm. "Sorry, he lives in the apartment in the basement. He must've forgotten she wouldn't be here tonight. He wanders up here on occasion. Jimmy!"

The old man sat up straight, his light snoring stopping abruptly.

"We got company."

Jimmy looked over at Bee and then rose so slowly that she thought she could hear his knees creak. "Oh, hi there, Miss Tyler." He cradled the chicken in his arms as he stretched a bit. "I wanted to make sure you were all settled, given the hour. Let you know you can always call on me if you need anything. I'm Jimmy, Clover's dad."

"It's nice to meet you," Bee said.

He shook her hand and then looked over at Knox. "What are you doing here so early?"

Knox shrugged. "Went for a drive. Couldn't sleep. Then someone tried to run me off the road." He gave Bee a sideways look that felt more conspiratorial than angry.

"I'm *sorry*," she said, playing into his joke. His bright eyes twinkled, and her heart sped up.

"Ah," Jimmy said. "Well, I'll go on ahead and get your bags then, Miss Tyler."

"Bee," she said, just as Knox said, "I've got it, Jimmy."

"No, no," Jimmy said, slowly making his way past the two of them. "I still got two arms and two legs. I'll just put Bennie down outside and get you set up, Miss Tyler."

Bee exchanged a quick look with Knox and then hurried on ahead. "I've got it, don't worry. And call me Bee!" She dashed past Jimmy back to her car and pulled out two huge suitcases and a large backpack stuffed with a handful of books she'd been planning to read for the past several years. They were smashed against her laptop, her tablet, a charger, a backup charger, and two mobile chargers, just in case. She didn't plan to work, but how else was she going to have access to the outside world?

When she was done, she turned to Jimmy with a smile as he watched her from the porch. "Okay, I'm ready."

He scratched the back of his head. "Well, let me carry just one thing, at least."

She acquiesced, handing him her backpack, and followed him to the bottom of the stairs in the foyer. She hesitated, looking between the set of bags she had dragged in, and then grinned sheepishly as Knox quietly took them from her and trudged easily up the stairs.

"Thank you!" she called to his retreating back.

Once the three of them reached the top, she was beckoned into a bedroom that was nearly the size of her studio. Across from the doorway was a large window, through which she could see the soft glow of the morning sun, a wintry forest of bare but beautiful oak trees, and a red barn with a roof covered in fresh snow. *Whoa,* she thought. *That's gorgeous.*

She stood there staring for a moment before Jimmy cleared his throat. The sound made her jump, and she turned back to him with a small laugh. "Sorry," she said. "Just admiring the view."

"Yeah, it's pretty nice," Knox answered. He stayed there for a moment, a whimsical look on his face, like he was remembering something. Then he shook his head. "Anyway, I should get going. Jimmy can help you if you need anything else."

"Oh," Bee said. "Okay. It was nice to meet you." She didn't know why, but she felt a little disappointed that he was leaving so soon.

As if sensing her disappointment, he glanced back at her. She couldn't guess what had gone through his mind as his bright eyes caught hers, but he was suddenly turning around and walking over to the balcony window. "See that little place that looks like a shed? If you need anything and Jimmy's sleeping or out wandering the woods with Bennie, just come on over and knock."

"I do not wander the woods," Jimmy protested. "You make me sound like I'm ancient and senile."

"You ain't?"

Jimmy made like he was about to box Knox, and Knox responded with a fake fighting stance, pushing the old man out into the hallway. Bee watched them both, amused, wondering at their relationship to each other.

Without meaning to, she wondered if she'd get to see more of Knox, get to more closely admire the stubble on his chin, the dark lashes that fell across his bright blue eyes, and the muscles beneath his parka . . . What kind of work did he do here? What exactly did he use those hands for?

"By the way," a voice said, cutting through the haze of her brain, and Bee remembered that she had not flown across the country for romance. Jimmy hovered in the doorway of the room. "Clover said to make sure I told you the house is yours; aside from this morning, I'll be sure to stay out of your hair, unless you need me, in which case just come visit the apartment door 'round the corner. Otherwise, welcome to Salem, Bee. I hope you have a nice rest."

Jimmy clicked the door shut behind him, and after a moment more of staring out the window, Bee let herself fall back onto the bed.

Rest, she thought. What a novel idea.

Chapter Four

Clover

Monday morning, December 11, 2023

Clover watched the hills that lay ahead of her, waiting like great mages of a strange new land, as the plane taxied to the terminal. She had thought, when she first landed at the airport, that she would feel some immediate transformation—a new sense of self or a weight lifted. But, mostly, she felt tired.

It had been a five-hour flight, after all. Her legs and neck were stiff, and while she was used to early mornings on the farm, the bright lights and loud chatter of the airport in Akron and now here in San Francisco were new for her.

Of course, she wasn't a complete country mouse—she'd been on a plane before. It had just been a while. Maybe a decade or so, if she counted, and she didn't want to count, because then she'd have to focus on the reason she'd left in the first place, which was that her farm—her family's farm—was all she'd ever truly known.

A year ago, that wouldn't have bothered her—or, well, it wouldn't have bothered her *so much*. She could've pushed it aside, shoved it down, gritted her teeth, and looked out on the business her family had built, the gorgeous house she had inherited, and the amazing man who loved her and been grateful.

But then Knox had pushed the question—and not for the first time. Not *would* she marry him. No, he'd asked that years ago. But *when*.

"Soon," she'd say.

"I know, baby, but when?"

When, when, when. He wanted an actual, tangible, near-in-the-future date.

And it was only when she tried to finally give him an actual, tangible, logistically reasonable answer that she'd realized . . . there wasn't one.

The blow might've landed more softly for them both if her mom hadn't died shortly thereafter.

I didn't raise you that way.

Clover took a sharp intake of breath. That's what her mother had said when Clover had tried to confide in her a couple months before she died. They'd been sitting in the hospital room and Mae Mills had asked why she couldn't just settle on a wedding date, maybe soon, maybe while she was still alive. Clover had tried to placate her mother, but that final plea broke apart the dam she'd kept contained all these years. "I have something to tell you, Mom," she'd started. "About Hailey Blackwell."

Of course her mother knew who Hailey Blackwell was.

Clover had grown up with her from preschool through high school, just as she had with Knox. It was a small town, after all, with family lineages going back generations.

Clover could still remember the day she'd met Knox properly. He was all of five, wearing an overlarge trapper hat and snow coat, and he was waddling through the heavy snow of his front yard, making huge, uneven tracks. A chicken had escaped its coop in Clover's yard, and Clover, freshly home from Sunday school and wearing nothing but a yellow sundress, had dashed out her front door after it, bones shivering and eyes watering. Knox had seen the chicken cross his path and jumped, holding it tight in his gloved hands. Then, seeing her shake in the cold, he offered her his trapper hat.

They were inseparable from then on, and everyone knew them as best friends: Knox and Clover, Clover and Knox, never the two shall part. When their parents joked about their eventual marriage, Knox would blush, and Clover would scoff, and then the two would run off together again, to make up stories in her parents' attic or play hide-and-seek in his family's stables. When he offered to train as their farm manager after the last one moved cities, it was clear to everyone involved that it was just another excuse for the two of them to spend even more time together, to plan even more adventures.

Then Knox's parents divorced. They were sixteen, and Knox's happy-go-lucky nature took a sharp turn. He was angry and lost, and his mom, feeling her own sense of defeat and darkness, sent Knox away for the summer, to stay with relatives in Cincinnati. It was the first time Knox and Clover had ever been apart. And that's when Hailey appeared.

The two had always seen each other in classes, and in the hallways, and at the same haunts frequented by all their class- mates. They would smile sometimes, maybe not others. They were polite at best. Then, one day, Clover walked into Hai- ley's summer job at the local Baskin-Robbins. They talked. They talked some more. Days passed, and then weeks, and Clover went from finding excuses to visit Hailey at her job to both of them agreeing to hang out after, to see a movie, to walk around the mall in the next town over, to sleep over.

Nothing happened, not really. Just two new friends getting closer. Maybe Hailey's gaze would linger too long on Clo- ver when she made her laugh. Maybe Clover's fingers would brush against Hailey's when they sat together on Clover's balcony, looking at the stars. Maybe, as they lay together at night, sharing a bed as friends do, limbs barely touching, Hailey's breath against Clover's neck, or Clover's lips near Hailey's ear . . . maybe these things would feel less like an accident and more like . . . maybe. Maybe more. Maybe yes. Maybe *now*.

Then, months later, Knox came home, all boyish and full of stories about his time away. He was eager to catch up, and so was she, but . . . it also meant less time with Hailey. It meant feeling like she'd lost a truth she didn't know she'd found.

It was the first week of school when everything changed. By then, something about Knox had shifted. Yes, he was a little taller, his voice a little deeper. But the way he looked at her, the way he spoke to her—all of that was different too. Softer, somehow, and more direct. Then one day, she'd been standing at her locker, fumbling with the code as she always did, when a deep voice tickled her ear.

"Hey, Clover."

She jumped about three feet in the air. She turned and looked at Knox, who had appeared behind her, his backpack slung across his shoulder, his morning apple half eaten in his left hand. She admonished him, as she always did, about being "so quiet despite being so damn big," and he laughed, as he always did. "Sorry," he said. "Didn't mean to startle you."

"You always say that," she said, glaring playfully as she turned to face him fully. "And you always do it."

He grinned as he took another bite of his apple, and Clover pretended to pout.

"You're so mean to me."

He laughed and rolled his eyes. "You're right. I don't know how you can stand me."

"Lots of love and whiskey," she replied automatically, exactly the way her mother would say to her father. She and Knox had heard it once when they were kids and adopted it as their own favorite saying. They'd made this exchange so often that at first it didn't occur to her why he was slowly moving closer, his hand now above her head as he leaned against the locker, all six feet of him towering over her, his blue eyes darkened with . . . Was it hope?

He took a deep breath, and she felt it in her lungs. "How much love?" he asked then.

How much love?

Clover had told Hailey about it hours later: Knox asked me out on a date. KNOX! she'd typed, because it was KNOX, her best friend, and not *Knox,* a potential love interest. But Hailey hadn't responded with either incredulity or polite needling, as Clover expected. Instead, she'd asked to come over that night, and sit on her balcony, and look at the stars.

"Clover," Hailey had said then, as they looked up at the moon, bare legs crossed and knees gently touching. "Do you love Knox?"

"Of course I do," Clover said, because she did.

"But do you *love* him? Like . . ." Hailey bit her bottom lip, and Clover pretended not to notice the way the skin pulled beneath her teeth. Instead, she focused on the streaks of auburn the moonlight made in her hair and how much she wished Hailey's brown eyes were looking at her and not at their shoes.

"Like what?" Clover asked, ducking her head down so she could catch Hailey's gaze. At night, when they were alone like this, Clover had always been amazed how clearly she could see the planets when Hailey looked at her, how clearly she could see other worlds.

"Like this," Hailey said, and suddenly her lips were pressed against Clover's. Her arm wrapped around Clover's back, keeping them both upright, and Clover was thankful, because in that second, she absolutely felt like she was going to fall. It was only in the quiet seconds that followed—breaths heavy, eyes hooded, and stars shining like beacons in the night as Clover pulled Hailey back in—that she realized that, God help her, she already had.

How much love? Knox had asked her. *How much love?*

But good Christian girls from Salem didn't kiss each other.

Hailey and Clover both knew that, and Clover didn't know why Hailey seemed to have suddenly forgotten, but she wasn't going to. That's what she'd told herself the next morning, when she'd gone over to Knox's house and told him, yes, she'd go out with him. And then, months later, yes, she'd be his girlfriend. And then, and then . . .

And then there she was ten years later, Knox Haywood's fiancée, while the girl she'd fallen in love with first had disappeared to a city where "good Christian girls" defined themselves. Hailey had texted her a couple weeks before graduating high school, months after Clover had stopped responding:

> I'm going to college in San Francisco.

> I miss you.

> I wish you and Knox the best.

This is what Clover had explained in the hospital, where her mother lay in bed, eyes boring into Clover's with sharp scrutiny. "I don't think I can marry Knox," Clover told her, unable to meet that piercing gaze. "I'm . . . Hailey and I were . . ."

"It was a summer crush," her mother said, waving her hand as if to dismiss the concept. She turned away and closed her eyes. "Girls always have crushes on each other. Teenagers explore, that's normal."

"No, Mom. It wasn't exploration. It was . . . I would move

heaven and earth for Knox. But I've *never* felt the way I did that summer with Hailey."

"So, maybe you'd be happy with another man then. You've been with Knox your whole life . . ."

"Mom, you're not listening to me."

"I am, Clover." Her mother sucked in a harsh breath. "And you're wrong."

"How do you know?"

"Because I didn't raise you that way."

That way. Those two words had made Clover's world smaller than she'd ever thought possible. So small she felt as if she were suffocating.

So, they moved on from the subject. Her mom felt it was settled. "It's just cold feet," she said to Clover, and to herself, probably, and Clover didn't push. Not while her mother lay in a hospital bed. They found something lighter, something buoyant. They found a way to laugh, that day, and those that followed.

But the problem was that no matter what her mom thought, she *had* raised Clover to be stubborn, principled, and forthright. So she had followed her heart and broken up with Knox anyway.

And then her mom had died.

And then her dad had had his heart attack.

And then, and then, *and then.*

Clover pulled her gaze away from the hills to look down at the baggage claim sticker she'd put on her boarding pass. She ran her fingers over the number, willing herself to feel something—some sort of pride, perhaps, for getting out of her funk and trying something new. But she also wondered, not for the first time, if she was stepping on her mother's memory by being here in the first place—the city her little high school crush had run off to.

She'd had jitters that morning, fears of falling from the sky or other great disasters. While that alone was frightening, what was worse was the brief flash of calm that followed, as if a part of her welcomed the thrill. Or was it the emptiness that would come after?

She hated not knowing what she was feeling, what she wasn't. And yet the one time she'd tried to be honest with herself and those she loved, it had blown up in her face.

That's why she kept waiting, staring out at the hills of San Francisco just past the tarmac, long after her fellow passengers had scurried from the plane and tracked down their luggage.

She wondered how long she'd have to wait.

"YOU SAFE? FLIGHT go smoothly?"

"All good, Daddy." Clover's flip phone pressed against her ear uncomfortably as the taxi rumbled along. "How is Bee—does she seem nice?" She shifted, keeping her eyes tracked on the green foliage that flashed by her window.

"Oh yeah, lovely girl. And I saw Knox this morning too."

"Mm." She leaned her head against the window as her dad rambled on, telling her about how Bee and Knox had apparently met on the road, and how he and Knox had talked a bit that morning about his moving plans, and how he was planning to go into town to run errands, and . . .

Clover felt the urge to hit the brakes, even though she wasn't the one driving.

"Knox is moving?"

She heard her father hesitate. "He didn't tell you?"

"No." She frowned. She had no right to feel angry or indignant. Of course Knox would want to move; he was probably as desperate to get away from the farm as she was. Still, he could've at least *told* her. What was next—a new job? Maybe he was trying to extricate himself from her life entirely. Maybe this was the first step.

"Clover?" Her dad's warm and concerned voice brought her back to herself. "You okay, baby?"

She squeezed her eyes shut and opened them again. "Fine, Daddy."

"You know, if you talked to him, I'm sure Knox would—"

"It's fine, Daddy." Her dad was one of the few people who had never suggested she'd made some sort of grave mistake by ending her engagement with Knox, but she didn't want to risk it. It was hard for some people to understand—how she could love him but not be *in love* with him. How she could still want to be part of the fabric of his life but also not be, say, the mother of his future children.

They didn't understand that, at the end of the day, he was still her best friend. Of everything she'd lost this past year, why couldn't she at least keep that?

Her father switched subjects and began talking about Bennie and how she'd started to befriend their horse, since the other chickens had rejected her. Clover allowed herself to feel amused and forced herself to focus on her father's cheerful tone and the steady movement of the taxi. Once he was satisfied that she'd survived the first part of her trip with life and limb and they exchanged their "I love yous," Clover turned her attention back to her temporary city. Knox was trying to move on with his life. She would try to do the same.

The trees disappeared into a complex system of highways and high-rises, and when the city came into view, the first thing she noticed was a cable car with a faded red body and brown roof passing by. She was surprised to see a few people actually hanging on to poles on the outside, just like she'd seen in movies. *Well, that seems fun,* she thought. She'd have to try one of those out before she left.

Soon her own car began to ascend, and she noted how steep the hills were as they traveled—up, up, up, up—toward a row of uniquely colored Victorian homes and what she assumed was the corporate headquarters of a local bank. She felt like maybe the taxi would dip backward at any second, and so would her stomach, but the car seemed to perch just fine on the side of the road.

"We're here," the driver said.

"Where?" she asked.

"Your destination," he said. "That's what the address says."

"Oh." Clover blinked, her eyes searching for anything that looked like it would hold the inside of Bee's apartment. "Of course. Thanks." She didn't actually know what it was supposed to look like on the outside—there weren't any pictures of that—but she assumed one of these picturesque homes that dotted the street must have a much more modern interior.

"That'll be eighty dollars," her driver said.

She winced. A part of her was convinced she should've taken the subway system, even if she'd never traveled underground in her life, but she knew she wouldn't have survived a trek up those hills, no matter how strong her legs were. She paid him in cash—a requirement she gave herself to stay on budget—and as he grabbed her bags from the trunk, she took a moment to breathe in the air and look around her.

She felt like she was standing on the edge of a new world, beneath a crisscross of phone lines. A steady bustle of cars climbed past her on the street. Clover imagined them as massive billy goats traipsing over the mountains with engines strapped beneath them. She laughed a little. This was kind of fun. Like she was an explorer on a grand new adventure.

Once the driver plunked the bags at her feet, she took one in each hand and began to walk toward the Victorian homes.

"Miss," the driver called after her.

"Yes?"

"The building is right there." He pointed at what she had thought was a bank, a concrete building more than fifteen stories high with towering glass windows and a doorman stationed out front.

"Oh," she said, breathless. "Thanks."

And she thanked the doorman too, when he silently opened the door for her as she passed into the lobby. Clover tried not to gape. Beneath a spiral glass staircase that led to a grand piano was a sitting room outfitted with six massage chairs facing a waterfall. Beside it was the entrance to a coffee shop, with the words CASTRO CAFÉCITO in cursive neon lights stationed above it.

This is a hotel, Clover thought. *This lady lives in a hotel.*

"Your name, please?"

Clover looked at the security guard who had appeared before her, trying to remember the directions Bee had sent to her. "Oh, I'm Clover. Mills. I'm a guest of Bee Tyler."

The security guard checked her answer against a clipboard and then went behind his desk, typing something into the computer. "Okay, thank you, Miss Mills. You know where you're going?"

"Yes, thank you, sir."

"You're welcome. Happy holidays," he said as he gestured toward the elevators to his left.

Clover mumbled the phrase in return and followed along, pressing the call button for the elevator and trying to subdue the rising sense of awe. When the doors opened, she was met with the scowl of an impeccably dressed Black woman. She was looking at her phone and completely oblivious to the woman with two huge suitcases standing in front of her.

"Um, excuse me," Clover said, sidestepping the woman who seemed like she was going to walk right into her.

The woman looked up from her phone, and Clover resisted the urge to take a step back. She was . . . well, she was stunning, even frowning as deeply as she was. Her slick, straight bob framed her round face, and her deep brown skin seemed to shine against deep-set bright brown eyes. Clover's tongue grew heavy, but the woman barely seemed to register her. She gave a quick flick of her eyes up and down Clover's fresh-off-the-airplane appearance and then continued walking.

"Okay," Clover muttered to herself. "Gorgeous *and* rude. Noted." She hoped she wasn't a neighbor. If she was, she'd be sure to steer clear.

She pulled her bags into the waiting elevator and pressed the floor number, though as the doors closed, she could still see the woman's retreating form, and honestly, she didn't mind the view.

She sighed and rolled her eyes up to the ceiling. "Sorry, Mom," she mumbled, and then laughed quietly to herself. It was a bad joke, but, you know, so was the last year. Clover chose not to focus on the lingering scent of jasmine the woman seemed to have left behind, and moments later, she walked out into a clean, brightly lit hallway with rows of white doors that led to what she assumed were million-dollar condos. Most were decked out in colorful wreaths—some in traditional Christmas colors and a handful in white and blue, which she assumed belonged to those residents who celebrated Hanukkah.

She glanced at the arrows indicating the apartment numbers to either side of her and double-checked the email she'd printed out the night before. Bee's apartment was supposed to be to the left of the elevators, so she started in that direction.

"No!" she heard someone shout behind her, followed by loud panting. "Oh my—I'm so sorry. Could you—?"

Years of chasing animals on her and her neighbors' farms had honed Clover's instincts. She let go of her bags and leaped toward the dripping furball that was now chasing its own tail, distracted apparently from its original attempt at freedom. The little pit bull didn't even squirm; it just hung limply in her arms, panting with a lopsided tongue as her owner, a tall East Asian woman, jogged toward her.

"You *suck*," the woman groaned as she took the dog from Clover's arms. Then she gave Clover a tired smile. "And you're an angel. Thank you so much for grabbing this little jackass. She hates bath time."

"Ah," Clover said. "No problem, I'm kind of used to it."

"You have dogs?"

"Chickens," Clover supplied. "And a horse."

The woman cocked her head, then took in the two bags at Clover's feet. "You must be visiting someone, then. Unless you're turning one of the condos into a farm."

"Not yet." Clover smiled. "And yes, visiting a . . . friend." Bee had told her that the building wasn't yet cozy with short-term subletters, so she opted to be vague.

"Did you get her?" someone else called from down the hall. While the first woman was lithe, with short black hair spiked with gel, the second was white, short and curvy, with long bright red hair and a tattoo that ran up her leg, just beneath her jean shorts.

"Yes, dear," the first woman responded. "This happens a lot," she said to Clover as the redhead ducked back inside the apartment. "I'm Dee, by the way. That's my wife, Leilani."

Clover tried not to react. *Wife*, she thought. That wasn't a word she heard thrown around by most women in Ohio. Or any woman, for that matter. She wondered if Hailey was married now or settled somewhere in the city. The thought made her happy and sad at the same time. Still, she smiled and offered her hand. "Clover. It's nice to meet you."

"You too," Dee said. "And this little terror is Miss Cleo." The dog continued to pant idly. "Thanks again for grabbing her. Leilani had just walked through the door, and—*bam*—Missy bolted. Most of the time, she just wants to get away from the bath, so it's not too hard to get ahold of her; other times, someone will be walking out of their apartment or going down the stairs, and she'll make a break for it, just because she can. She's a wily one. Anyway"—Dee took a breath—"I appreciate it. We're just down the hall, obviously, so, you know, if you need anything while you're here, give us a shout."

"Thanks," Clover said, watching as Dee scolded Miss Cleo like a parent with a toddler. It reminded her of her dad and Bennie, in a way that both warmed her and made her cold.

She already missed her dad and the animals, but it was too late to worry about that now. She grabbed ahold of her bags once more and finally made her way to Bee's apartment. It was easy to find once she turned the corner. Bee had told her to look for an apartment with a little red mailbox out front, seated on a wood-carved red-and-white candy cane.

Cute, Clover thought.

She reached in and pulled out the key Bee had left for her. Then she took a deep breath and opened the door.

A view of the Castro District greeted her from across the room. There were more windows than walls, and in every direction Clover looked, she could see the city.

Holy shit.

The pictures didn't do the apartment justice. They had shown a small four-hundred-square-foot studio with nice, updated fixtures, but that was about it. They'd shown the view too, but Clover had assumed those were just bonuses from Google Images: examples of what she'd be able to see *when she was outside.* But here she was, on the tenth floor of a luxury high-rise, looking out across the entire city of San Francisco.

She felt like a queen or a mogul.

Clover walked to the window directly in front of her and looked down. Beneath her was a tennis court, a pool, and a small dog park, all of them enclosed on the premises. Clover didn't have a dog, but here, she could suddenly imagine herself with one of those tiny handbag Chihuahuas, chauffeured alongside her as she took in spa treatments and ordered cocktails by the hot tub.

She pressed her forehead against the window and allowed herself a moment to take all of it in—the view, of course, but also the fact that she was here, in a brand-new city, in a hotel that pretended to be an apartment building, and for the first time in her entire life, she was actually on her own. It felt so much better than being surrounded by people she'd always known, and who had always known her, and still feeling completely and utterly alone.

Clover walked away from the window and to her bags, dragging them to the queen-sized bed on the right side of the room. She needed to focus on something else—anything else—because the shock of hopefulness she suddenly felt was not only terrifying, it was electrifying.

This was what she'd been waiting for.

For once, Clover heard a different memory of her mother's voice in her head as she put her bags aside, sat on the bed, and took stock of her surroundings. *Okay, girl. The day is early and the chickens are fed. What are you going to do next?* She smiled to herself, even as the fond saying put a little pain in her heart.

Then she put on the lightest jacket she owned and ventured back out into the world.

Chapter Five

Bee

Monday evening, December 11, 2023

Bee wasn't used to having so many places to sit. It was a weird thought, but the only thing her brain seemed to be able to latch on to after she'd passed out that morning, hibernating following her long flight across the country. She'd drafted a text to her sister, deleted it, considered calling her parents, panicked, and then turned her attention to the absolutely massive house that she could call her own, at least for now.

It wasn't that space was foreign to her. Her parents, after all, had a small mansion that they had boasted about since Bee and Bethany were in diapers. But living in the heart of the tech community, Bee had long since traded comfort for luxury, convincing herself that a gorgeous view and an accessible coffee shop would more than make up for having precisely six feet of space to move around in.

Okay—she was being a little bitter. She loved her studio. It was cramped and outrageously expensive, but it was *hers,* something she'd had to fight for the many times her parents had offered help with a mortgage on a larger place in exchange for their many strings, or, God forbid, the handful of times they'd suggested she move in with *Bethany.* Bee shuddered. No, she would take her own place any time.

Still, it was nothing like Clover's country house, with its cozy accoutrements: a foyer with a gold chandelier and clean wooden stairs that led to Clover's bedroom, a master suite with a balcony that overlooked the forest beyond and a claw-footed tub in the bathroom. Though the house clearly had history, it was one of deep love and care. Every update seemed thoughtful, every detail purposeful, every corner clean.

Past the stairs on the first floor was the living room, which had windows on every side, allowing light to pour in during the day and now revealing starlight as dusk came. There was a TV mounted above the fireplace, against a backdrop of exposed, weathered red brick that looked perfectly unpolished. The room was sectioned off by a family couch with the comfiest cushions Bee had ever lay on, and behind it was an oak desk and a full wall of books, like something out of Bee's childhood dreams of stealing into Belle's home at night and ripping out her library with a forklift.

And then there was the kitchen that Jimmy had recommended she spend some time in that morning. Bee didn't *really* cook. Microwaving and ordering in were much more her specialties, but there was something about the sheer size of a kitchen like Clover's—something that promised a generation of family memories, of high school study sessions around the table in the kitchen nook, of holiday dinners planned and prepared at the huge island in front of the six-burner stove. It was a chef's kitchen, made wholesome with love. When she'd first seen it, her gaze had locked on to the catalog of height milestones scribbled on a wall beside the refrigerator.

Clover at three.

Clover at six.

Clover at thirteen.

In Bee's family, appearances were everything, and part of the child-parent contract she'd signed out of the womb was making sure she was never idle, or at least never seemed to be so. Starting in junior high, she'd been president of the debate club, editor in chief of the newspaper, regional vice president of the honor society . . . an endless list of little feats to fill her résumé. Her parents kept a record of her progress by tracking awards and titles.

Clover had simply had to grow.

And if Bee's parents saw her now, lazing about and flipping through channels on Clover's television—she had *cable!*—they'd probably send her a bill for the investment they'd wasted all these years. They were going to be *pissed* when they found out she wasn't coming to their Christmas Eve dinner.

Sighing heavily, she reached for her phone. She had been keeping it on airplane mode as if disconnecting herself from incoming calls and alerts would also shield her from the anticipation of her family's ire, but now she turned it back on, pulling up the text message to Beth that she'd begun drafting earlier that afternoon.

Hi sis, it read. Just wanted to let you know that I'm out of town. Won't be back until after Christmas. Not answering emails till then. Love you!

It was short and sweet and would absolutely get her killed. She deleted it and tried again: Hey Bethy! It's Bee, obvi. So . . . totally last minute, but I realized I needed a breather, and so I packed up my bags to take a quick vacay in Ohio!

Ugh, no. Why was drafting a text message so much harder than writing ad copy?

Because you suck at both, her inner critic whispered into her ear, laughing. Bee groaned and fell back into the cushions of the couch. Maybe she could ask Ayana to cover for her, suggest she'd struck up some deal between their companies and sent Bee on a covert mission to . . .

Bee let out another heavy sigh. Eventually, she'd just have to tell her family that she was gone. Whatever excuse she gave, short of a terminal illness, would be met with fury, and she'd have to deal. She didn't want to, but it's not like she hadn't before. But she also didn't have to do it *right now.*

That's right, she told herself. *No need to rush. It's day zero; you just got here.*

Instead, she decided to dial Ayana, which was the sane thing to do, given that her best friend was officially the only other person in her life who knew she had left the city.

"Hey, girl!" Ayana's perky voice soothed Bee's anxiety almost immediately.

"Hey," she said. "I'm alive and in Ohio."

"Glad to hear it. How's the Vacate so far?"

"Honestly?" Bee looked around the massive living room.

"Utterly ridiculous. I haven't had this much space in at least a decade. The house is gorgeous, and my swap-mate's dad is seriously the sweetest. He lives in the apartment downstairs. And the *farm manager . . .*" Bee bit her tongue. She hadn't meant to bring him up.

"Uh-huh?" Ayana prodded.

"He's cute," Bee said simply.

"Oh, really? Because it sounded like you were about to say he was *foine.*"

Bee laughed. "I mean, he's definitely easy on the eyes. But that's not why I'm here." She settled into the cushions of the couch. "I am not in the market for a vacation boo."

"Why not? Summer doesn't have a monopoly on flings."

"I am on hiatus."

"Fine. I accept your hiatus. Actually, speaking of men you're not at all interested in—guess who I just saw on the invite list for the Christmas Eve Eve party?"

Bee rolled her eyes so hard she felt the muscles strain. *Roger.* They'd dated off and on since she moved to San Francisco, and it took only the fourth time of him cheating on her for her to realize that she was wasting her time. "I thought he quit tech so he could manage his father's yacht business."

"He's high up at a new VR company now. My assistant must have added him on accident."

"Gross." The idea that she'd have to hobnob with him at future tech events nearly made her gag, but she sucked her teeth instead. She'd never been in love with Roger, and it was safe to say he had never been in love with her either. But he had represented everything that she was expected to want:

well-mannered, attractive, successful. Every excuse he made when he was caught texting another woman, or out partying late with a pretty colleague, or having dinner with "a friend" was one she had been all too willing to accept, if it meant she got to keep the fantasy of their romance for anyone who looked at them. At the very least, he'd been nice to her, even if he'd never been *good* to her.

"I'm not exactly thrilled to rub elbows with him either, but business is business, I guess," Ayana said. "Just be thankful *you* get to spend your holidays across the country."

"Oh, I am. Very much so. Thanks for the encouragement, by the way."

"Always. I'm rooting for you. Hot farm manager or not."

Bee laughed. It was good to remember who she did have, even when it felt like she was entirely alone. Her memories flickered back to the fateful Christmas when her parents had first suggested that she and her sister should work together. The one when they'd told her that writing for fun was a waste of time. When Beth had readily agreed to partner with her, Bee thought it was the first sign that the relationship they'd let unravel during their late teens and early twenties was on its way to being stitched back together.

Now Bee was terrified to text her.

She looked up at the ceiling and decided to think about Ayana's business instead. "How's the planning for the holiday market?"

Ayana was all too excited to switch gears, and Bee welcomed the comfort of work that had nothing to do with her.

When they eventually said their goodbyes, Bee let her phone drop. Finally feeling somewhat content, she reached for the remote beside her and flipped through the channels until she landed on her favorite Christmas film, which featured Tori Spelling and Tia Mowry battling for top spot in a caroling competition. She allowed herself to sink into their ridiculous rivalry for the next thirty minutes, only startling out of her comforting haze when she realized there was singing that wasn't coming from the TV.

. . . when you're sleeping / He knows when you're awake.

Bee turned the TV down and rushed to the window, pushing back the curtains she'd drawn earlier.

There were carolers walking down the street, dressed in what Bee's mom would call their Sunday best, in a variety of green and red. It was dark out, but whoever was leading the small procession—a little blond boy—was carrying what looked like an electric lantern. Behind him was a mix of teenagers and adults, just a handful of both, singing a medley of Christmas classics that immediately made Bee feel like she was in the heart of her very own Hallmark film.

She looked around for her coat and her boots, then dashed out the door. It was only when it slammed behind her that she realized she didn't actually know what she was doing—it was neither Halloween nor Mardi Gras. One did not throw candy or beads at carolers. But as she headed toward the street, she noticed others coming from their houses, wrapped in coats and blankets, gloved hands holding cups of something steaming and, Bee imagined, decadent. Some leaned against one another as their own voices murmured along to the chorus. Even Knox, she realized, was standing across the way, chatting up a happy-seeming family.

She took note of his relaxed posture: one hand in his pocket, the way he threw back his head and laughed when one of the older boys said something she couldn't hear. She had to admit—even in the dark, the man was easy on the eyes.

When he saw her, he smiled and raised a cup of something in a toast. She blushed and waved back.

"Figured you'd need these," a voice behind her murmured. She turned as Jimmy ambled up to her, a pair of gloves in his hands. "Heard the door to your place slam and figured you came out to see the town's famed carolers."

"Famed?" she asked, thanking him as she accepted the gloves. Her fingers were, in fact, freezing.

He nodded. "Yeah, we love 'em out here. Look forward every year." Though the carolers had stopped on the street, allowing the neighbors to crowd in just a bit more, he was already turning around and heading back to his apartment. "Enjoy yourself, Miss Bee," he called behind him.

She turned her attention back to the carolers, to this neighborhood she was a part of, however briefly. It wasn't going to last, this little dream she'd found herself in. But that didn't mean she couldn't fall in love with every single moment of it.

She just had to give herself permission.

Chapter Six

Clover

Monday afternoon, December 11, 2023

So, just hold on tight, okay, especially when we hit a bump or two along the way," the man with the mustache said as Clover held on to the pole of the cable car for dear life.

Although he was short, with slicked-back black hair and a heavy Mexican accent, the man felt just like her dad, reminding her with the cautiousness of a father to be safe, and to pay attention to any cars or trucks that passed, and not to sway too much with the movement of the cable car lest she fall off.

"Okay, so you're good, then?" he asked again as the car began to move.

"Yes, thank you, sir," she said, smiling at him warmly.

"Okay, very good." He waved at her and moved back toward the spot next to his wife, who looked like she was more than used to her husband playing dad to every young tourist who looked like she had a death wish.

As the car moved, Clover leaned into the wind that rushed against her face and the clash of city noises that surrounded her, testing her senses—snippets of conversation, the sharp honk of passing vehicles, the shouts of pedestrians rudely cut off in the intersections. The cable car shot down a steep hill and then slowly climbed another.

Knox would love this, Clover thought. For the briefest moment, she considered sending him a text and describing the streetcar to him, and the apartment she was staying in, and the hills all over the city. She wanted to tell him everything, and hear his absurd commentary and silly jokes, and laugh about how expensive everything seemed.

But he wouldn't want to hear from her. And even though he didn't know about Hailey, and Clover had no intentions of trying to contact her anyway, she felt guilty about being in her city. Like a betrayal by osmosis or something.

The fact that it was just as bright and full of holiday cheer as it would have been in Salem made it worse somehow. Her world had changed completely during this time last year, and yet the holidays had the audacity to come back around and follow her across the country. Only this time, she wouldn't have her mother or her fiancé or even her father. There'd be no Motown Christmas music playing throughout the house as her mother set about planning the guest list for the holiday party, and as her father and Knox competed to see who could make the grandest holiday display on the farm. She wouldn't get to taste test the famous mac 'n' cheese or hand deliver the invitations she'd been tasked with carefully crafting every year since she was old enough to navigate the streets on her own, first with a rusty old bike and then with the family car. She and Knox wouldn't spend hours in the breakfast nook, planning what they'd add to the community tree at the annual holiday tree lighting.

This year, she was alone. And yet, there were still Christmas trees being decorated, lights being strung, and festive music being played throughout the streets. Her only solace was hearing one of Kelly Clarkson's sad Christmas breakup songs blasted through the speakers of a young woman's red Mini Cooper as she made her slow and steady trek up Taylor Street. *Merry Christmas, to the one I used to know,* Kelly sang with all the anguish Clover felt in her soul. It was the perfect soundtrack to the one and only Christmas-related location Clover would allow herself this trip.

SHE LIFTED ONE leg and then the other, wiping beads of sweat off her brow. Just when she thought the street might rise straight into the sky, she finally began to see the hint of a plateau, gleaming gray stones beckoning her onto a flat plain and sweet, sweet relief.

Grace Cathedral loomed far above her, its spire reaching into the sky and its steps leading to large oak doors, its presence grand and intimidating as she supposed any historical site should be. The path to its door, up another few rows of stairs, was lined with bright yellow holiday lights that glinted against the darkness like fireflies. Bee had listed it as a holiday must-see, and even Clover couldn't resist the visit. She hated to admit it, but the walk was worth even this—this grand plane of gentle Christmas warmth beckoning her into the hallowed halls of the savior.

When her mother had died, Clover had gone to church every day for a month. Then it faded into a few times a week. Then just Sundays. And then . . .

She wasn't protesting. She didn't blame God or anything like that. It's just that—well, the *people*. The pitying looks, the unwelcome pats on the back. At first, she'd felt cradled by her community's love and support; they loved her mother as much as she did, after all. Many of them had even known her longer. But then news of her breakup with Knox spread, and the hugs got tighter, and their words of support got preachier, and Clover began to feel claustrophobic.

They thought her breakup with Knox was a symptom of her heartbreak, a misguided attempt to control her life in the face of something as shocking and uncontrollable as a terminal illness. They didn't know that she'd been thinking about it for a long time, that she'd wondered if her love for this man hadn't *always* been a powerful kind of platonic.

She took each step slowly, amazed still by the sound of the city that surrounded her, here at this historic place of worship, holding court among a kingdom of cars and monuments and steep vistas. At the doors to the cathedral, she paused, breathing in the peace and the chaos, and breathing out the anxiety she felt. Then she opened the door.

What greeted her was more gorgeous than she could have imagined. The ceiling must have been at least thirty feet high, with stained-glass windows that brought in hints of color amid the pale white stone, with gold sconces of light that led down to the pulpit. In the entrance hall, a large white tree glowed with shimmering white lights, and just beyond it, she could hear the church choir rehearsing.

They sounded much better—and bigger—than the carolers in her neighborhood.

Careful not to disturb them, Clover stepped around the Christmas tree and took a seat in one of the pews. A few people were scattered throughout the hall, some with eyes closed and bodies hunched forward. Others were scrolling on their phones, as nonchalant as if they were merely waiting for the credits of a film to finish rolling. In the far corner, near the front, a man was weeping. She could tell by the way his shoulders shook.

She supposed she wasn't the only one for whom a cold December night could bring painful memories, no matter what state she was in. She settled into her seat and closed her eyes. Listened to the man's sniffles, the choir's hymns, the steps of people coming and going. She thought of how happy her dad would feel when she told him that yes, finally, she'd seen the inside of a church. She thought of how sad her mom would be if she knew she hadn't been going at all, how disappointed she'd be if she learned that the holiday traditions she'd worked so hard to build were thrown away for something as superfluous as a solo trip across the country.

She thought about her cousins and her aunt and uncle, whom she wouldn't see for the holidays for the first time ever. Her friends back at home, whom she'd pushed away months ago.

She thought about Knox.

And she wondered, though she tried not to, what they all would think if they had known about Hailey, or heard about her new neighbors Dee and Leilani, or found out that she'd started off her first morning in San Francisco tongue-tied at the sight of a rude but gorgeous woman.

The thought jolted her eyes open. She looked around again, as if caught, and only then realized that her phone was buzzing. She checked the caller ID. Knox was calling her.

Flustered, she grabbed her belongings and stood, hurrying just outside the doors of the church. Then she flipped open her phone. "Hi," she said. "Everything all right?"

"You paid me extra this month," he said without preamble.

She frowned, stumbling awkwardly away from the entrance as an elderly couple tried to squeeze around her. "I'm sorry?"

"You paid me extra this month," he repeated. "I'm just letting you know. There might've been a clerical error."

"Oh. No." Clover relaxed. So, the farm wasn't on fire and her dad hadn't collapsed in a field somewhere. "I figured, since we have a guest in the Big House and you offered to look out for her for me, that the least I could do was give you a little bonus."

He didn't respond for a long while. "It's not really a big deal," he said finally. "You didn't . . . I don't know how I feel about that."

"I was just trying to do something nice," she said, "since it's the holidays and all." *And I broke your heart right before Christmas last year,* she didn't say. "Plus, it *is* an extra duty, technically. Like workin' overtime or something."

His laugh sounded a lot like disbelief. "Overtime?" he said. "Clover, if I got paid for all the 'overtime' I've done on this farm over the years, I could *buy* my own house."

Clover bristled. "If you want more money for the work you're doing—"

"That's not what I meant—you know what? Never mind. I appreciate you being thoughtful, Clover. I hope you're enjoying your trip."

She'd barely responded with "Thanks" before the call ended.

"What the hell?" she muttered. A woman passing by her with a small baby wrapped in her arms shot her a frown, and Clover put her hands up. "Sorry," she said, although she was finding that she was starting to get mighty sick of apologizing. It was like everything she did required an explanation to somebody.

She looked back at the church and then shook her head. Even when she was doing something right, she was doing something wrong. Why couldn't people, just for once, accept what she did, no questions asked?

Irritated, she left the steps of the church, feeling more and more like leaving Salem was the best Christmas gift she could've given herself.

Chapter Seven

Bee

Tuesday afternoon, December 12, 2023

The snow settled and shifted in the wind as Bee rocked back and forth in her chair. She was on the balcony of her host's bedroom, wrapped tightly in a heavy blanket, on top of her fleece pajamas. She felt like a princess in a snow globe or an old lady who had just retired. Either way, she was feeling calm and centered, nursing a steaming cup of hot cocoa as the sound of the chickens squawking wandered to her through the snowfall. After the carolers left the night before, she'd gone upstairs and drawn herself a bath, before going straight to sleep.

She'd slept late. Her phone was still off. And now here she was, still doing not much of anything. It felt amazing. Lifesaving. Necessary.

Weird.

Okay, maybe a *little* scary.

She took a sip of her hot chocolate, focusing on the taste of melted marshmallow on her tongue. Then she set her cup down on the small table beside her and stretched her arms luxuriously above her head. She closed her eyes and tried to rock herself gently into an early afternoon nap.

Back and forth, back and forth . . .

It should've felt soothing, but something was keeping her awake.

A little knot tied into her stomach.

Back and it would grow taut . . .

Forth and it would tighten . . .

She took a deep breath. *No,* she thought. *Absolutely not.* But even as she tried to force herself to relax, her fingers began to twitch, and her jaw began to work itself as if possessed by an angry spirit.

After a tense battle of wills against herself, she finally set both feet on the ground and thrust herself to the edge of the seat in a huff.

She was restless.

Goddamn it.

Irritated, she thrust the blanket away and hurried back into the bedroom, closing the sliding door behind her. She wasn't really sure what to do, even as she riffled through her baggage and picked out a pair of skinny jeans, a simple black tank top, a cute pair of pink earmuffs, and a wool coat she'd gotten on sale at Anthropologie.

This is what Ayana couldn't understand—that *failing to* work was only half of her problem. The other part was *not* working. Her brain was instead in some sort of limbo of half action, unable to rest but also incapable of productivity. Like if she could only *just* . . . then she *might* . . .

The sentence was never finished, never filled in.

So, there she was, actively inert.

Fully dressed, she sat at the edge of the bed, her fingers tapping out a rhythm on her knee. She could try to read, but the plane ride had convinced her that was still a lost cause. She *could* try to work—after all, the setting was serene, the quiet peaceful. Maybe this was all she needed: stillness away from the bustle of the city.

She pulled her laptop out of her backpack and opened it. Then she closed it immediately. Groaning, she flopped back down on the bed and looked at the ceiling, wondering if she'd be able to pick out the different animal sounds if she breathed quietly enough.

Was that a moo? she wondered. *Are there cows here?*

Clover hadn't mentioned any, but Clover hadn't exactly been chatty in her emails. Aside from some basics about the house, and a general note that animals on the farm existed, much of what Salem had to offer was left to Bee's imagination.

"Although she had mentioned something about a tree lighting . . ." Bee muttered. And the farm manager. Knox. With his bright blue eyes and boyishly curly brown hair, and that smile . . . What was he doing right now anyway?

Bee sat up. He *had* told her that if she needed anything, she could let him know . . .

Sure, she thought. *That works.* She could ask him about the tree lighting and what else people did for the holidays. That was totally reasonable.

She grabbed her phone and set off down the stairs and out the door, toward the cabin Knox had pointed out to her the other morning. As she did, she was surprised to see Jimmy out in the chickens' pen, bent over and humming what sounded like "Midnight Train to Georgia."

"Good afternoon, Mr. Jimmy," she called to him from behind the wire fencing.

He jumped up, pulling his newsboy hat off and pressing it to his chest. "Good God, I thought you was my daughter." He laughed and righted the hat back on his head. "She'd kill me if she saw me out here doin' any kind of work. Good afternoon to you, Miss Bee."

"You can just call me Bee."

"And you can just call me Jimmy." He winked, and Bee smiled.

"Jimmy it is, then. What are you doing?"

"Oh, just giving some extra love to some of our more passive chickens. Most of the girls get along just fine, but a few like to puff up their feathers and enforce the pecking order. Like Mabel." He leaned in close and whispered, "Stay clear of her."

Bee chuckled a little but stopped when she noticed his arm start to shake. He was holding on to a green pail of what Bee assumed was chicken feed, and the feed began to spill as Jimmy started coughing. She snatched the pail from him and placed a steady hand on his back, but he waved her away and stood up straight.

"Mabel ain't dead, and yet her spirit can haunt ya. I bet the old hen is a witch in retirement." His laugh turned into another cough, but he shook it off and reached for the pail, thanking her as he headed back inside. "Anyway, enough excitement for the day. I hope you enjoy your stay, Bee—and don't worry about me! Just an old man fightin' off age."

Bee watched him go with a small smile. He seemed nice enough, and who was she to tell him to take it easy? Still, she could understand why her swap-mate wouldn't want him outside working in the cold. She wouldn't tell on him, of course, but she thought she might want to keep an eye on him. God forbid an old Black man die on her watch.

She kept walking past the chicken coop and rounded the corner to Knox's cabin. Up close, it seemed cozy—real logs, from what she could tell, and a little porch with a dusty black welcome mat. She hesitated for a second, feeling odd about disturbing someone without prior warning. In fact, it had probably been nearly a decade since she had actually walked up to someone's door to see if they were home. These days, she shot off a DM and waited for a reply. Now she knocked gently and then took a step back, trying not to shiver in the cold. After another moment, she knocked again, and when she still heard no reply, she knocked harder and pressed her ear against the door.

Still nothing.

She blew out her lips and took a look around. She could go back to the house and . . . sleep? Watch TV? Maybe Jimmy would want to play a board game.

Bee groaned, feeling increasingly like she wanted to pout and stomp her feet. Instead, she pulled her coat tighter, adjusted her earmuffs, and turned around. She was not going to give up! She had a mission, and she would succeed at it. She squared her shoulders and trudged away from the cabin and in the opposite direction of the Vacate home toward . . . er . . . what looked like woods. Deep, scary woods that led to God knew where.

That was fine, though.

Pretty, even.

Snow-scattered branches and cute little animals burrowing into their homes beside tiny campfires underground, or whatever woodland creatures did to keep warm. Either way, it was fine. She would be fine.

She continued walking until she heard a dull *thud-thud-thud* just a few meters ahead of her. She walked toward the sound and found what she was looking for: Knox, hair askew and breathing hard, with an axe high above his head.

Well, it wasn't *exactly* what she was looking for.

"Hey!" she said, feeling absurdly giddy. Her persistence had paid off—she hadn't felt like that in a while. "I found you!"

Knox paused with his axe above his head, apparently startled by the tiny Black girl who had just emerged from the trees. He took a step back and let the axe fall to the side, wiping his hair from his face. He was wearing a thick half-sleeve parka over a black-and-green-checkered flannel with his sleeves rolled up, and his jeans looked worn and muddied. He'd obviously been hard at work, and she felt a little bad for interrupting him. He actually looked kind of . . . upset.

"Are you okay?" she asked before she realized it was none of her business.

"Huh? Oh." He cleared his throat and wiped his hands on his shirt. "Yeah, I'm fine. Just . . . thinking."

"About chopping wood?"

He looked at the woodpile like he'd never seen it before in his life. Then he chuckled. "It's just what I do when I'm stressed."

"So, you *are* stressed," Bee pressed. She clasped her hands behind her back as she took a few steps forward.

This time he full-out laughed. "Yes, I suppose I am. Not much to do here in the wintertime except wait for the ground to thaw. But I've always figured, if I'm gonna be stressed, I might as well make myself useful, given that it's the dead of winter. Speaking of, I believe I owe you and Jimmy a delivery of firewood."

Bee smiled. *If I'm gonna be stressed, I might as well make myself useful.* A man after her own heart.

"Were you out on a walk?" he asked.

"I was looking for you," Bee said, and then resisted the urge to cover her mouth. "I mean, that sounds . . . I just meant that I saw you weren't at your cabin, so I thought I'd do a little exploring. It was nice—the snow in the woods and all that."

"Ah." He stood there with one hand still holding the handle of the axe. A few seconds of silence passed until he spoke again. "So . . . what did you need?"

Bee blinked. "What? Oh! Ah . . ." Her query about local holiday happenings seemed a little trivial now, given the fact she'd trudged through snow and forest to find the man, who was trying to have his personal time to decompress, but she really didn't have any other reason to be bothering him. "Are there any cows around here?"

He blinked.

She waited.

"Um, yeah," he said. He scratched his chin, and Bee tried not to note how handsome he was with just a shadow of stubble. "Not here. Too expensive to keep. But there are some just down the road."

"Oh, okay." She paused. "I thought I heard some. Earlier. In my, er, Clover's room."

He nodded. Then: "A lot of people have animals around here. Some of them are useful for the holidays. The Blankenships nearby have a petting zoo, and there's the annual tree lighting at Lester's Christmas Forest." He thought some more. "There's horseback riding."

"Horseback riding?" Now, *there* was something new and exciting. Bee hadn't ridden a horse in years, if perching on a saddle while a man led the horse around in a circle for three minutes at the local fair counted as "riding." "I would love that! Are there stables nearby, or would I have to drive there?"

"There's one nearby," he said. "And we have a horse at the farm, though you may have to ask Clover about that." He looked at the wood on the ground. She was clearly distracting him from his task.

"Can I help?"

He looked back up at her. "With the horse?"

"No," she said, laughing. "With the wood. Can I help you with it?"

He chuckled and shook his head. "Of course not. You're a guest. I'll, uh, finish up here and then bring some of the wood up to the Big House."

Bee held up her hands, feeling a giddy burst of determination. "I'm a quick learner, I swear. Er . . . not that I'm trying to get in your way or anything."

Knox gave her a once-over, clearly assessing her fitness for manual labor. She wondered in that moment if her fluffy pink earmuffs were maybe just a little bit of overkill with this outfit. "It's . . . not exactly easy."

"Even better!" Bee rolled her shoulders and cracked her neck a couple times to prove her point. Then she bounded over and stood in front of the pile of wood he'd been chopping. "Where do we start?"

His lips quirked to the side. "You ever hold an axe?"

"Never in my whole life."

"Great. Let's start there."

He instructed her to come to his side of the woodpile and stand a few feet away. Then he placed a heavy piece of wood on his chopping block, picked up the axe, hefted it over his shoulder, and brought it down with a loud crack. He did this a few times, making sure she was watching his movement. Then he handed her the axe and let her take hold, waiting until she was comfortable with its weight before he let go completely.

"Okay, you ready?"

"Yup!"

"Good. Now lift it just like I showed you and—wait, you're holding it too high on the—no, now it's too low. Here, wait a second." He walked closer, a little to her left, and grabbed on to the handle of the axe. "Bring your hands up to here. Good. Now lift, like this." He lifted the axe so that it was between them. "You good? It feel all right?"

Bee followed his instructions closely, her mind thoroughly on the task at hand, but as he moved behind her, his arm brushing against hers, she felt her heart beat just a little bit faster. *It's just been a while,* she told herself. *But damn he smells good.*

"Bee?"

"Uh-huh?"

"I said, does it feel all right?"

"What?"

"The axe?"

"Yeah! Absolutely. A little heavy, but nothing I can't handle." That wasn't entirely true. The axe was heavy as hell, and Bee couldn't remember the last time she lifted anything heavier than her luggage, but she wasn't about to tell Knox that.

"Okay, good. So, your hands should meet each other at the bottom of the swing, and your top hand goes back up as you're lifting it again."

She did as she was told, praying the axe came down on the wood and not somewhere infinitely less pleasant. She closed her eyes as the axe stuck in the wood, not splitting it exactly, but at least she hadn't lost a foot.

"A little harder next time, a little more momentum, but you got the gist!"

Impressed with herself, Bee swung harder and faster the

second time, missing the first cut but managing to break off a few splinters.

Knox was trying hard not to laugh.

"Hey!" Bee huffed, already starting to feel warm and sweaty. "I'm not doing too badly."

"You're honestly not," he agreed. "I mean, the point is to actually split the wood in two, but if you hit it another ten times, that'll do the trick."

Bee glared at him playfully. "I said I'd help with the wood, not that I'd do your job for you. I am, *after all,* a guest."

"Oh, I see. And this is entertaining you?"

"Supremely."

Knox laughed. "Great. Then, uh, I'll just go over here and wait, if that's all right with you."

"Thank you."

Bee steadied herself over the wood, lifted the axe again, and this time managed to—oh, wow, she missed completely. Knox began to laugh so hard he had to cover his mouth, but that was okay with her. At least he was starting to warm up.

He let her pretend to chop wood for another twenty minutes before she was finally worn out, and then she relinquished the axe and was only the slightest bit *miffed* when he chopped her piece of wood with barely a thought.

"I started it for you," she called from her spot against a nearby tree.

"Oh, absolutely. Couldn't have done it without you."

"That's right."

He shook his head, but he didn't seem to mind that she

stuck around, watching as he chopped what seemed like an endless supply of wood for the next hour and occasionally offering to show him how a real pro should get it done.

Finally, he decided he had enough wood for a delivery, and together they walked back through the forest toward the Big House.

"So, how long have you been working here?" she asked, carrying exactly two logs while he carried the rest.

"About twelve years," he said.

Bee stopped, totally unable to cover her shock. "How old are you?"

He quirked an eyebrow in her direction but kept walking. "Twenty-seven. You?"

"A lady never tells," she answered, sticking her nose up in the air. Then she hurried to catch up to him. "Twenty-nine," she said. She liked the way he smiled at her, even if it was clear he was trying to hide it. Like he thought she was cute.

Bee hid her own smile, though she couldn't deny the butterflies in her chest. "I imagine you haven't always been the farm manager, though. Unless you were a child prodigy."

"No," he said. That was it. Just no. Bee quickly got the hint that he wasn't interested in talking about his life on the farm. That was okay. She switched gears.

"So, tell me about this tree lighting ceremony. What does one wear? Do I bring pie? Do we gather around and sing like the Whos from Whoville?"

He started laughing again, and Bee found she was starting to really like the sound. "Yes," he said. "Exactly like the Whos from Whoville. But we have to be quieter this year, since last year some guy dressed head to toe in green came and stole all our stuff."

Bee tried to bite her smile into the side of her cheek, but Knox's eyes sparkled at her again, a knowing smirk playing on his lips. This was too easy, talking to him like this. Like they'd known each other for years. She wondered if he was like this with all the girls—charming and funny and warm. Or was she sparking something in him too? After her experience with Roger, she felt inclined to be cautious, but there was something about Knox that made her feel bold.

They continued to banter and chat lightly about the town as they finally approached the Big House. By then, she was sweaty and covered in dirt and wood, and she felt like she could sleep for days. Her muscles ached, and God knew how she *smelled*, but the whole chopping wood thing had done the trick. She had done enough for the day, and she was ready to go back to her room and pass out.

"You hungry?" Knox was hovering by the entryway as she started to drag herself up the stairs. As if in response, her stomach made a desperate cry for help, and in that moment she remembered that she actually hadn't eaten yet today. She looked back at Knox sheepishly.

"Maybe. Can you recommend a place to order from around here?"

He looked at her like he was weighing a decision. Then: "I could whip something up. If you want." He added the last part like a boy asking a girl to be his date to the prom—casual but full of nerves.

Bee wet her lips in thought and pretended not to notice when his eyes dropped to her mouth. "That could be nice."

"Y'all okay?"

Knox jumped like someone had shoved hot coals under his feet. "Hi, Jimmy," he said.

Jimmy eased himself between the doorframe and Knox, so they were both standing there in front of her. "Didn't mean to startle you two. Just wanted to check in before I settled in downstairs."

Bee wasn't sure why she felt like she'd just been caught sneaking a boy into her room, but she was blushing nonetheless. "I'm all good, Jimmy, thank you."

"I was just about to give Bee some recommendations for takeout," Knox said. He didn't look at her.

"Takeout? Oh-ho, let me tell you something, Miss Bee, I don't think anyone in all of Salem would disagree that I make just about the best corn bread and mashed potatoes on the East Coast. I'd be happy to put something together for you."

Bee tried to catch Knox's eyes, but it was clear that his offer had expired. "I'll see you both later," he said. Then he left, just like that.

"I'm okay, Jimmy," she said. "Thank you. I'll just look something up, if that's okay."

"Okay," he said, seeming a bit confused. Maybe he too had noticed the sudden change in mood. "Well, as I've said, I'm just below if you need anything. You have a good afternoon, Bee."

"You too, Jimmy," she said. She waited until she was sure

the door was shut, then she hurried up the stairs. She didn't know why she felt so upset—so a random guy she'd just met had offered to cook for her, then pretended like he hadn't. That was . . . okay, no, that was weird. And Bee didn't have time for weird. That was *not* what she had come here for. She walked to the bathroom and turned on the shower, waiting for the water to get hot. Then she peeled off her sweaty snow clothes and forced herself to enjoy the sting of a hot shower. It had been a good day thus far, she told herself. The house was beautiful, the snow was enchanting, and the company was . . .

Well, Jimmy was nice.

She didn't need to think about Knox, and his axe, and his—

Okay, let's not get carried away, Bee reprimanded herself. But as she stood in the shower, letting the steam and heat roll over her, she did begin to wonder if that's not exactly what she had come here for.

To be completely and totally carried away.

Chapter Eight

Clover

Tuesday afternoon, December 12, 2023

The special today is a half vanilla chai and half regular chai, and a shot of espresso with a house nut mix milk blend."

"Could I just get a black coffee, please?"

"Absolutely, sweetie. Love your flannel, by the way."

"Oh." Clover looked down at her outfit. It was the barest variation of what she'd worn the day before. When she'd gotten home from her day of adventuring last night, she'd passed full out on her hostess's bed and woken up with bad breath and wrinkled clothes. Then she'd showered and thrown everything back on, except for her underwear. Compared with the people in the building's coffee shop, she felt like a walking potato sack, but the sentiment was nice. "Thanks," she said. "I like your tattoos."

"Pokes by Stokes," the barista said. "That's my girl—she's a

self-taught tattoo artist down in Oakland. You can follow her
@stokeypokey if you want to look her up."

"Oh," Clover said. "Thanks."

"Mm-hmm. Was that large or small, by the way?"

"Uh, small."

"Hot or iced?"

"Hot."

"Gotcha. We'll call you when it's ready."

Clover nodded and moved toward the group of patrons
who were waiting for their drinks to be made.

"One bi chai! One bi chai at the counter! Half vanilla, half
regular?"

Clover nearly tripped over her own feet as a familiar woman
with a smart bob walked up to grab her order. In that moment, she couldn't tell what made her more nervous: the name
of the drink or the hot woman from yesterday who was back
to haunt her.

Her coffee order was next, and Clover was grateful for the
distraction, though she couldn't stop her eyes from catching
the curve of the woman's lips as the dark maroon slid over
the open slit of the coffee cup lid as the woman walked out
of the coffee shop. Like yesterday, she seemed to be scowling
at her phone, and Clover couldn't help but mentally suggest
that maybe it'd be better for her mood if she, you know, put
it away.

Not that it's my business, she thought, as she picked up her
own drink and left the coffee shop.

To her surprise and delight and horror, the woman was
now waiting in front of the very same elevator that she'd

come out of the day before. Clover wondered if the woman would recognize her, given that she was wearing . . . the exact same outfit. *Please don't recognize me*, she thought.

As the elevator doors opened and they both stepped inside, Clover tried to work off her nerves by offering a polite smile, but the woman didn't seem to notice. Instead, she continued tapping away at her phone with neatly trimmed nails painted a neutral color that aligned with her smart, shoulder-length bob and the plum dress that hugged her curves nicely. *She's so* pretty, Clover thought. *Really pretty.* She surmised that she'd be only an inch or two shorter than the woman, if not for the black stilettos that helped accentuate the woman's—

Clover cleared her throat and willed the doors to open quickly, suddenly feeling all kinds of warm. When they finally freed her from her cage of anxiety, she hurried into the hallway and made a beeline toward Bee's apartment.

Unfortunately, the woman followed in her direction.

Clover slowed her steps and took a deep breath. There was no need to panic—truly, nothing to panic *about*. So some stranger was attractive. So they were both getting off on the same floor and walking in the same direction, giving Clover enough time to realize that the perfume she picked up on in the elevator wasn't only a sweet jasmine scent, but had gentle notes of sandalwood that made Clover want to touch her and experience it against her own skin.

So what?

"Excuse me." The woman broke through Clover's thoughts, and Clover realized they were both standing in front of Bee's door.

"Oh. Um, yes?"

"This is my sister's apartment."

Clover blinked in surprise. "Oh." *Oh.* No wonder she looked familiar. She hadn't exactly pored over Bee's photo, but the resemblance was obvious, even with Bee's long faux twists and the woman's short, straight hair. It made her wonder if Bee was out in Salem making people trip over themselves, like her sister was doing to her.

"So you might have the wrong apartment," the woman continued. "Or are you visiting Bee?"

"No," Clover said quickly, feeling embarrassed and ridiculous and *why was she so damn flustered?* "No, I'm staying here for a few days. I'm Clover." She put her hand out.

"Bethany. Beth." The woman shook Clover's hand, but she was frowning again. "You're staying here? Alone?"

Clover shifted, feeling defensive. "Yes," she said.

"So, where is Bee?"

Shouldn't you know? Clover wanted to ask. *She's your sister.* Instead, she put on a pleasant smile. "She's at my home—in Ohio. We switched houses using Vacate." Clover paused, realizing she might have to explain exactly what Vacate was, but before she could open her mouth again, Beth had already pressed her phone to her ear, a muscle in her jaw nearly ready to burst. Clover stood there awkwardly as she heard the phone ring until something that sounded like an automated message responded. Instead of leaving a message, Beth gripped the phone in her hand and glared at it so hard that Clover was certain it was going to fling itself into the nearest fire.

"You have got to be fucking kidding me," Beth said to herself. "That's why I couldn't get ahold of her yesterday. I'm going to kill her. I swear to God."

"O-kay." Clover turned toward the door, feeling that the hot, stoic woman was hot, stoic, and maybe a *little* terrifying. "Well. I'm going to go inside now."

Beth's head snapped back up as if she'd just remembered that Clover existed. "Actually, do you mind if I come in? She has something I need."

"No, sorry—I'm really not comfortable with that. Maybe if you hear from Bee later, she can let me know if it's okay?" *Or she can email you.*

Beth looked at her with her mouth slightly ajar—clearly, she wasn't expecting a no. Maybe she just wasn't used to hearing it. Clover put on a sweet smile, feeling an odd sense of triumph. Beth might be attractive, but she couldn't just barge into what was currently Clover's private space and take God knows what. If she and her sister were having issues, that wasn't Clover's business, and she didn't want to get thrown into the midst of it if Beth took something she wasn't supposed to.

Beth squared her shoulders and pocketed her phone. "Sure. I'll get in touch with Bee and stop by later." She gave Clover a curt nod and turned on her heel. Apparently, Clover was dismissed.

Well, okay then.

Clover rolled her eyes and let herself into the Vacate. For the most part, she had had mostly pleasant to neutral interactions with people, but it was nothing like her community in Salem. People here always seemed to be in a rush, just barreling on over to this task and the next one, to the point that some of those people—ahem, *Beth*—didn't seem to notice that other people existed. Whatever warm and confusing feelings Beth had inspired in her at first finally started to dissipate. Mostly.

Okay, not at all, but that didn't matter. Beth was hot but rude, and even if she were a saint, none of that would matter. Clover wasn't here for romance. She was here for . . . well, for herself.

She wandered over to the open view of the city, where she could see the expanse of buildings spread before her like flowers in a field. Immediately, she felt herself begin to calm. It was eerie, the effect the city had on her. One second she felt her blood pressure rise to the sun, and the next she felt like a dot within the skyline. It was unsettling.

But she kind of liked it.

As she stared and sipped her coffee, a distant buzzing began to echo throughout the room. She figured it was either bill collectors or her father, but when she checked it was a text from none other than Bee. I am so sorry about my sister, the text read. I know you're still just getting settled in. Would it be okay if she stopped by some morning this week? Just real fast.

Clover sighed. Sure, she responded, that strange feeling in the bottom of her stomach returning again. So, she'd be faced with the attractive grumpy lady once more—just what she needed. She didn't envy whatever relationship the two sisters seemed to have with each other; it didn't seem particularly copacetic.

Being an only child herself, Clover had often wondered

what it might be like to have a sibling—someone she could share her thoughts and fears with. Sure, she had her cousins just down the street, and Knox had been her confidant for most of her life, but she knew it wasn't the same. Having your lover be your best friend was a fairy tale for some, but for her, it had started to feel suffocating. No matter how true she wanted to be to herself, part of the relationship contract was that she'd have to compromise part of that for someone else.

At least, that's how she had started to feel.

But her mom had softened part of that feeling. Even without a sibling, she could always go to Mae Mills for advice—about school, about her relationship, about clothes, about anything. Mae had been the person Clover felt her most authentic self with, the person who knew Clover's innermost feelings—even if she didn't agree with them.

Now Clover didn't have anyone save for her dad, and she feared any new information she might share about herself with *him* would just result in another heart attack.

Her thoughts wandered back to Knox. If they'd never dated, would they have stayed friends all these years? Could she have been her most authentic self with him? Clover liked to think so. It wasn't, after all, like she'd kept *so* much from him. He knew everything else about her, from how she took her coffee in the morning and at night, to her fears about the farm and keeping it from going under, now that she was its inheritor. And she knew that coffee made him jittery at night, and that he loved to sing, and that one day he would be the very best father to someone's little girl.

She'd never told him about Hailey, but that was all, that

was it. How was she to know that the memory of that summer would stay with her all these years later? If she tried to tell him now, she wondered if he'd understand. That she could love him as much as she had, as deeply as she had, and still wonder if maybe loving a woman would feel more . . . right?

She took another sip of her coffee to find that she was down to the last dregs. She knocked it back like a shot and threw the cup in the trash by Bee's tiny kitchen. It was the only thing about the apartment that wasn't particularly grand—simply functional. It didn't exactly inspire Clover's usual penchant for cooking, and besides, she hadn't had the chance yet to fill the fridge. From what she'd seen, it looked like that wasn't something that ever made the top of Bee's list either.

Her stomach grumbled. It was early yet, and she still had more of the city to explore. She could grab something quick and easy from one of the *many* other cafés down the street. And maybe explore some of the thrift shops she'd seen too. After all, given that she was going to see Beth again, she wanted to demonstrate that she did happen to have more than one set of clothes. Not that she cared what Beth thought. She was pretty, sure, but also very stylish, and if Clover thought about it, so were Dee and Leilani and most of the people she'd seen as she'd wandered the city. Everyone was so individual, so confident, and it made her wonder if that was something she could experience for herself. If one day, maybe soon, maybe here, she'd be able to look in the mirror and recognize the person she saw looking back.

Chapter Nine

Bee

Tuesday evening, December 12, 2023

If Bee could smash her phone into a thousand tiny, microscopic pieces, she would do it in a heartbeat. In fact, the only thing stopping her now was the knowledge that somehow, some way, her sister would find a way to reach her, be it through carrier pigeon, a voodoo doll, or a robot army fixated on her exact coordinates. Beth was relentless, so proven by the *thirteen* text messages she'd gotten from her until Bee finally called her back.

"You have to tell them," Beth was saying now. Her tone was characteristically flat, although Bee could feel her ire radiating like a flame to her skin.

"I *will*," Bee insisted.

"When? You didn't tell me you were going to be gone, and we *work together*. I don't think Mom is going to settle for a text an hour after dessert is served."

Bee glared at the ceiling, trying not to feel so much like the chastised little sister, even as she wore the bunny slippers she'd bought as a pick-me-up at the airport. In fact, after having engaged in actual real physical labor with Knox, she'd showered and then decked herself out in her fluffiest pajamas, prepared for a peaceful, inactive evening of scrolling through Netflix until she was alerted to the alarming fact that her sister and Clover had met. No one should have to meet Beth on her bad days. She'd hardly recommend they meet her on a *good* day. Of course, Bee would be hard-pressed to know what days those were.

She sucked in a deep breath. Her sister wasn't awful. This was a natural response that Bee had fully been expecting. But *God,* she was just *so*—

"I will tell Mom and Dad tomorrow, Beth."

"Why not just call them now?"

"Because I'm busy. I have . . . things to do." *Like emotionally prepare myself.*

Beth didn't sound like she believed her. "Sure. Fine. I just need the purple dress for Ayana's Christmas Eve party."

"I know what dress you need; I already texted Clover that you'll stop by in the next day or two."

"Great, thanks."

"And it's Christmas *Eve* Eve, December twenty-third, so not actually—"

"I know, Beatrice. We've been going to this party for four years now."

"I know, *Bethy,* I was just making sure—"

"Is that seriously the most important thing we need to discuss right now?"

"What else do we possibly need to discuss?"

There was silence on the other end. Bee held her breath. She pictured Beth rolling her eyes and pursing her lips to the side. She imagined her sitting prim and proper in a smart black dress at her kitchen island in a high-rise in the Financial District, holding a cup of black coffee while she scrolled through the *Wall Street Journal* on her phone.

What was most disturbing about this picture was that Bee couldn't get complete details—everything was blurry and unfocused. Beth had moved somewhere new in the last few months, and while Bee had an address, she actually hadn't visited. She didn't know what Beth's kitchen looked like, let alone what her daily routine was. For all she knew, Beth was wearing footie pajamas and sipping sugary cereal from a bowl of Froot Loops while sitting in a hovel in the woods.

When they were kids, Bee and Beth used to tell each other everything. They'd do each other's homework, share in each other's chores, and if one of them forgot some task their parents had appointed her, they'd cover for each other. But as soon as high school hit, things got harder, more competitive. Maybe it was because their talents had become clearer. Beth was on a more clearly successful path, and Bee . . . well, Bee just fell behind. Beth became the hardworking, no-nonsense sister, and Bee was the flighty one. Period, end of story.

It had been their parents who insisted they work together, with their father's seed money of course, but Bee never felt like she was working with family. She was just a cog in a fucked-up machine.

The distance that grew between the two of them had bothered Bee for a long time, but it seemed like Beth preferred it that way. So, Bee stuck to the picture she had: Her sister, perfectly poised and utterly frustrating. Her sister, who was so much like their mother she wondered if *they* weren't actually twins.

"Nothing," Beth said finally. "I'll let you know if anything comes up with work, but the holidays are approaching, so I guess we're not completely fucked if you're gone for a while."

"Great," Bee said. "Thanks." Then, because there was something in her that wanted to salvage this conversation: "Feel free to borrow anything else you need for the party."

Beth let out a breathless laugh. "Bye, Beatrice."

"Bye, Bethy."

When they hung up, Bee felt her entire body relax. She slumped onto the bed and let her phone drop beside her. It was a crappy call, but not one of their worst. All in all, she would call that a win.

Now all she had to do was tell her parents and then cancel her phone plan. Har-har.

She could imagine the conversation with ease: *Bee, have you any idea how you've utterly disgraced the family?* She imagined a snooty British accent to mimic her mother, although her mother was from Chicago. Something that sounded like a Disney villainess seemed more appropriate.

She'd have to be much more delicate when she spoke to her parents. No shortness, snapping, or talking back. Nothing that would get her disowned, no matter what they said to provoke her. But of course she wouldn't do that anyway. She would never. Bee was a good girl, just like she was raised to be, and she was *responsible,* dammit. She took a vacation without telling anyone; it wasn't like she'd stolen trade secrets or made the stock market crash. At most, she was going to miss the family Christmas Eve dinner, *God forbid,* and Ayana's networking party.

They would all survive without her.

She sighed. Later. She would worry about it later. She reached over to the nightstand, grabbed a couple bobby pins, and pulled her hair into a loose bun atop her head. Then she took a deep breath and headed back downstairs, determined to enjoy a night without the voices of her family in her ears.

THE NEXT MORNING, she got ready without checking her phone even once. She had an entire day ahead of her in a sunny, snowy town completely absent of everyone she knew, and she was going to enjoy every goddamn minute of it.

Twenty minutes later she found herself walking down the staircase and heading toward the windows, where she pulled opened the curtains with a flourish that made her feel royal. She began to peruse Clover's collection of books, thinking that *this time* she might find the inspiration to read, when she heard someone singing the Temptations' rendition of "Rudolph the Red-Nosed Reindeer" just outside the window.

She peered outside and saw Jimmy hunched over in the brisk morning air, attempting to run after another mob of hungry chickens. She knew she should leave it alone—the man knew what he was doing, after all. Still, the idea of her sitting and reading while he worked outside didn't sit right with her.

Resolutely, she donned her thick red scarf and coat, marched past the kitchen to the foyer, and threw open the door, a blast of deep chill shuddering through her body. If she was this cold, she couldn't imagine how freezing Jimmy must be. She rubbed her gloved fingers together and crunched through the snow toward the chicken coop, where she saw Jimmy attempting to push Mabel away from a small group of chicks.

"Jimmy!" She didn't know why she had a scold in her voice. It was his home; he could do as he pleased.

"Well, good morning, Miss Bee," he said, straightening up stiffly, a deep smile adding to the wrinkles around his eyes. "What are you doin' up so early?"

"I could say the same to you," Bee said teasingly. "Aren't you freezing?"

"Nah, girl. I got long johns, a thermal shirt, and a vest under this coat. I'm doin' just dandy."

Oh. Bee felt a little sheepish. Of course he was better dressed than her for this kind of weather. Even so, she still had at least forty years on him. "Well, I'm glad to hear that, Jimmy. But listen, as your guest, I would absolutely love to learn more about the chickens and the coop. Will you show me how to feed them?"

Jimmy gave her a dubious look while Bee offered her most winning smile. Then he let out a heartwarming cackle and held out the green pail of chicken feed. Bee crossed over the little gate and took it from his hand, and the two of them spent the next fifteen minutes tending to the chickens as Jimmy explained who had first dibs, whom she had to keep an eye out for, how often he fed the chickens and around what time.

"It's really not too hard a job," he was saying now, after he'd told her where to put things away. They walked arm in arm back to the house, and Bee waited patiently as he took his time up the steps. Once inside, he led her to the kitchen and made her sit as he tended to the coffee. "Don't think I don't know what you're doing, young miss," he said, filling the kettle from the faucet and placing it on the oven burner. "I was an army man, you see. I know schemes and trickery when I see 'em!"

Bee put a delicate hand to her chest. "Schemes and trickery? I would never!"

"Uh-huh." Jimmy stared her down, but he couldn't fight the twinkle in his eyes. "You and my daughter, boy. Can't do nothin' with you gals around."

"Sounds like you've got a daughter that loves you very much."

"I sure do. Sure do." Jimmy nodded to himself. "A little too much, I think, sometimes. Though I guess change can do that to a person." He scratched the back of his ear and looked out the window to the front yard. "She used to love Christmas decorations, boy. Couldn't get enough of the lights and the music. Speaking of—do you mind?"

She gave her blessing as he wandered out of the kitchen, and a moment later, Bee could hear "The Little Drummer

Boy," by the Jackson 5, start to play. When Jimmy came back in, he was carrying what looked to be a photo album.

"Thought you might be interested in seeing some of the history of the house," he said.

Bee smiled, scooching over to give him space at the kitchen table. "This is my wife, Mae—short for Mabel," he said. "We were married for thirty-eight years. I was twenty-six; she was twenty-three." He pointed to a faded color photo of a young woman with short, soft pressed curls. It was clearly a staged photo, one of those glamour shots that used to be popular back in the day, but she looked stunning nonetheless, with a sweet smile and sparkling eyes.

"She's beautiful," Bee said.

"She really was," Jimmy said, and Bee's heart ached for him. He pointed to another photo. This time, Mae looked older, a little more tired—her hair was pulled back into a tight ponytail, and she was holding a pale crying baby in her arms. "That's Clover," Jimmy said. "She was white as a ghost when she was born. I looked at Mae so crazy those first few months." He chuckled to himself. "But that girl is mine, through and through. Stubborn, prideful, resourceful—sweet like her mama only if you ain't lookin'."

Bee looked at the photos wistfully, listening to Jimmy as he flipped through the photo book, sharing so much of his family with pride and joy. Though she smiled, she could feel the strain of the conversation tugging on the corners of her lips and the tears behind her eyes. If she thought hard, she imagined there might be some photos of her somewhere at her parents' house that weren't tied to graduations, to news-paper clippings, to award announcements, to evidence of her productivity or her value. She was sure she'd seen a few photos of her laughing, maybe her and Beth playing tag, at some point, before grades started being issued for their various intellectual performances.

Bee bit back her bitterness. It wasn't that she wasn't loved—she had it better than *a lot* of people, she knew that. She came from a family with a lot of money, and she made a lot of money (and she'd lost a lot of money, but she wouldn't think about that for now). At best, she had champagne problems. But it didn't stop her from thinking about her family's constant assessments: inquiring as to whether the dress she'd worn to the bimonthly family dinner was prop-erly pressed and from an appropriate designer; question-ing why she'd want Marley hair or Senegalese twists when she could afford the upkeep of a customized wig or pro-fessional sew-in with long, silky hair imported from Brazil. They inspected the whiteness of her teeth and the neatness of her manicured nails.

Bee was meant to be perfect, and she wasn't. She never would be. But that didn't stop her from trying.

The kettle sounded. Jimmy closed the photo album and stood up. "Milk and sugar?" he asked.

Bee acquiesced, not bothering to ask if he might have oat or soy or whatever. She wasn't vegan and a hint of lactose wouldn't kill her, even if she was intolerant. When he fin-ished preparing their pour-over coffee, he handed her a cute little mug shaped like a llama. Then he took a deep whiff of his black coffee. "Nothing like the smell of a good dark roast," he said with a sigh.

Bee took his cue to inhale. She liked the smell of coffee just fine, but there was something about having it here in this gorgeous country house with a gentleman who could be her father—well, not *her* father, given the warmth and gentleness—that made the scent even sweeter. In that moment, she decided to forget about her family. *I'm supposed to be relaxing,* she reminded herself. *I'm allowed to do that.* She accepted Jimmy's toast as he clinked his mug against hers and then watched as he wandered over to the love seat and sunk down deep with another satisfied sigh.

"You and my daughter," he mused to himself. "Can't do nothin' with you gals around. But don't you worry"—he wriggled deeper into his seat and leaned his head back, his fingers still wrapped around the handle of his mug—"Jimmy's still got some work in him yet. Don't you worry."

Within moments, Bee heard the unmistakable hum of the old man snoring. Quietly, she made her way to him and gently took the coffee from his fingers, placing the mug on the table beside him. Satisfied, she returned to her coffee and let herself sink into the sound of Jimmy's sleeping as she watched another bout of snow flurry past the kitchen window.

Chapter Ten

Clover

Wednesday afternoon, December 13, 2023

Clover stared at herself in the window of the piercing studio, her index finger gently brushing the brand-new stud on the right side of her nose. She hadn't thought she would actually do it—the idea had occurred to her briefly yesterday, when she'd gone thrifting, but she was never one to act on impulse. And yet, here she was. *Pierced!*

Of course, plenty of girls at home had piercings and some even had a few small tattoos, but it wasn't common, and often those girls had "history"—minor scandals whispered about in school halls or beyond church walls. Now that they were all reaching thirty, those scandals were hardly newsworthy, but they had nonetheless cemented them as different.

Clover wondered if that's what she was now. Different. *I didn't raise you that way,* she heard her mother's voice echo in her ear. She brushed it away with squared shoulders. She was here. She was doing this.

Back at the condo, she grabbed another coffee from Castro Cafécito, feeling a mixture of relief and disappointment when she didn't run into one particularly frustrating twin. Then she headed back up the elevator, where she saw that the flag on the little red mailbox outside her door was raised. She pulled down its door. Inside was a rolled-up flyer:

HOLIDAY MAKERS' MARKET
6 P.M. TO 10 P.M.
UNION SQUARE

"Oh, hey, you're home!" She heard Dee's voice behind her.

"Yeah." Clover smiled. There was something about her neighbor that felt warm and friendly. By her feet was the little escape artist who had united them the day before, panting lazily as Dee firmly gripped her leash.

"I tried to stop by earlier, but you were out—whoa!" Dee peered closer at Clover's face. "Is that new?"

Clover blushed and resisted the urge to touch her nose. "Yeah. Just got it a couple hours ago."

"Looks great!" Dee said. Then she leaned forward conspiratorially. "If you're also in the neighborhood for some new tattoos, I know a few people who can hook you up." She winked and leaned back. Clover chuckled softly.

"One change at a time, I think."

"Makes sense, makes sense. Sometimes I go a little hard when I'm into things." She pointed to her right shoulder. "After I got my first tattoo, I decided I should go ahead and get a full sleeve. Hurt like a bitch, but I loved it." Then she pointed to the flyer in Clover's hand. "Also! I passed that around weeks ago but wanted to give you a personal invite, since we're neighbors now. Leilani will be selling her wares there."

"Oh," Clover said. She felt guilty for having wanted to crumple the paper and toss it in the bin. If she remembered correctly, Bee had mentioned something about it in her emails, and Clover had been just as uninterested then as she was now. But her neighbor looked so earnest that Clover was willing to reconsider.

"No pressure, of course, but if you're looking for something fun to do tonight, might be worth it."

"Oh, it's tonight?" Clover peered more closely at the flyer. She'd been a little tired from the day's adventures—but one more event couldn't hurt. Besides, she liked Dee. She'd spent so much of her life with the same group of people. It was refreshing to make friends with someone new. Plus, her cousins would want some sort of souvenir from her trip, and she figured it might be nice to do *one* holiday thing while she was here. "Sure," she said finally. "I'll see you both there."

"Great!" Dee beamed at her. "Okay, I gotta get this one back inside," she said, nodding at the still-panting pit bull that was now lying down. "See you in a bit!"

Clover waved goodbye, and when she got inside, she looked at the small handful of bags she'd acquired from various thrift shops throughout the city that day. It probably wasn't much for someone who actually lived in these condos, but for Clover, it felt like a mix of fortune and promise.

Two days ago, she would've thrown on whatever was in her bags and hoped for the best. Hell, two days ago she wouldn't have even considered going back out with the sun so soon to set. But now? Well, now Clover was feeling a bit more bold.

And she had the clothes to match.

As darkness took hold of the city, she shrugged on her new leather jacket and disappeared among the streets and shops until she found herself in a cluster of dogs and strollers and outstretched hands holding steaming cups of something sweet, as folks caught up with friends and chatted up the vendors.

Holiday lights snaked through the trees that surrounded them and popped up as oversize reindeer and angels and a large menorah that was more than twice her height. Though certainly larger than the holiday markets in Salem, she was surprised nonetheless by the coziness she felt, here in a city she was certain anyone could disappear into and get lost.

Okay, so maybe she missed celebrating the holidays a *little* bit. As she traversed the rows of little shops, she could admit to feeling sort of warm and fuzzy and—holy shit, it cost *how much* for a sugar cookie? *One* cookie? What else did they want, the promise of her firstborn child?

Unable to contain her shock, Clover wandered deeper into the tent she'd glanced at, wondering if the chocolate was flecked with gold and the caramel-covered apples promised ever-lasting youth and glory.

"Are you okay?"

Clover looked up to find a tall Black person wearing a

yellow beanie and an oversize sweater vest with a grinning Grinch sewed onto it. They were standing behind the product table and staring at her with apparent concern.

"You look a little . . . pale," the person continued.

"Why are these so expensive?" she asked, noticing too late the touch of awe in her voice.

They laughed. "Um . . . well, it *is* San Francisco. I think our prices are pretty competitive with the other stuff you'll find here . . ."

Clover blushed at the directness of her question and took a step back, realizing that she had been hovering over the peanut butter–covered pretzels like Columbo trying to solve a mystery. "Sorry," she mumbled. "I'm visiting from Ohio, and I'm just not used to prices like these. Not that I think your stuff is *over*priced . . ."

"No worries." The person chuckled again. "The city is expensive. I actually live out by Fruitvale, across the way. It's a little cheaper, at least."

"Yeah," Clover said. "I've noticed it's a little expensive here. My budget's had to stay tight for me to feel like I'm having any fun."

"Well, here," the person said. "Have a cookie on me."

"Oh no, I couldn't."

"Please. It's the holiday spirit. Just do me one favor?"

Clover eyed them warily. "What's that?"

"Go ahead and check out the booth with the redhead. She's a friend, and she's selling some dope art."

"Redhead?" Clover figured there was more than one

redhead selling wares at the night market, but Dee *had* said her wife would be setting up shop tonight. "Her name wouldn't happen to be Leilani, would it?"

"Yeah! You know her?"

"No, not really. But, um, I met her wife yesterday. Dee? The condo I'm staying in is on the same floor as them."

"No way! Well, in that case, I'll walk you over. I'm Mo, by the way. They/them pronouns." They pointed to a brown-skinned South Asian woman with short, curly hair farther down the tables beneath their tent, who was packaging up some sweets for a customer. "That's Bailey, my girlfriend. She/her."

Clover shook their hand and then gave a little wave to Bailey, who'd looked up when she heard her name. "I'm Clover," she said. "Um, I use she."

"Dope," Mo said. They gave their girlfriend a kiss and then guided Clover through the web of tightly packed stalls and fairy lights. "How long you here for?"

"A couple weeks," Clover said.

"Visiting friends?"

"No."

"Family?"

"No." To their credit, Mo didn't seem fazed by Clover's short and increasingly antisocial responses. Still, Clover felt that things would get awkward real quick if she didn't offer any information of her own. "I thought it'd be good to take a vacation from my farm for a bit, on my own. Try some new things, see some new places. This is my first time in San Francisco."

"A farm?" Mo said. "Oh, you gotta meet my friend Gilly. She runs a farm outside the city—it supplies some of the bougie-ass restaurants around here, actually. Where is—Gilly!" Mo stopped at a booth full of colorfully clothed crocheted creatures and winked at Clover. "This is her side gig." Then they cupped their mouth and shouted toward an East Asian beanpole of a person wearing an elf's hat and green combat boots. "Hey, Gilly, this is Clover! She's from Ohio, and she's a farmer. She's visiting San Francisco for a few weeks!" The person Mo had called Gilly looked up and waved. She finished her transaction with two grinning teenagers who were now holding their crocheted gifts to their chests, then came over to greet Clover and Mo.

"It's Gillian, Mo, and hi, Clover. I'm Gillian. Pronounced exactly like I've said, with a *juh* sound, no matter what Mo says."

"Gillian," Mo said, so that the first syllable sounded like gills on a fish.

"I hate you."

"Hey, Clover," said a voice behind them, and Clover was a little relieved to see Dee.

"Hi," she said. She was surprised when Dee gave her a quick hug, but she returned it warmly, just before Mo pulled Dee into a headlock and rubbed the top of her spiky head.

"Happy holigaaaays," they sang merrily. "I was just about to show Clover to Leilani's booth."

"They wanted to stop and torture me first," Gillian deadpanned.

"You know it's your favorite kink," Mo said.

"Why are you like this?"

"Leilani's booth is actually pretty packed right now," Dee cut in, and Clover was once again thankful for the interruption. It wasn't that she didn't like Dee's friends—quite the opposite, in fact. They were just so . . . *different* from her own back at home. It was taking her a moment to adjust.

"Packed how?" Gillian asked.

"One of the tech companies here has a setup right next to Lei's table. I guess they're trying to do a holiday promotion or whatever."

"Gross. Can we get no peace even at Christmas?" Mo sighed dramatically.

"I'm sorry my people cause you so much suffering," Dee said, rolling her eyes.

"You work in tech?" Clover asked.

"Yeah, most of the people in our building probably do, to be honest. Though not all at the same company. We can still head over to Leilani's booth, though. The tech folks have free hot cider."

"I *guess* I'm in," Mo muttered.

"I was talking to Clover," Dee responded, while Mo covered their heart and pretended to die.

"O-kay," Gillian said. "Well, I've got to man the station here, but you three have fun. It was nice to meet you, Clover."

Clover barely had time to say, "You too!" before Mo and Dee had ushered her back through the market, toward what was indeed a pretty large and imposing crowd. People were whispering and pushing their phones ever higher. From what Clover could see, they were all standing around trying to get photos of some white man in a full red Santa suit, complete with the white beard. Even the adults were enthusiastic.

"It's some internet personality," Dee explained. "In partnership with Vacate."

"Oh!" Clover said. "That's the app I used."

"Makes sense," Dee said, just as Mo shouted, *"Make way! Make way! Lesbians coming through."*

"Why are they like this?" Dee muttered, echoing Gillian, though Clover could see a hint of a grin on her face even as her own heart stammered in her chest. She wasn't used to being in a group as . . . well, "loud and proud" as this. With a bit more poking and prodding, they were able to make their way through to Leilani's booth. It managed to still have a few customers, despite the attention the Vacate booth was taking up.

As Dee went to greet her wife, and Mo went to body slam her or whatever their greeting of choice would be, Clover noticed that one of Leilani's patrons seemed awfully familiar.

"Oh, it's you," the woman said as she turned in Clover's direction. Perfect bob, dark brown eyes, an impossibly sultry voice—

Stop it! Clover chastised herself, certain that her brown cheeks were a bright shade of red as Beth quirked an eyebrow at her.

"What are you doing here?" Beth continued.

"I'm . . . shopping," Clover responded. "For the holidays." What the hell else would she be doing there?

"You look different," Beth said. She tilted her head to the side. "Did you get a nose piercing?"

Clover swallowed. She didn't know why it bothered her that Beth seemed so perceptive. Dee had noticed too. Still, she felt defensive or . . . something else she couldn't place. She touched her fingers lightly to her nose. "I'm not sure how I feel about it yet," she said.

Beth didn't respond, her attention back on a collaged painting of a Black woman with long black braids draped in royal purple. "How much for this?" she asked Leilani.

"The print is a hundred," Leilani answered. "Six hundred for the original."

Beth looked back over at Clover, studying her for a moment and in a way that made Clover feel as if she were the painting Beth was considering. She couldn't help but hold her breath as Beth's dark eyes swept over her. "What do you think?"

Clover forced herself to look at the painting, though pulling her gaze from Beth was a task she hated to admit was difficult. "It's stunning," she said. She gave Leilani a genuine smile. "Truly."

"I'll think about it," Beth said to Leilani. Then, without another word to Clover, she turned and walk away. Clover wondered at her severely underdeveloped social skills. Still, she couldn't help watching her leave.

"Are you enjoying the market?" Leilani asked her, as Beth walked straight up to the internet Santa at the Vacate booth next door and shook his hand, then continued to greet and chat up the other important-looking people at the booth. Though she wasn't in business attire this evening, she still looked so remarkably put together: a stylish little brown bag, black boots, black jeans that fit her snugly, and a long black trench coat over a low-cut red tee that hugged her curves. Beth might have been hard to talk to, but dammit if she wasn't easy to look at.

"Clover?" Leilani asked again, and Clover realized that she hadn't answered.

"Yes," she squeaked.

Leilani chuckled and looked toward Beth. "She's the one who doesn't live on our floor, right?" she asked Dee.

"Correct. The twin," Dee confirmed. Then she winked at Clover. "Neither of them is hard on the eyes."

To Clover's surprise, Mo didn't say anything. Instead, they grinned ear to ear and gave Clover a huge thumbs-up. Somehow that was way worse. "I'll take you over there," Mo offered suddenly, and before Clover could think to protest, she was being shuffled along to the Vacate booth, past a line of agitated-looking fans. "Hey! You're Beth, right?" Mo asked without preamble.

The cup of cider in Beth's hand paused at her lips. "Excuse me," she said to the reindeer-dressed Latino she'd been speaking to. "Yes," she said, turning fully to Mo. "And you are?"

"Mo!" They stuck out their hand, and Beth shook it with a tight smile. "This is Clover, you two met earlier, at my friend's wife's art booth. She's staying in your sister's Vacate."

"*You're* Clover?" someone shouted from behind them. Another Black woman with long locs appeared, wearing a silver dress and dangling gold earrings. "I'm Ayana, Bee's friend. Do you hug?"

Did she hug? It wasn't really a question people asked her, but she supposed she wasn't opposed to it. "Sure," she barely managed to say before Ayana pulled her in with a strong grip around her waist. It honestly made Clover blush, which was horrifying, because Beth was now looking at her with what seemed to be . . . a smirk? Clover had yet to see anything resembling a smile on Beth's lips. She wasn't sure how she felt about that.

"I am so glad you're here," Ayana was saying. "I hadn't had a chance to reach out yet, but I was planning to check in with you since—"

"She owns the app," Beth finished dryly.

"*Since* you're staying at my best friend's house and you're new to the city." Ayana shot Beth a playful glare, and Beth just shrugged and sipped her cider.

"Ayana loves strangers," Beth muttered. "Hence the app."

"Ignore her," Ayana said with a sigh. "A few of us were actually just about to sneak over to the ice rink they've set up near the menorah. Would you like to join us?"

Without meaning to, Clover looked at Beth, whose perfectly sculpted eyebrow was lifted in appraisal. She was clearly amused by Clover's discomfort and curious to see what would happen next. That was interesting, Clover thought. Was Beth the type of person who reveled in *other* people's social awkwardness? If so, did that make her callous? Did Clover care?

Ugh, Beth was frustrating, and Clover didn't even know why it bothered her so much.

"I'm okay," Clover said, just as Mo said, "We'd love to!"

Clover widened her eyes at Mo, who just shrugged and

winked. Then they bent toward Clover and whispered, "Actually, I gotta get back to my booth. But I'll send Dee over to chaperone!"

"I don't need a chaperone," Clover whispered back, but it was too late. Mo was already jogging back toward Leilani and Dee, turning only once to give Clover an overenthusiastic thumbs-up.

"Old friend?" Beth asked, and Clover's heart nearly stopped. She didn't realize she was so close to her.

"Um, no. New, actually. I just met them tonight."

"Ah." Beth nodded thoughtfully. "They seem a bit much."

At this, Clover bristled and stood up a bit straighter. "I actually think they're great."

Thankfully, Ayana returned from wherever she'd disappeared to, just in time to pop a warm cider into Clover's hand and begin ushering her and Beth out of the booth, while a few other colleagues followed suit. "Santa Claus is covered and my wife is already over by the menorah, snagging one of the tables for those of us who don't know how to skate. Let's go!"

Before she knew it, Clover was pushed through the crowd again, surrounded by yet another new group of people. When they reached the table and took their seats, Ayana introduced her to her wife and colleagues. It was fine, Clover supposed, but she really hoped Dee was actually coming. Of everyone she'd met over the past two days, Dee felt the least like a stranger, and she could really use a friend to keep her from stumbling over her words, especially in front of Beth.

Not that it mattered, really, since Beth was back on her

phone, scrolling or texting or sending emails to important clients.

"Clover, I grabbed you a seven and an eight, if those seem right?" Ayana asked, now laced into her own pair of rental ice skates as she held up two pairs for Clover to examine. "Do you know how to skate?"

"A little," Clover said, though that wasn't entirely true. She'd grown up amid snow and lakes of ice her entire life, and ice-skating had once been one of her favorite winter pastimes, next to sitting outside the house with her family and Knox, and laughing with the neighbors.

"I can show you," Beth said, though her tone sounded as flat as usual, as if she'd already decided that Clover was going to need a lot of help. Clover pushed her tongue into her cheek and gently plucked one of the pairs from Ayana's hand.

"I'm fine," she said. "Thanks." She was still feeling defensive about Beth's remarks about Mo and didn't feel the need to spend more time with her than was necessary, no matter how hot she was or how good she imagined Beth would smell if she was pressed up against her. *Keep it together, Clover!*

She followed Ayana and her fellow Vacate colleagues onto the rink, and smiled as more than a few people stuck to the sides or tried out their footing like baby giraffes on long legs. Idly, she began to skate backward, making long, smooth strides on the ice.

"Whoa," Dee shouted as she and Leilani finally appeared, both skating wobblingly toward her on their rental skates. "You're a natural."

Clover blushed and shook her head, happy to see that her new friends had come to join her. "It's nothing," she said.

"You're joking," Ayana said from behind her. "*I* definitely can't skate backward. Not without falling on my ass. What else are you keeping from us, Miss Ohio?"

Clover looked around at her small audience, and as she did, she caught Beth's eyes—just for a moment, before she glanced away, slowly and methodically lacing up her skates. *Well,* Clover thought, *if the people want a show . . .*

She pushed her heel backward and spun into a wide circle, before coming back to its center and spinning into a tight twirl like a ballerina. Then she pushed her arms out in front as she floated backward again, her back leg lifted into the air, just like her mom had taught her. Of course, Mae Mills didn't have any professional ice-skating experience herself; she'd merely learned from YouTube videos and hours of detailed review of the Winter Olympics, as a tiny toddler Clover hopped up and down, begging her mom to teach her how to do what the princesses did on TV. Since Mae didn't know, she learned it herself and then taught it to Clover, spending hours on the ice after farm duties were done, before dinner, and between homework, until Clover felt as beautiful and powerful as any princess.

That's my baby, her mom would shout from the sidelines. *I taught her that!*

Suddenly, Clover felt her leg slip. Her vision blurred as tears struck the corners of her eyes, and all at once, she felt her body tip backward, her arms flailing.

Just as she thought her little show would come to a terrifying end, she felt strong hands grab her waist and her back pressed against a woman's chest, a sweet scent of jasmine bringing her back to reality. "I've got you," Beth's warm voice murmured in her ear. Her hands held tightly to Clover's waist. "Are you okay?"

Clover willed herself to breathe, but she couldn't remember how to. Her heart was fluttering in her chest. "Yes," she managed to croak out.

"Good." Beth made sure Clover was steady on her feet and then crossed in front of her. "Here," she said, holding out her hands. Clover grabbed them, and Beth pulled her forward, keeping her eyes on Clover as she guided her back to the sidelines. Clover had never had the mere touch of someone's hands make her vision change, and she was tempted to blame it on the sudden panic attack she'd just experienced. But she had to admit, seeing Beth's bright brown eyes stuck on hers, brow furrowed in concern and concentration, was not helping her feel any more calm or centered. It was, however, making her feel warm, and safe, and utterly, disastrously confused. She struggled for something to say to break the spell, though her heart screamed at her not to. "I . . ." she started. "I'm sorry."

"Why?" Beth asked.

"I don't know." She blew out a breath and then laughed, finally breaking eye contact. "Thank you. For catching me."

For the first time ever in recorded history, Beth seemed to get shy. "I saw you lose your balance," she said with a shrug.

"Were you watching me?" Clover had meant it as a joke, but Beth's silence made her heart race. *Why would she be watching me?* Clover was a decent skater, but she wasn't *that* good. Unless Beth was looking at her for a different reason, but that couldn't be . . .

Her thoughts were cleared with the sudden appearance of a water bottle in her face as Dee, Leilani, and Ayana surrounded her, peppering her with questions about if she was feeling hot, or cold, or tired, or hungry. When they were finally convinced that she wasn't on the brink of death, she looked up to see that Beth had moved away, making small talk with a few of Ayana's colleagues, who had come off the ice to congratulate her on her quick reaction.

Soon her friends returned to their normal friendly banter, and Clover willed herself to listen, and to respond, and to enjoy the company of these new people who seemed so eager to share themselves with her and invest in her well-being. They were kind, clearly, and full of so much life. A kind of life, perhaps, that she'd never allowed herself to consider. So, she *did* listen—absolutely. And if her gaze sometimes wandered back over to Beth, who, sometimes, maybe on accident, seemed to look back at her, Clover's new friends were kind enough to pretend not to notice.

Chapter Eleven

Bee

Thursday morning, December 14, 2023

Now that she'd gotten the hang of driving through the streets of this small little town, Bee felt marginally more confident that she wouldn't die in a snowbank. In the light of a brighter morning, she could better see the neighbors' houses—their imposing sizes, their huge front yards, their aging paneling and chipped fences, and the tire swings and dog toys that suggested rich and busy family lives.

Bee had traveled a lot in her life, though less so with the demands of her business. Still, aside from college, she'd actually never stayed anywhere more than a week or so, if that. It was strange, sinking so fully into a life so unlike the one she was used to living—and one where so many people seemed content to stay.

The day before, she'd asked Jimmy about the notches in the kitchen wall that had marked Clover's height, and he was all too happy to tell stories about his little girl growing up, and scraping her knees, and scorching brand-new pots. She'd lived in that house all her life, until now, and even Knox had spent half his life on that farm. Meanwhile, the moment both she and Beth turned eighteen, they were nearly crawling out of their skins with desperation to leave home.

She was sure she was romanticizing things—everyone had their struggles. But for her, right now, the loyalty of her swapmate and those around her made Bee curious. She was eager to explore more about what it might mean to be satisfied, instead of constantly striving for more, better, shinier.

What did it mean to feel content?

Jimmy too had lived in Salem his whole life, and to hear him tell it, a contented life started with a full stomach. "It's like knowing where you're going to get your next meal," he'd said. "If you're not constantly searching, full of fear and anxiety, you can focus on what you've got in front of you."

"So, if I have DoorDash ready to go at all times, I'll reach nirvana?" Bee had quipped.

Jimmy had laughed. "I reckon it's less expensive to know how to cook a thing or two yourself. You know that saying: If you give a man a fish, he'll eat for a day. If you teach a man to fish, he'll—"

"Eat for a lifetime," Bee chimed in.

"Exactly."

"Too bad I don't know how to cook."

"Oh, well, Miss Bee," Jimmy had answered with a gleam in his eye. "We can fix that right here and now."

Though she insisted she was still too tired and jet-lagged

to attempt anything more than a Hot Pocket, Bee promised Jimmy she'd think about a cooking lesson or two before she left. Then he'd invited her to a game of cards, and before she knew it, the afternoon became early evening. She found herself disappointed when he retired to the apartment below the Big House, and for the first time in nearly a decade, Bee found herself missing her parents.

But despite her promise to Beth, she didn't call them.

Not last night and not this morning, but today. She would call them today.

But first, she had errands to run. Real ones this time.

The mom-and-pop market Jimmy had recommended to her the night before was nestled between an old movie theater and a little café that boasted brunch and artisan coffee. Bee made note of the coffee shop immediately. You could take the girl out of San Francisco, but . . . What she wouldn't give for an overpriced latte.

She parked and headed into the grocery store, immediately taken with the cozy decor and the little pictures of the family who apparently owned the place, all smiling faces cuddled in close with various farm animals.

"We like to share a bit of family pride here," an older gentleman with a dark green apron said with a chuckle.

Bee ducked her head, embarrassed to be caught staring like some sort of tourist, but the man came over to her jovially, deep creases in his white, weather-worn skin and reindeer antlers atop his thinning white hair. "I'm Bob," he said, offering his hand. "Technically, I own the place, but don't tell my wife." He laughed happily and then gestured to the store. "If there's anything I can help you with, don't hesitate to ask. We got everything you need here, short of, I guess, furniture. And tools. And maybe if you needed, I don't know, really highbrow literature. Hmm. Maybe we don't have everything. But we got enough! Unless you're hankering for a particular strip of beef . . . We're not really a butcher." He shook himself out of his mutterings and then beamed at Bee again. "Well, hey! If you need it, we probably have some of it. No, that's a terrible pitch . . ."

He wandered off, and Bee stared after him, feeling both charmed and confused. She reached into her pocket and pulled out her phone, double-checking the recipe she'd researched that morning. She wanted to surprise Jimmy soon—proof that she'd been listening to his sage advice.

Still, as she wandered the aisles and tried to parse the different brands and labels, she wondered if she hadn't bitten off more than she could chew. The recipe—a chicken stew—had *seemed* easy enough, but given that she was having trouble telling the difference between parsley and chives, she realized that she was maybe a little less up to the task than she'd suspected. It was a feeling she had grown a little too used to these days, and she *really* didn't like it.

Before she allowed herself to sink into an anxiety spiral, she put the phone away and tried to focus on what was in front of her. Was there anything she already knew how to make? That pie crust seemed appealing—how hard was it to bake a pie? She considered it, but didn't trust herself with the science of baking. Maybe a side soup was more manageable. Her sister was a decent enough cook; maybe she'd deign to answer a text from Bee that wasn't about work, or their parents, or the stuff of nightmares.

Or maybe not. Best not to tempt fate.

As she thought through the options of what a multiverse version of herself might concoct on her own, she found Bob again, this time sweeping the floor of the pasta and beans aisle. "Hi," he said, as if genuinely happy to see her again. "Oh, hey, what do you think about this: 'If you need it, we want you to have it.'" Bee couldn't stop the laugh that escaped her lips, and Bob sighed in defeat. "I'm not very good at this slogan business."

Bee thought for a minute. "What about . . . 'Your first stop when you need to shop.'"

Bob's eyes widened. "Hey," he said. "Hey, that's pretty good!" He muttered it to himself a few more times, emphasizing each word differently.

"Thanks," Bee said, although she thought it could still use some work. "Speaking of needs, I'm thinking about making . . . a dish. Of some sort. I'm not much of a cook, but thought I'd make something for the family I'm staying with."

"Oh, that's easy." Bob grabbed two cans of red beans and handed them to her. "You ever made chili?"

"No."

"Well, it's about the easiest thing you can imagine, and it only takes two pots—one for rice and one for the chili. Easy peasy." He gave her a quick recipe, pointing out what she needed in that aisle and directing her where she'd find the rest. "Oh, what family are you staying with?" he asked, just as she thanked him and returned to her ingredient-finding quest. "I know pretty much all the locals here."

"Do you know Jimmy and Clover Mills?"

"Oh," Bob said quietly. "Knox's girl."

Bee smiled politely as Bob shook his head.

"Terrible thing, them losing Mae like that. We get our eggs and chickens from them, but after Mae passed away, well . . ." He sighed. "Let's just say some of the conversation has dried up. Seems to be all business these days; the Mills girl ain't much for talkin'. I hope they're doin' all right. It used to be the highlight of our Christmas to head on down to their annual party and just catch up with everyone, you know, all the locals and the other businesses here. We were a tightknit group, I'd say. Haven't heard from them in a while, though, aside from when they stop by to make their purchases."

He bowed his head for a moment, and Bee let the silence hang. Then he cleared his throat and gestured to Bee's shopping cart.

"Since you're a friend of the family, I'll give you a nice discount, okay? And anything you need, you just let ol' Bob know. I'm here to help." He pulled her into a tight hug and then walked away shaking his head sadly.

Once again, Bee felt dazed, but her heart was full. If the rest of the locals here were anything like Bob, this was a town that loved fiercely—they took care of their own. It wasn't often Bee got to feel so enveloped in such warmth, and what a shock it was to experience it in such a small, unassuming place, amid the brisk winter winds.

As promised, Bob gave Bee a hefty discount that she

felt guilty for accepting. Then he pushed an entire roasted chicken and two bottles of white wine into her arms, before letting her go with a pat on the shoulder and a request that she give the Millses his and his wife Jean's love.

After dropping off the groceries in her rental car, she locked the door and scurried quickly into the coffee shop next door, her tongue already tasting the hundreds of calories in her extra-sweet vanilla latte. A white barista with blond hair wrapped in a stylish bun greeted her from the cash register, while two burly-looking young white men stood behind her, pouring various coffees and syrups into paper cups. There was a short line ahead of her, but Bee didn't mind the wait. Like the grocery store next door, the decorations inside here were warm and inviting, like a small mountain lodge scented with roasted coffee beans and freshly made paninis.

To the right of the coffee bar were several small tables; students seemed to huddle together over some, catching up on their winter readings, while others lounged in front of the fireplace, chatting animatedly with their friends and partners.

"At least it gives other businesses an opportunity to try new things," the Black man in front of her said with a shrug. "I'm looking forward to seeing the talent show here."

"Yeah," the white woman with him said with a sigh. "I mean, that party was just so majestic, though, with all the little decorations and that gorgeous house. And the farm's owner was such a sweet lady too. But yeah, at least there will be a little something to participate in this year."

"Don't sound so disappointed," the man teased.

"I grew up watching the chorus sing while everyone laughed and mingled. It's just sad that the first year I'm actually *part* of the chorus, the whole tradition has changed."

Bee listened with interest—this was the second time she was hearing about a beloved local Christmas party getting canceled, and it seemed unlikely that they weren't talking about the same special house she was currently staying in.

She watched as the couple took their coffee and scones and joined another group of people seated around the stone hearth on floor pillows. She realized upon closer examination that she recognized a few people—they must all be from the chorus she'd heard a few nights before.

The memory of the neighbors all outside, singing together, made her little city-girl heart grow two sizes. Once she received her coffee order, she found a spot near them, wondering if she'd learn more about the house she was staying in, or perhaps their enthusiasm for creative expression would rub off on her. Either one would suffice.

"So," the woman from the line began, and Bee leaned in, sensing from her tone that she'd hear some *chisme*, as Ayana would say. "How are you and *Knox*?"

The blonde to whom the woman had spoken flipped her curls coyly and sipped her coffee. "I don't think it's any of your business, Lacey."

"Stop torturing us and tell us the details, Taylor!" another woman, South Asian and smiling brightly, chimed in. "How'd the date go?"

Bee bit her lip. This wasn't exactly what she was hoping to hear, but, as they say, be careful what you wish for.

"I . . . I don't know," Taylor said. She huffed and leaned back on her pillow. "I don't know if he knew it was a date."

"What do you mean?" Lacey asked.

"He was just so . . . *nice*. The whole time we were together, he was . . . distant. Kind, as always, funny, as always, but he didn't, like, try anything. It felt like we were just . . . hanging out."

Bee tried to stifle her satisfaction with a sip of her latte, then chastised herself. *You don't care,* she lied to herself. Badly.

The man from the line spoke up. "Do you think he's still hung up on Clover?"

At the mention of her name, the group went quiet. Then Lacey spoke up. "They *had* been together since we were kids. That's, like, most of all our lives."

"And I adore Clover," the South Asian woman said now, speaking with a gentleness Bee couldn't identify as genuine or not. "But she left him kind of suddenly. Maybe he's just taking things slow for now."

"Or playing the field," the man said, and Lacey smacked him lightly on the shoulder.

"He's not *you*," she scolded, and he wrapped an arm around her waist.

"Aw, babe. You know I only have eyes for you now."

"Took you long enough," she muttered.

"We've been together for, like, four years," he said.

"And I asked you out in eighth grade!"

"Well, I hope Knox doesn't make me wait that long." Taylor sighed dramatically, and the group she was with laughed.

Bee wished she felt just as merry, but her heart was starting to ache. Not only was Knox currently taken, but he had previously been taken by her swap-mate. In her mind, that made him permanently off-limits.

Just as she considered getting up and leaving, her phone buzzed. She was thankful to see a friendly face pop up on the screen.

"Hey, A," she said with a sigh.

"Hey, B!" Ayana answered. "Why do you sound so miserable? Ohio too cold for you?"

"No," Bee said. She didn't want to admit that she was feeling sad over a boy she'd known for eight seconds, so instead she came up with the next best answer. "I'm planning to tell my parents tonight that I'm out of town."

"Oof," Ayana said. "Good luck."

"Thanks. What's up?"

"Just wanted to thank you for suggesting that YouTube celebrity to me a few months ago. Our booth at the holiday market was the belle of the ball."

"I'm sure the free swag didn't hurt."

"Probably. I saw your sister too. She came over and schmoozed with us for a bit."

"Did she curse you out for convincing me to use your app to skip town?"

"She probably did in her head, but no, she kept it classy—didn't say a word about you."

Somehow that actually made Bee feel worse. "Great," she said. "Well, I'm glad the event went well. Sorry to miss the next one too."

"No, you're not," Ayana said.

Bee laughed. "I'm not, no. All things considered, I'm actually enjoying myself here in the snow. There are cows and chickens and thousands of miles between me and my family, and most of my clients. It's a good holiday so far."

"Good! Glad to hear it. Oh! I almost forgot—I met Clover yesterday too. Nice girl! Beth saved her from almost dying."

"She what?!"

"Clover almost fell on the ice at the skate rink, but all good. No concussions."

Bee couldn't resist rolling her eyes. Her sister always swooped in to save the day. "Well, that's good," she said. "Thank her for me."

"Done and done. Anyway, I was just calling to check in on you and thank you again for your help. You know to call me if you need anything." As they said their goodbyes, Bee realized how much lighter she felt.

Once again, Ayana had put things in perspective for her, albeit unknowingly. Bee had meant what she said—she *was* enjoying herself here in Salem. One boy's taken heart wasn't going to change that. Even so, she knew that if she was really going to relax, she'd have to stop putting off the one call she'd been avoiding since she got there.

She pulled up her mom's name, feeling her heart beat faster with every ring.

Just when she hoped that the heavens were smiling down on her, her mom picked up. "Hi, Beatrice. What do you need?"

"Hi, Mama," Bee said. "I wanted to tell you something."

Chapter Twelve

Clover

Thursday morning, December 14, 2023

The caller ID displayed a number she didn't recognize, but Clover had already pulled herself out of bed. Preemptively annoyed, she cleared the sleep from her voice and answered with a deep and hopefully menacing voice. "Hello?"

"Hello?" the caller responded, and Clover thought she could recognize the unnecessarily dry huffiness. "Is this Clover?"

"Who's calling?" Clover asked, suddenly feeling shy.

"This is Bethany, Bee's sister. We met the other day."

Clover ignored the rapid beating of her heart and threw herself back onto the bed. "Hi, yes," she said. "I remember you saving me from sudden death."

She thought she could hear Beth smile, even on the phone. "Something like that," Beth said. "Bee said it would be all right if I stopped by. Did she let you know?"

"Yeah," Clover responded, though honestly, Bee could've

told her a marching band was scheduled to perform in the living room, and she wasn't sure she'd remember. A lot had happened over the past three days.

"Great. I'm almost there. I should be up in about ten minutes."

You have got to be kidding me. "Sure thing," she said, and then groaned out loud when the line cut out. Ten minutes— that was barely enough time to fix her hair, let alone find something halfway decent to wear.

Not that she *needed* to look halfway decent. She didn't care what Beth saw her in—not really. It's just that, well, Beth was so put together. Clover didn't want to appear like she was a slob in comparison, or worse—just some girl from a farm in the middle of nowhere. That was all. *Well, at the very least, I can brush my teeth,* she told herself. She rolled out of bed and made her way to the bathroom. When she was done, she fluffed out her hair and examined her outfit. She was in a white tank top and a loose pair of black sleep shorts that were . . . well, they weren't *that* short—if she stayed like that, would it be inappropriate? Too risqué? Maybe risqué was the right vibe today.

What am I even thinking? she scolded herself. She took a few more minutes looking in the mirror, then decided that she didn't want Beth to think she'd been waiting for her. She turned on the TV in Bee's apartment for the first time since she'd arrived and quickly flicked through the streaming options. *The Best Man Holiday* jumped out at her, and Clover tossed the remote down triumphantly. It was her favorite movie, and the perfect distraction for when Beth's intimidating presence filled the room.

A second later, there was a knock at the door. *Damn*, she thought, and quickly double-checked the mirror to make sure there wasn't anything stuck in her teeth. Then she strode over to the door with a frighteningly giddy sense of anticipation.

Unsurprisingly, Beth was wearing another glamorous outfit, this time a deep purple blouse over a fitted pencil skirt. Gold studs sparkled from beneath her chic bob, and when she looked at Clover's morning attire, her eyes seemed to widen. Clover leaned against the door and tried for a casual smile that didn't reveal her nerves. "Hi," she said.

"You don't have work?" Beth asked, and Clover tried not to slam the door in her face.

"I'm on vacation," she said. "Which is . . . why I'm here."

As usual, Beth didn't respond. She had turned her attention back to her phone, and then she took a step forward.

"Yes, please do come in," Clover said, her sarcasm hardly masked. She sat heavily on the bed as Beth's heels clicked against the hardwood floor toward Bee's closet. Clover allowed herself just one second to follow the seam trailing up Bee's tights through the slit of her skirt, before mentally smacking herself upside the head and doing the one thing she never did: grab her phone to distract herself.

"Oh," she muttered.

Beth turned to look at her, her fingers lingering on the fabric of a purple dress. Clover didn't know why she cared, as she clearly wasn't talking to her, but Beth seemed to be waiting nonetheless.

"My . . . friends texted me. The ones I met yesterday. They invited me out tonight."

"You're going out with people you just met?" Beth asked, an eyebrow raised. "Is that what you're going in?"

"No," Clover managed through a tight smile. "They just texted me." She gestured to her bag on the floor. "I'm sure I have . . . something to go out in. I think. Although I didn't really plan *to* go out." She mumbled this last part to herself, now staring hard at her luggage and thinking through the potentiality of her outfits. She'd bought a couple of nice shirts and that dress from the thrift shop . . .

"You can wear Bee's clothes," Beth offered casually.

"I'm pretty sure that's against the rules of my stay here."

"Half of them are mine anyway." Beth sighed as if Clover were the one imposing ridiculous suggestions on her. She paused and glanced at the TV. "You like that movie?"

Clover frowned. "What's wrong with it?"

"Nothing," Beth said. "It's not exactly my favorite."

"It's a classic," Clover asserted.

"Even when all the men lip sync to New Edition for some strange reason?"

"*Especially* then."

Beth chuckled and turned back to Bee's closet. "Got it," she said. Then, much more quietly, she said, "You're cute," and it was so low, Clover would've sworn she was hearing things. Maybe she was. She wasn't really sure what to say in response, so she just sat there, on the bed, while Beth spent the next few moments flicking through coats and dresses. Then she pulled out three options and laid them on the bed, all without putting down the dress she'd come for. "These will fit you, I think, and they're pretty cute. Feel free to grab any of the coats. Bee won't care. It gets cold here at night."

"I—thank you?" Clover could barely hold her surprise, though Beth was already walking out of the apartment. "Bye?"

But Beth had gone, leaving three expensive-seeming cocktail dresses and a bewildered young woman in semi-risqué pajamas in her wake.

THOUGH THE OUTFITS Beth had suggested were all well and good, Clover could dress herself, thank you very much. In the dress she'd bought earlier that week, with hoop earrings she already owned, Clover stepped into the cool night air, an electric feeling already thrumming in her skin.

She hadn't been out on the town in a very long time. Visiting tourist attractions and holiday markets was all well and good, but it was something else entirely to be dolled up with a group of friends. And while, yes, they were all people she'd only just met, Clover felt oddly comfortable with them. They felt like a different sort of home.

When Clover entered the swanky, brightly lit one-room restaurant, it didn't take long to find Dee and Leilani, who were with Gillian, the crochet vendor she'd met the night before. They were seated around the little bar carved out in the middle, with a familiar face at the center.

"You made it," Mo said as they twirled two bottles of liquor in both hands and then took turns pouring them in a neat row of glasses. Dee and Leilani pulled Clover into one warm hug after another, while Gillian reached out and shook her hand. Mo reached over last, their tall frame bent nearly in half over the bar.

"Yeah," Clover said, sounding as surprised as she felt. "I guess I did. Thank you for inviting me."

"Our pleasure. It's only, like, your fourth night here, right? Figured you'd want to visit the hippest bar in the city," Dee said, gesturing to the finely dressed people all around them. It seemed to be an all-ages crowd, from college kids clearly on their first date behind them to an elderly group of friends having a raucous ball somewhere to their left.

"Is . . . this your bar?" Clover asked Mo, after they'd handed water glasses to a new set of patrons who'd just sat down.

"Nah," Mo said. "Just my night gig. My friend runs the place, though. She just got back from out of town, so she's busier than usual tonight."

"I'm her supplier," Gillian chimed in. "For the vegetables and stuff, anyway."

"Oh, right," Clover said. "You're a farmer too." That was sort of nice, actually, to meet someone in her line of work in a city so different from her own. She wanted to ask Gillian how she liked it, but she was distracted by Leilani whispering something into Dee's ear. Dee pulled away to look into Leilani's eyes, and then they rubbed their noses against each other, like lovers in their honeymoon stage.

"Gross," Mo cut in, slamming a shot glass down in front of them. "Get a room." They winked at Clover, who found herself blushing—although she wasn't sure why. She was used to couples being cute. Up until a year ago, she and Knox had been just such a couple, the one everyone had said would last until old age and beyond. In that moment, Clover felt a tug of sadness, her fondness for the man who'd once been her fiancé grasping at her heartstrings and threatening to thrust her back down memory lane.

"How'd you two meet?" Clover asked instead, but Mo shook their head, lifted the shot glass in their hand, and nodded to the ones they'd put in front of Clover, Dee, Gillian, and Leilani.

"Shots first, personal questions next—unless you don't drink, in which case I apologize for the temptation."

"I drink." Clover laughed. "Trust me."

They said cheers to that, and then Dee and Leilani launched into their love story, which involved lust at first sight across a crowded lesbian bar in the heart of Oakland. "We'll have to take you there," Leilani promised, as Dee nuzzled her ear and the two giggled into their drinks. Mo took Clover's order, while Gillian then shared her version of events, which included Dee crying at her apartment at four a.m. over a personal pizza because her ex had posted something searing on Instagram.

Lei cut in to include an anecdote about pet-sitting and morning bagels at the local queer café, which then tied into how Mo had run into *their* ex who'd just started working there. By the time everyone's food had arrived, Clover felt as if she'd learned everyone's romantic history, which felt far messier and more exciting than her own.

"What about you?" Gillian asked between bites of her dinner. "You got someone back home waiting for you?"

"Or excruciating details we can trauma-bond over?" Mo

shouted as they shook a tumbler of liquor and crushed ice for a couple beside them.

"Well," Clover said, "I broke up with my fiancé at the end of last November and then my mom died a week later."

The four of them went silent, looking at her and then exchanging looks with one another. Then Dee pulled her into a bone-crushing hug, and Gillian called out, "More drinks! Unless you don't want them!"

"Oh, I think I could do another one," Clover said. "Or two."

Clover insisted she could hold her liquor, but Mo cut her off at three, and that only made Clover like them more. As it happened, Clover could shoot whiskey with a gang of truck drivers if anyone wanted to bet money on her, but she was happy to be buzzed and feeling high-spirited as she, Dee, Gillian, and Leilani waited for Mo to grab their coat and clock out for the night.

"Okay, how are we feeling, fam?" Dee asked as she draped her arms around Leilani and Clover and led the five of them down the street. "Tired? Wired? What's the plan?"

Gillian bent her head toward Clover. "We can walk you home if you want, Clover."

Clover thought about it, but honestly, she couldn't remember the last time she felt this good. "Maybe," she said, tilting her head up at the stars and trusting that Dee was going to keep her from walking into traffic. "What else is on the agenda?"

"I seem to remember Leilani promising us a lesbian bar," Mo chimed in. They pulled out a piece of gum and popped it into their mouth. They shook the pack toward Clover, and

Clover shook her head. "I'm tryna quit smoking," Mo offered by way of explanation, shoving the pack into their back pocket. "So that I don't die young and shit."

"Solid plan," Gillian said.

"Let's do it," Clover said. "The bar, I mean."

Mo whooped. "One car to Oakland, coming right up!"

And that's how Clover found herself squashed between three lesbians and a nonbinary person in a tiny Honda Civic at eight o'clock at night on the Bay Bridge, looking out over the expanse of inky darkness that spread out above and below them, stars reflected from the sky to the water to the city buildings beyond.

Within half an hour, they arrived at their new destination, Clover having now learned where each of them grew up and how they'd all arrived in San Francisco. Dee and Gillian were born there, Leilani grew up in Oakland, and Mo had traveled across "the wasteland of the West," escaping Tulsa and then Fresno, to wind up down the street from their two best friends "and Gillian," to which Gillian stuck out her middle finger and the two pretended to tussle in the car.

Clover told them her brief and simple story, which was that she'd spent her entire life in Salem, having met the man she'd planned to marry back when she was only five. She feared that they'd judge her for that—something so basic and dull—but they only asked more questions: What did she like about growing up on a farm? What was it like to experience snow every year? Did she have horses? Did she like her town?

Someone asked Clover why she'd chosen to vacation in

San Francisco, and it was the first time that night that her
tongue turned to lead. She thought back to the night she'd
signed up for Vacate all those months ago, after her mom
died, after her engagement ended, when she'd thought she
might as well burn it all down and start over.

If she'd told her old friends she'd traveled to San Francisco because of a girl, they would have looked at her like
she was insane. Her new friends, however, would probably
understand.

"I knew a girl in high school who moved here when we
graduated," Clover said. "Our town was a little . . . too small
for her. She told me she thought she'd be happier here."

Her friends exchanged looks with one another. "Were you
two close?" Leilani asked.

"She kissed me on my balcony beneath the stars our junior
year of high school," Clover said. She tried to make it sound
nonchalant, but her heart was thundering in her ears. "It was
before Knox and I were officially . . . together." She didn't tell
them that it was the kiss with this girl that had pushed her
into Knox's loving, heterosexual arms. She couldn't tell them
something even *he* didn't know.

Hell, *she* hadn't known it—not really. It was just something
that nagged at her: the kind of truth that pokes and prods
at you for years until, one day, your fiancé asks you to put a
wedding date on the calendar.

This part she didn't say out loud. The last time she'd been
that honest with someone, she'd died, and Clover didn't want
to be responsible for the deaths of four people she'd just met
and their Uber driver.

"Anyway." She cleared her throat. "I came here because I . . . well, it seemed like it would be . . . safe here." She wasn't sure she was making herself clear, until Mo reached over from the front seat and squeezed her hand.

"I know what you mean," they said. "Tulsa wasn't safe for me either."

Clover thought she might cry, but instead she squeezed Mo's hand back and let herself be distracted by the blast of music and loud hum of conversation that drifted into their open window as their Uber pulled up to the bar.

Once inside, the five of them huddled on a row of low fake leather benches situated across from the karaoke screen. Two women were singing loudly and off-key to Keith Urban's "I'll Be Your Santa Tonight," while a man in a large feathered black overcoat danced around them like a bird in a mating ritual.

"It's lively tonight," Leilani called over the music.

"I can see that!" Clover shouted back, confused and delighted by the scene in front of her. She was pretty sure she'd never been around so many colorful people in all her life, and she was shocked by how comfortable she felt. She was one woman among two dozen scrunched together under low lights and in high spirits. She could be anyone, she realized suddenly. Anyone at all.

This bar, and this city, and these people—her friends—would accept her exactly as she was.

"Dope!" Gillian said, as the dim glow of her phone lit up her face and she sipped a glass of water. "Our friend is here; she just got out of her taxi."

"What friend?" Clover asked.

"The one who owns the restaurant," she said. "Oh, there she is."

Gillian stood, and Clover watched as she bear-hugged a thin brunette wearing a green utility jacket over skinny jeans and black wedge heels. Clover felt her throat go dry and her vision start to blur—she hoped it was the alcohol. She hoped to God it was the alcohol, or else she was having a heart attack, or a delusion, or . . .

Gillian led the woman over, and she smiled politely at Clover, brown eyes glinting against smooth olive skin, pink glossed lips parted amicably: "Hi, I'm Hailey."

Clover's mind flashed back a decade ago, to when she was a teenager beneath the stars on her balcony, to soft kisses and promised secrets pressed against another girl's lips.

Hailey's eyes widened in sudden recognition. "Clover Mills?" Hailey said. "Oh my god, is that you?"

Chapter Thirteen

Clover

Thursday night, December 14, 2023

Time slowed. No, it sped up. Clover wasn't sure. She was absolutely unsure about everything in her life at that exact moment, and it was only Gillian's surprised "You know each other" that pushed her soul back into her body.

"We did," Hailey said. She and Clover looked at each other with uneasy smiles, and then, with awkward laughs, they fumbled into a hug that Clover feared would kill her on the spot.

Mo threw their head back and let out a delighted cackle. "*Amazing.* Just fucking *incredible.* Oh, Clover." They threw an arm around Clover's shoulders and pulled her in for a quick side hug. "You have made my entire fucking week. Drinks!" They threw their hands into the air and turned in a circle like a gladiator announcing a battle win. "Drinks for everyone!"

"I'll get them," Hailey said as Mo continued to laugh like a mad person drunk on power.

"Me too," Clover said. Hailey raised an eyebrow, but Clover avoided her gaze, instead taking the opportunity to grab everyone's orders.

"Shall we?" Hailey asked, and when she slipped her arm through hers, Clover didn't pull away. Together they walked to the bar, pushing through a gaggle of wasted gays, and waited for the bartender to notice their existence. "So," Hailey said. She pulled away so she could look at Clover properly.

"So," Clover said.

Hailey gestured around. "I'm surprised to see you here."

"In San Francisco, or at a lesbian bar?"

"Um . . . both." Hailey giggled, and Clover felt her heart speed up. Hailey looked exactly as Clover often imagined she might, grown and confident, with brown eyes still big with questions. If she stared too hard, Clover knew she'd get lost in them—in the depths of dark brown, in the expanse of questions left unanswered. She made a feeble attempt to get the bartender's attention, and when that failed, she attempted nonchalance instead.

"Just . . . curious, I guess. About the city. I'm here on vacation."

"Ah." Hailey nodded with far too much certainty. "Curiosity. Of course."

Clover frowned at the implication, and this time she channeled her irritation into a forceful heave up onto the bar, leaning over it with an arm high in the air. This time, the bartender came to them, and Clover gave their order.

"So," Clover said, dusting herself off. "You have a restaurant!"

"I do," Hailey said.

"It's nice. I was there earlier, with Gillian and Mo and everyone there." Clover waved in the direction of her new friends.

"How do you all know each other?"

"Oh—we, um . . ." Clover thought back to the stark difference between her social life yesterday morning versus this evening and explained how she met the ragtag group of queers she was now out partying with.

"Sounds about right," Hailey said, and laughed. "Dee is the biggest extrovert on planet Earth, second only to Mo, but that's just when they're in a good mood. They both make friends fast."

"How'd you meet them?" Clover asked, thankful for a normal flow of conversation.

"College," Hailey said. "Well, I met Mo in college, after they transferred from someplace in Fresno. Then they introduced me to Leilani, who introduced me to Dee, who introduced me to Gillian, who's my supplier for our produce." When the bartender put down her drink, Hailey grabbed it and took a quick sip. "What about you? How's the farm?"

"It's okay," Clover said. She wasn't sure how much information she'd want to blurt out all at once. In any case, none of it seemed as glamorous as having a restaurant in the heart of San Francisco. "My, um . . . my mom died recently, and then my dad got sick, so I've just had to focus on getting some of the business under control."

"Oh, Clover, I'm so sorry."

"It's fine," Clover said. "I'm fine. Things are just a little bit hectic. Hence, you know—I'm here! To reboot a little."

"Well, I'm sure Knox is being helpful, at least. Last I heard, you two were engaged, so cheers to that!" Hailey said, lifting her glass in the air.

"Oh." Clover hesitated. "Where did you hear that?"

Hailey faltered. "Instagram, I think. Someone from high school posted about it."

Of course. God, she hated the internet. Clover bit the inside of her lip, wondering if she should correct Hailey or not. It felt . . . dangerous. "We were engaged," she said slowly, trying out the words. "But we . . . aren't . . . anymore."

The rest of the drinks came.

Clover grabbed the two nearest to her, and Hailey grabbed the others. They walked back to their group of friends, who greeted them enthusiastically, and Clover could tell immediately that she and Hailey were going to be gossip fodder for *weeks*.

"So," Dee said, her arm draped lazily around Leilani. "How do *you two* know each other?"

Hailey and Clover exchanged a glance. Then Hailey winked and crossed her legs—two things that made Clover's brain short-circuit. "Old friends," Hailey said. "We go way back."

Chapter Fourteen

Bee

Thursday night, December 14, 2023

*H*ave yourself a merry little Christmas, let your heart be light . . .
Bee mouthed the words to herself and let herself be carried away by the simple melody, the old-timey chorus, and the orchestra playing in the background. Her parents loved Frank Sinatra nearly as much as they loved the Temptations, and she knew every pause and warble of every holiday song he'd ever sung.

It was the one part of the family holiday traditions that she loved, and possibly the only one she'd miss this year: Frank's record spinning as they sat around the table, holding hands and thanking God for the food they were about to receive. Then Dad would pop a bottle of champagne, and they'd all be quizzed on their yearly achievements. As Bee waited for her turn, she'd inevitably start to panic, hot flashes of pain gripping her chest, and her head starting to ring. So, she'd focus on Frank's voice—or Bing Crosby's, when he made an appearance—and the gentle warble of their baritone voices would help her keep all the little pieces of herself from breaking off.

She felt that now, in the inviting warmth of Clover's living room. Quiet, and slow, and whole. And she stayed like that, even as the music changed and Nat King Cole's soothing voice took over, then was replaced with "Last Christmas," by Wham!, and a slew of other classics. She did nothing but listen and let herself be.

If she'd been back home, another scene would be playing out, Bee was sure. One where she paced the floor of her tiny condo, fingers clenched in her hair, tears fighting their way down her cheeks, as a hired car from her mother waited out front and her phone rang, demanding that Bee answer, that she give in, that she submit. But Bee was across the country, address unknown. Snow falling, cows mooing, and the radio playing as wood crackled in the fireplace.

I could stay here forever, Bee thought. And she felt, for the first time, that maybe she would. But no—she was certain she'd find something here that made her an anxiety monster too.

Still, suffice it to say that the call had not gone well. Her sister had gotten her capacity for icy judgment and sharp appraisals from someone, and she was not nearly as skilled as their mother. If Beth had an edge to her, their mother was a blade.

"What's really going on, dear?" her mother had asked. "Are you sick?"

"No," Bee answered. "I just needed a break."

"A break?" she said. "A break from what? Your sister told us about the recent issues with the company. Sounds like you should be working harder, honey, not resting on your laurels."

"Okay, Mom." Bee rubbed her face.

She had let her mom berate her some more, with the occasional interstitial of "Well, I hope you're warm there" and "Do you need me to send an extra coat?" It was the type of whiplash Bee had grown accustomed to: the surprising reminders that her mom did love her, in her own way. It just got lost in the utterly desperate need to demonstrate that their family was superior to all others.

When she was finally able to convince her mom that she was neither dying nor sick and that yes, in fact, she was *still* not planning to come home for Christmas dinner, her mom switched tactics and put her dad on the phone. His method was offering money to tide her over and suggesting that she needn't travel across the country to run away from her problems.

"If the business is failing, honey, we can help with the investments," he said.

Bee gritted her teeth and declined, and then again, and then again, until, finally, they both exchanged strained "I love yous" and hung up.

She had sat back in her seat at the coffee shop and taken a few slow breaths. She hoped that was enough to get them out of her system for a few days. Sometimes hearing their disappointment live and in action actually reduced the buzzing in her head, like a junkie getting their fill. She was both repulsed by and addicted to their criticism; at this point, she wasn't sure what she'd do without it.

"Probably experience normal emotions like joy and satisfaction," she muttered out loud.

But her mother's final words stuck in Bee's head: *You always find a way to disappoint me, Beatrice.* And yet she wondered why Bee didn't want to come over for dinner. Funny lady, her mother.

She shifted from her position on the couch and laid a book from Clover's library that she had been attempting to read facedown beside her. When she was younger, reading had easily been one of her favorite pastimes; it was what had made her want to be a writer, after all. But even that was something tinged with the expectations of her parents—something personal that was expected to be turned into something profitable.

If you're going to be a writer, you have to be a great one. Do you think you're on the level of James Baldwin or Gwendolyn Brooks? Are you going to be published in the New York Times *like—like that Roxane Gay person? What exactly were you planning to do with an English degree? And second place in some silly city writing competition? How many people are even in Poughkeepsie anyway?*

Abruptly, Bee stood. Warm as the living room was, it was beginning to feel stuffy, closed in. She needed air.

She donned a set of warm winter outwear and ventured outside, grateful for the moonlight and the quiet hum of conversation from a pair of neighbors across the street who were enjoying a late-night bonfire. She sat on the steps and looked up at the stars, singing Nat King Cole quietly to herself and willing the wind to wipe away her memories of the last few conversations with her family.

"You've got a nice voice."

Bee jumped, and Knox chuckled.

"Sorry," he said. "Clover hates when I do that."

"You could've been a spy in another life," she said. Though she didn't mean to, her gaze couldn't help but sweep over him, her skin growing warm. What was it about this guy that made her heart beat so fast? "Where are you coming from so late?" she asked, in an effort to change the subject.

"Rehearsal," he said. He pointed to the guitar case strapped onto his back. In the darkness, she hadn't noticed it until now. "The chorus asked me to accompany them on some songs for a performance they have coming up."

"At that talent show?" At his surprised look, she elaborated: "I went to the coffee shop this morning. Overheard some people talking about it."

"Ah." He nodded. It seemed for a moment that the conversation would end there. She prepared to wish him a good night, but then he cleared his throat. "Do you think you'll perform anything?"

She laughed harder than she meant to. "Absolutely not."

"Why not? I meant it before—you didn't sound half bad."

"Because I was half singing under my breath. Believe me, you don't want to hear me try to bust out a real ballad. It won't go well."

He grinned. "Something else, then. I'm sure you've got something up your sleeve." He gave her a playfully inquiring stare, his eyebrow and chin raised, like he knew what she was hiding and was patiently waiting for her to admit it. God, he was charming.

"Fine," she said with false annoyance. "I write, a little bit. I mean, that's what I do at home. But it's mostly, like, web copy, and blah blah blah. I don't really write creatively anymore."

"But you used to?"

"In college," she said. "A little after, I guess. A little before. I've got poems and stories shoved in a closet somewhere."

He nodded, this time his head down like he was listening hard and trying to solve a problem she had presented to him. Then he lifted his head like an idea had struck him. "You could read something."

"I'm not performing!"

He put his hands up as he laughed. "Okay, okay. Sorry. All my friends are doing something at this show, so I guess I'm just used to being the hype man. It's the big event of the season, besides the tree lighting."

Bee thought about everyone's disappointment around the Christmas party Clover's family used to throw. She wanted to ask him about it, but it didn't seem right at the moment.

"I'll cheer you on at the performance," she said instead.

He touched the back of his neck, then. It made him suddenly look like a young boy. "I'll look forward to it."

His eyes stayed on hers as another moment of silence passed between them, and Bee fought to tamp down the electricity coursing through her chest. *This is just the way he is,* she told herself. This is what Taylor and her friends had been talking about earlier that day—he was a charming guy just out of a years-long relationship. If he was doing anything, it was playing the field, just like Roger would do, and Bee wasn't looking for games.

She wasn't looking for anything.

She stretched and stood. "I should get to sleep," she said.

Knox blinked. "Of course, yeah. Sleep well, Bee."

"You too, Knox."

She wrapped her coat tighter and walked quickly back inside.

HOURS LATER, SHE lay staring up at the ceiling above her bed, all too aware of the fact that it was long past midnight. But the day's events haunted her, keeping her head filled with too much information to process into a good night's sleep. Taylor, and Clover, and Knox, and all the details of their lives and the ways she'd crept inside them were enough to keep her mind preoccupied, but something else was keeping her mind racing.

You could read something.

The idea that Bee could do anything creative these days was nearly laughable; chopping wood with Knox the other morning had been the most unique thing she'd done in years. But . . . there was something inspiring about seeing Knox with his guitar tonight and hearing the enthusiasm with which the chorus had talked about singing earlier that day, once they were done gossiping about Knox's love life. None of them were professionals, so far as she knew, and the talent show was merely an opportunity to share themselves with one another. No prizes or accolades were up for grabs.

What would she have to lose if she did share . . . something? If anything, she could get something back: that spark she thought she'd lost so many years ago. What did it matter if it never made it into the *New Yorker* or the *Paris Review*?

Pushing the covers off her, she riffled through her purse, finding a crumpled napkin from the coffee shop, then a pen. She cleared off space on Clover's side table and began to write what came to her.

You're wasting your time, a voice whispered in the back of her mind.

She kept writing.

You're going to embarrass yourself, it whispered again.

But she didn't stop. Not this time. She forced herself to keep writing, crossing out words and scribbling into the edges of the napkin. When she was done, she looked at her handiwork. It looked like a serial killer wrote it, or maybe a hostage forced to write out her own ransom letter, but at least she'd done it.

She wrote something for herself.

Take that, Mom.

Chapter Fifteen

Clover

Friday morning, December 15, 2023

The first thing Clover did when she awoke was check her phone. It was something she never did as soon as the sun streamed through her windows, but she needed to make sure last night was real. That she had indeed somehow miraculously, magically, impossibly run into Hailey Blackwell. And that Hailey Blackwell had asked her to dance.

She sank into the memory. Someone—clearly a stressed-out millennial like themselves—was singing karaoke to "I'm Not Okay (I Promise)" by My Chemical Romance, and it was not the least bit a romantic, festive, or particularly rhythmic song to dance to. Although the song had come out when they were still kids, it had been one of their many summer-before-senior-year anthems and they knew that song *well*. Hailey took Clover's hand, and they jumped up and down together, screaming, *I'm not o-fucking-kay,* at the top of their lungs like the seventeen-year-old girls they had once been. Then they collapsed into each other's arms in a fit of giggles.

Hailey's cheek had brushed against Clover's; then her lips pressed against her ear, hot breath tickling her neck. *Give me your phone,* Hailey had said. *I want to give you my number.*

If Clover had been a braver person, she might've kissed her right then and there. But she wasn't *that* drunk. Instead, she did as she was asked and handed Hailey her phone, sending back a text to confirm Hailey had hers too.

Now, as Clover checked her phone, she was desperate to see if Hailey had texted her again.

Breakfast? Hailey had written.

And Clover suddenly realized she was starving.

At the café Hailey had recommended, Hailey was already seated, dark sunglasses perched on her head as she scrolled through her phone. Today, her hair was pulled up into a bun, with wisps of waves that framed her face. When she saw Clover, she broke out into a smile.

"Hey!" she exclaimed. She pulled Clover into a tight hug without hesitation, and Clover let herself enjoy the embrace.

Honestly, it was weird, as if no time had passed at all. Clover could remember every sensation she'd ever experienced more than a decade ago in Hailey's presence, every rapid heartbeat, every shiver down her spine. It was like she and Hailey had been tucked away inside a frame, and now that they were both here, their friendship resumed as normal, a living portrait of what they used to be.

It was only one summer, she reminded herself. But oh, what a summer it had been.

"It's nice to see you," Clover said as they took their seats.

"Yeah," Hailey said. "Wow. I can't even believe you're here. And we had so much fun last night! Just like old times." At that, Clover blushed, and Hailey covered her own smile with her hand. "Well, you know what I mean."

Clover picked up the menu, and Hailey took her cue.

"What are you thinking?" Hailey asked.

Clover mulled over the breakfast menu with its fanciful items. Then again, what did she expect with the word *Slut* in the restaurant's name? "I think I'll do the Beast with Two Backs," she said.

"Solid choice," Hailey said. "I'm a fan of that one myself." She winked at Clover, and Clover blushed again. She'd have been telling a bold-faced lie if she said she hadn't spent a fretful night *not* thinking about that very thing. What made it worse was that her brain couldn't seem to focus on one thing. Beth's tight skirts and cool gaze kept popping in uninvited.

Well, all of it was uninvited. Clover had tried desperately then, as now, to not think about anything lurid. Instead, she kept her focus as Hailey offered her a warm smile.

"So," she said breathily. "You're here!"

Clover laughed. "I am. Although, I admit, I'm probably just as surprised as you are."

"What brings you here exactly?" Hailey laid her cheek on one hand. "If I remember correctly, I think you once called San Francisco a den of sin."

"I didn't say that!" Clover gasped. "Did I?"

Hailey grinned. "Yes. If there's absolutely anything I remember from my life in Ohio, it's that."

Clover felt her skin grow hot, though she didn't know if it was from amusement or shame. She didn't remember saying those exact words, but she remembered when Hailey had told her that she was going away for college. It had broken Clover's heart, though she'd already broken Hailey's by then.

Clover had made her choice, and now here she and Hailey were a decade later, two adult women in a café across the country from where they'd met. Clover's heart fluttered; she wondered if this was a second chance. She didn't even know she'd wanted one, but she'd wondered about Hailey for years since that kiss—and she'd wondered about herself. There were so many questions she'd refused to ask herself, and yet they were always there, just beneath the surface.

"I'm sorry," Clover said suddenly, and Hailey shook her head.

"We were kids," she said. "I mean, I'd be lying if I said it didn't mess me up bad." She looked down at her menu. "I cared for you a lot," she whispered.

"I know," Clover said. "I did too."

Hailey looked at her, a brightness in her eyes, and it broke Clover's heart to think that, for so many years, it was possible Hailey hadn't known. But why would she? After their kiss, Clover had stopped answering her calls. For all the years Clover had spent questioning herself, she wondered if Hailey had questioned herself too—questioned if she'd miscalculated their relationship or Clover's affections for her. God, what hell that must have been for her.

"I'm so sorry," Clover said again. "For just leaving you high and dry like that. For just—"

"Disappearing one day and showing up on Knox Haywood's arm?"

Clover swallowed, but Hailey reached across the table and grabbed her hand.

"It is okay. Seriously. Honestly, seeing you at a lesbian bar last night immediately healed up any wounds that might have still been open. I mean, that was pure gold. Plus"—and at this Hailey bit her lip—"it was pretty nice to dance together too."

Clover smiled at the memory of their bodies pressed against each other the night before. "Yes, I suppose it was."

"What can I get you ladies?"

Hailey smiled up at the waitress. "I think we're both going to have the Beast with Two Backs."

As they waited for their food, they caught up about what their lives had been like in the decade that had passed, and how funny it was, the little world they all lived in, that a chance encounter with total strangers could lead to two old friends reuniting. When their orders came, Hailey finally asked about Knox, and Clover was honest.

"I knew marriage wasn't what I wanted," she said. "Or, at least, marriage right now. To . . ."

"A man," Hailey finished, and Clover laughed.

"I guess."

"He'll be okay," Hailey said, taking a bite into her breakfast sandwich. "It's not easy losing you"—she gave Clover a little smile—"but he'll bounce back."

Clover cleared her throat and picked up her sandwich. "What about you?" She took a bite, willing herself to be brave. "Are you seeing anyone right now?"

This was the first time their whole meal that Hailey looked at a loss for words. "Messy breakup," she said after a moment. "On again, off again. Off right now. It doesn't look like it'll work out."

"I'm sorry," Clover said. She was being genuine, but she'd be lying if a part of her hadn't felt a spark of hope. Maybe her church folk were right. The Lord did work in mysterious ways and whatnot. She hadn't been ready ten years ago, but maybe she was now.

Hailey excused herself to the bathroom, and Clover glanced out the window. A Black woman with a short bob passed by, and Clover felt her heart speed up involuntarily, but no, it wasn't who she thought it was. Why would it be? Why should she care? She shook her head and reached for her phone, surprised to see a text from Knox. A stab of guilt pierced her. What would he say if he knew all the things she'd kept from him over the years? They weren't in love anymore, but even so, she still loved him, still wanted him in her life. The question was: Would he want the same?

She opened the text.

Hi Clover. Wanted to ask you about inventory for the spring. It looks like the quantity of eggs we were expecting is low...

"Oh my god, Knox," she muttered. She scrolled past his long update, which he could've emailed for the love of all things holy, until another text popped up right after.

Tree lighting's tonight, btw. We'll miss you there.

Clover sighed. The tree lighting was another one of those Mills family traditions, and Knox was always eager to find two new ornaments to add to it every year, one representing something he wanted to bring into the year, and the other, something he wanted to let go of. It was a fun way to bond with their community, and this year, she was missing out.

Hang something up for me? she typed back.

She watched as the ellipses on her phone indicated he was typing. They appeared. Disappeared. Appeared. Then:

I will.

"Everything good?" Hailey asked when she returned.

Clover pocketed her phone and smiled at her. "Absolutely," she said.

They fell back into easy conversation until the check came. Clover offered to split the bill, but Hailey insisted, and Clover let that warm feeling wash over her again. They grabbed their coats, and Hailey looped her arm through Clover's. "So, Clover. What do you have planned for the day?"

Clover thought about it. "I'm totally free."

Hailey grinned. "Perfect."

Chapter Sixteen

Bee

Friday night, December 15, 2023

How is it?"

Bee watched anxiously as Jimmy took a tentative taste of her chili. As Bob had promised, it wasn't outrageously difficult for her to concoct, and while she'd tasted it herself, she was still worried that she was going to, somehow, send Jimmy to the hospital with food poisoning.

Jimmy considered the taste. "Mm-hmm," he said. Then he took another bite. "*Mm-hmm.* Okay, now!"

"You like it?"

"Absolutely."

Bee released the breath she'd been holding. "I'm so glad. I don't think I've cooked in almost a decade."

Jimmy shook his head. "That's a damn shame, because you ain't half bad. I could eat this every night." He took a few more hearty bites of the chili, nodding with each swallow. "Mm-hmm, mm-hmm, mm-hmm!"

Bee laughed as she settled into her seat and began to eat. "Now you're just playing it up. I know it's not that good, Jimmy."

He pretended to ignore her, scooping another helping of rice into his bowl. "Hurry on up and enjoy your hard work."

She obliged and was pleased to admit that she agreed with Jimmy. It *wasn't* half bad. "Thank you for encouraging me to make use of this beautiful kitchen, Jimmy."

"Thank *you* for inviting me to dinner."

"It's the least I could do," she said. "You've been such a gracious host."

"Technically Clover is hosting you," he said as he chewed. He paused and then released a deep sigh. "I hope she's doing all right in that big city by herself."

Bee put her hand on his. "I bet she's doing great. From what you've told me, she's a sharp lady. And San Francisco is a great place. There's a lot to do."

"Yeah," Jimmy said. "I just hope it's worth missing the holidays over."

Bee considered him thoughtfully. She figured that if she had a dad like Clover's, she couldn't imagine missing the holidays with him either. But, if what she had heard was true, she also couldn't imagine living on the same plot of land as her ex-fiancé. She could understand needing a little space from that.

"Speaking of the holidays," Bee said with as much tact as

she could muster, "how would you feel about going with me to this famed tree lighting that everyone keeps talking about?"

Jimmy smiled. "I appreciate you, Bee, but I've been sort of avoiding the holidays myself with Mae gone, and then Clover . . ."

"I understand," Bee said with a long-suffering sigh. "I suppose I'll just have to go by myself. Alone. In a city I don't know. With people I don't know. Alone."

This time, Jimmy laughed. "I mean, I s'pose I wouldn't be much of a gentleman if I let you go alone."

Bee shrugged, though her eyes sparkled. "It's up to you."

"Well, then," Jimmy said. "I guess we should get going."

THEY TOOK JIMMY's car to the tree lot, and when they arrived, Bee was overtaken with surprise. There was a massive tree in the center of the lot, at least four times her height. It was covered in mismatched decorations, a fact she found puzzling until she realized people had brought their own ornaments. Every so often a person would walk up to it and add something to an available spot on the tree, either appropriate to their height or farther up, using the sturdy set of freestanding stairs beside it. Occasionally, a group of teenagers would rotate the stairs, so that each side of the tree could be accessed.

It was an unusual sight, and one that made Bee fall even more in love with the little town she'd found herself in. Sure, she'd seen huge, fancy trees before, but they were usually in the middle of a big mall or some other, more official location, and no one was ever allowed to touch them.

Here, it was meant to be touched. Everyone made it their

own, in some special way. She watched as two siblings, a boy and a girl, approached with their mother, a Black woman with graying dreadlocks. She couldn't tell in the dim light of the yard what they were adding to the tree, but she could hear the children squabble, with one shouting, "It was *my* turn, Kendrick!"

Though she didn't recognize this family, she was surprised as she looked around to see so many people she did recognize. Of course, she hadn't actually spoken to most people yet, but she'd seen people out and about, whether it was her neighbors down the street, or folks at the coffee shop, or members of the chorus.

Jimmy, of course, was another story. As they both ventured into the crowd, the dreadlocked woman descended upon them. "Jimmy Larue Mills," she said. "Now, I did not expect to see you hear this evening, 'specially after you told me about fifteen times that the only thing you'd do this season was come on over to dinner. Hi, baby, I'm Janine. Janine Latrice, Jimmy's sister." The woman introduced herself so quickly that it took Bee a moment to realize she was speaking to her.

"Hi. Hi! I'm Bee. I'm, uh, staying with Jimmy. Well, at the house Jimmy lives under. I mean—"

"Oh, you're the young lady who swapped houses with Clover. Well, isn't that nice! Oh, she's so pretty." She smacked Jimmy's shoulder with enthusiasm. "How are you enjoying your stay, honey?"

"It's really lovely here," Bee managed to say, before the woman shouted behind her.

"Kendrick, Simone, stay with your father! I just discovered a missing person!" With no other explanation to her children, she grabbed Jimmy's hand and dragged him into the center of the crowd, with Bee following quickly. They walked through a maze of Christmas trees to a small wooden storefront with the words LESTER'S CHRISTMAS FOREST written in blocky black letters on a long stretch of canvas out front.

"Lester!" Janine shouted, pushing Jimmy out in front of her. "Lester, look who's here."

"Jimmy!" Another Black man about Jimmy's age came out, a walking stick in his hand. "I thought I wouldn't get to see you this evening. How you doin', old man?"

Though Jimmy had barely gotten a word in since being accosted by his sister, he looked genuinely happy as he accepted Lester's hug. "I'm doin' okay, Lester. Can't complain."

"How's Clover?"

"All right. Bee here is the young lady she's swapped houses with." He stepped aside, and Bee and Lester shook hands. "Bee assures me that she should be enjoying herself out there on the West Coast."

"I hope so. You know, a young lady like that should be careful. Without a man like Knox by her side, she could see herself in some trouble."

"Now, why would you bring something like that up, Lester?" Janine cut in.

"I'm just saying—"

"Jimmy!" This time, Bee recognized the person approaching them. "Boy, am I glad to see you out and about. And you!"

Bob turned his megawatt smile to Bee. "Well, it's sure nice to see you again too. Do we have you to thank for getting this old geezer out of the house?"

Bee blushed and shook her head, just as Jimmy proudly proclaimed, "Well, she just about demanded it. Said I ain't a gentleman letting a girl go out alone by herself."

"Here, here!" the men said. Janine winked at her, then began to pull Jimmy back toward the crowd.

"The kids will want to say hi to their uncle," she said.

Though she was invited to tag along with them, Bee politely declined. She felt satisfied that she'd convinced Jimmy to venture into the evening with her, but now that he was with his friends and family, he didn't need a stranger glued to his hip.

She wandered back to where she'd seen a table of free refreshments and helped herself to some hot cider in a thin paper cup. She gently blew away the steam so that the liquid wouldn't burn her tongue and watched as more people added to the tree and children ran along, playing tag and screaming, *"He sees you when you're sleeping! Ahhh!"* at the top of their lungs.

One pair of giggling and gleeful children led her gaze to a young blond woman sporting red earmuffs and a sparkling red coat. It was Taylor, from the coffee shop. She was chatting with the same group of friends Bee had seen earlier. She hadn't meant to stare, but she supposed she wasn't too stealthy, as she was the only person standing by herself. The woman caught her eyes and then pinned her with a kind smile. Before Bee could think to extract herself, Taylor approached with her hand out. "You're Bee, right? The woman staying at the Mills residence?"

Bee took a quick gulp of her hot cider and silently cursed when it scalded her throat. "Yes," she croaked out. She cleared her throat. "I mean, yes. Hi. You sing with the chorus, right?"

Taylor looked pleasantly surprised. "I do! I take it you've seen us come past the house a few times."

"Yeah. You all sound amazing." Actually, if Bee was honest, Taylor sounded a bit off-key, but she didn't need to tell her that.

"Thank you," Taylor said brightly. "Oh, it's a shame what's been going on with the Mills family recently. It must be awful what Mr. Mills is going through right now, with Mrs. Mills gone and his daughter just up and left right before Christmas."

"I'm sure she had her reasons," Bee answered. She didn't know Clover beyond the few emails they'd exchanged, but there was something about Taylor's tone that made her feel defensive on her behalf.

"Oh, I'm sure she did," Taylor said. "I can't imagine what the holidays must be feeling like for her too." Though it was an afterthought, Taylor seemed genuinely saddened. Bee tried to soften her tone.

"Yeah, it's . . . not easy for some people, I bet. Not that I really know anything about Jimmy or Clover. I've just heard little things here and there."

"Of course!" Taylor said. She had the decency to look a bit chagrined. "Here I am blabbing about their lives like you and

I are old friends. I'm not really used to new people around here. Although I do figure that since Clover's gone past Christmas that you'll be here until then too, is that right?"

"Yeah, exactly. We swapped with the same schedule, so I will, uh, *also* be skipping the holidays with my family, I guess."

"Well," Taylor began, "if you need anything, I'm just down the road from the Mills house. You can ask Jimmy for my number, and I'll be happy to help." Before Bee could respond, Taylor's eyes lit up at something behind Bee. "Hi, Knox!"

Bee swore she felt her heart stop. She took a deep breath and turned to see Knox approaching them, his head covered with a ridiculous-looking hat. It was dark green with ear flaps and trimmed with white fur.

"What are you wearing?" she asked.

He looked offended. "What do you mean?"

"On your head!"

"It's a trapper hat!"

"Are you going hunting?"

"It's cold!" he huffed dramatically, and stuck his hands under his armpits for added effect. "This is a very functional hat for this weather."

"If you say so," she said, rolling her eyes but still unable to hide her smile.

"Well, it seems like you two have clearly become acquainted," Taylor said. Both Bee and Knox turned to her abruptly. "Hi, Knox," she said again. "It's nice to see you."

"It's nice to see you too," he said. He gave her a quick hug and then turned back to Bee.

"How'd your writing go last night?"

"What makes you think I wrote anything?"

"I was just kind of hoping."

"Knox, you will not see me perform on that stage."

"You could show off your axe skills. I'll bring the stump."

"Well," Taylor cut in, her bright smile dimming. "I think I'm gonna go see when the lighting will start. It was nice to meet you, Bee. I'll see you at rehearsal, Knox."

"Oh," he said. "Okay, I'll see you then."

As she walked off, Bee couldn't help but nudge him. "I thought you two were dating."

He looked at her, bewildered. "Who told you that?"

"No one! I just . . . heard some things, is all."

Knox frowned and touched the back of his neck. She was beginning to notice he did that when he was uncomfortable. "Taylor and I have been friends for a long time. And she's a nice girl. But she's looking to settle down with someone, and that's not really something I'm looking for right now."

"Because you just got out of an engagement."

Knox's laugh was dry. Then he let out a little whistle. "Wow, word really does travel fast. You been here, what, six hours?"

"At least seven," Bee said. He chuckled. "We don't have to talk about it," she continued. "We can talk about other things—like what you put on the tree this year."

He smiled and ducked his head. "Something old," he said. "And something new." He looked up at the tree, but his gaze was distant. "The tradition here is to let go of the past and look toward the future. It's a Christmas tree and kind of a . . . New Year's tree too, really. And I've been stuck in the past for about a year now. So, just trying to figure out what's next for me." He looked back at her. "What about you?"

She blinked. "What about me? I didn't bring anything."

"If you had something to put on the tree, then."

Bee thought about it for a moment. "Honestly," she said, "if I put something on there, I think it'd bring the whole thing crashing down."

He laughed. "Join the club."

"Okay, folks." Lester appeared in the middle of the crowd, this time holding a large megaphone. "Now's the time. Everyone come on over and make sure you can see."

Knox gave Bee a sideways grin. "You ready?"

"One hundred percent," she said.

"Three," Lester said.

"Two!" the crowd joined in.

"One!"

The tree lit up like a blast of sunlight, setting the lot aglow in soft gold, green, and red. Some people, Bee noticed, were wearing sparkles like the ones on Taylor's coat, and they glistened too, like walking fairy lights.

Bee couldn't contain her delight. She smiled wide and clasped her hands to her chest, cradling her now-empty paper cup like a well-loved child. She probably looked a little ridiculous, a gleeful tourist overwhelmed with the Christmas spirit. But she didn't care. "It's gorgeous," she said.

When Knox didn't respond, she looked over at him and was surprised to catch his eyes. He looked away. Cleared his throat. "I should check on Taylor," he said.

She squinted at him, but nodded nonetheless. "Sure."

"Have a good night, Bee."

"You too, Knox."

She refused to watch him go. Instead, she kept her eyes trained on the tree and her ears tuned to the laughter and conversation that surrounded her. This was what she'd come here for, after all: to finally feel something close to inspiration.

Chapter Seventeen

Clover

Friday night, December 15, 2023

By the evening, it seemed like Clover and Hailey had traversed the whole of the city, and while Clover's legs were killing her, she hadn't felt so alive in months. With every memory they shared and landmark they visited, she felt like a whole new person. Like someone who had chosen this life instead of stumbled upon it.

"Wow, you and Dee weren't lying," Hailey said when they finally approached Bee's building. "This is seriously a hotel."

"It's a little ridiculous," Clover agreed.

"You should see my place," Hailey said. "I'm like a pauper by comparison. Dee and Lei have been trying to get me to see their new place for a minute. I think it's about time I do." She nudged Clover's shoulder. "I bet it's a nice break from the farm." She paused. "Not that the farm is bad, obviously. It was like visiting something from a fairy tale when we were kids."

Clover smiled. It was cute, seeing Hailey fumble a bit. She thought about letting her sweat a little more, but instead she said, "You can come up if you want to see it. Compare and contrast a little." Her heart hammered in her chest.

"The farm to the hotel, or my shack to your condo?"

"Both. Either."

Hailey gave her a slow, appraising look that made Clover's hopeful little heart dance. "I can't," she said finally. "Gotta get back to the restaurant. Busy night tonight. If I miss it, Gillian will kill me."

"Aren't you the boss?"

"That's what they say."

Clover dipped her head to hide her disappointment, but she understood. This was her first time taking a break in what felt like years. She knew exactly what it meant to be "the boss."

"It was good to see you, Clove," Hailey said. She kissed Clover's cheek. "Let's hang out again before you leave?" She said it as a question, and Clover nodded quickly.

"I'd like that," she said.

They hugged, and as Clover let Hailey go, she thought, with a little bit of surprise, that this might be the last time she ever would. She floated back up to Bee's apartment, feeling as if all the pieces of her life had clicked into place. She was *meant* to be here. She felt it in her bones. When she got to her door, she hesitated, then changed her mind, walking back over to Dee's door and knocking.

"Hey!" Leilani said when she answered the door, holding Miss Cleo back as she frantically tried to jump on Clover.

"Fancy seeing you here. Come in, come in." She ushered Clover inside, and Clover was engulfed by the smell of warm bread and cinnamon.

"That smells amazing," Clover said.

"Thanks," Dee answered as she came out of the small kitchen that mirrored Bee's. "First time making challah, so I'm really hoping it doesn't suck."

"Challah?" Clover asked.

"Jewish bread," Dee answered helpfully, while Leilani rolled her eyes.

"That is one way to describe it," Leilani said, swatting Dee playfully on the arm. "We're celebrating Hanukkah. It's the last night."

Clover felt like her brown skin might go white. "I'm so embarrassed," she said. "I should have checked or something before interrupting your holiday."

"Dude," Dee said, "not a problem. The more the merrier. Our door is always open, especially during Jewish holidays."

"It's the way of my people," Leilani said. She bid Clover sit down as she asked her what her beverage of choice would be. "We also have sparkling water, because Dee has no taste buds."

"Ouch," Dee said, though she was mostly fumbling with the oven by now.

"I'll take wine, thank you," Clover said. "You're sure it's okay? I just thought I'd stop by, since last night was such a whirlwind."

"Oh, you have to tell us literally everything." Dee stood up and pointed an accusatory oven mitt in her direction.

"Nothing happened!" Clover laughed. "We had breakfast this morning and then kind of wandered the city today. It was nice."

"*Nice?* You ran into your high school sweetheart and it was *nice?*" Dee said incredulously.

Clover couldn't help the shock wave that went through her body. Her entire life, *Knox* had been known as her high school sweetheart. The idea that someone else could hold that title felt jarring. Wrong, even. She shook her head. "Not technically my high school sweetheart," she said. "But yeah, a girl I've thought about for a really long time. It was surprising how easy it was to talk to her. And she's single now."

Leilani and Dee exchanged glances. For a moment, Clover forgot that they knew Hailey. She wondered what they knew.

"Isn't she?"

"She is," Dee said quickly.

"For now," Leilani muttered. Dee shot her a look, and Leilani gave Clover an apologetic smile. "Sorry," she said. "This is what happens when your friends know all of your business."

Clover nodded, thinking of her friends and family back home. She knew exactly what Leilani meant.

"I'm still glad you two ran into each other," Dee said. "Who knows, it could be fate."

"Could be," Leilani agreed. "You never know."

Clover didn't want to share how much she hoped they were right. Instead, she looked over at the window opposite the living room. Dee's apartment was technically more functional than Bee's—it had, at least, more than one room besides the kitchen. But it felt a little less grand, with two small windows instead of Bee's huge one overlooking the city. But against the darkness outside, Clover's eyes caught on the menorah, whose nine candles lit up the corner of the room, leaving a warm glow.

"That's really pretty," she said.

"Thanks!" Leilani said. "I got the menorah at a flea market last year." Her smile hinted at a little bit of nerves. "To be honest, this is only our second year celebrating Hanukkah together." She shrugged. "I'm still getting back into the swing of things."

Dee walked over to Leilani and put her arms around her. "Technically, I grew up as a Buddhist, but I haven't been to a temple in, like, nine years." She rubbed Leilani's shoulders. "It's okay, babe."

Clover smiled. "I went to church for the first time in nearly a year this week, and that's only because my dad begged me to."

"Heathens, the lot of us," Dee said.

Leilani grinned. "At least we're heathens together, I suppose."

Clover nearly snorted, covering her mouth. She wasn't used to being so callous about this sort of thing, but it didn't feel sacrilegious. Dee's point was that they were all trying their best, and she felt, for the first time in a long time, sitting here with her new friends as they drank wine and broke off a piece of challah together, that maybe her best was enough.

Chapter Eighteen

Bee

Saturday morning, December 16, 2023

Bee leaned her head back against the booth cushion and took a deep, steadying breath. Before she and Jimmy left the tree lighting last night, Bee had quietly pulled Bob aside and asked if he might have any recommendations for a quiet place to work. After her brief meeting with Taylor, she was entirely uneager to run into any familiar faces at the coffee shop again.

He recommended a Denny's just a few minutes out of town, so she'd woken up early the next morning and hopped in the car as soon as she was dressed. She didn't want to lose the momentum she was so unused to having. Now she was in a corner booth tucked away by the bathrooms, her notebook and pen laid out on the table in front of her.

She still hadn't written anything, though. She supposed

she was waiting for some of that magic from last night to seep back into her fingers.

"Well, if it isn't Miss Bee first thing in the morning," the waitress said to her as she approached.

Bee smiled up at Jimmy's sister. "Good morning, Janine! I mean, Mrs. Mills—"

"Oh, that's my maiden name, sweetheart. Technically, it'd be Mrs. Evans now, but you can go ahead and call me Janine."

"Janine it is. I didn't know you worked here."

"I work down at the hospital, actually, but I'm picking up some shifts for the holidays. Christmas ain't but nine days away, and I've got a couple things on layaway for the kids." Janine cocked her head at Bee's notebook and pen. "You gettin' some work done?"

"Oh, not really." Bee blushed. "Just jotting down some thoughts and ideas."

"Well, don't let me stop you. Can I get you anything—coffee? Cream and sugar?"

"That would be nice, thank you."

"Of course, sugar." Janine turned toward the kitchen, and then, seeming to think better of it, she turned back around. "By the way, I wanted to thank you for getting Jimmy out of the house last night. I haven't seen nearly enough of my brother these last few months. And I like to think he really enjoyed himself, being around some friendly faces."

Bee waved her hand politely. "I didn't do anything. I just needed the company."

"Don't we all, baby." Janine winked at her and then walked off.

Bee turned her attention back to her notebook. She had no idea what to write. Whatever chicken scratch she'd scribbled a couple days before had a few nice lines, but she was determined to put something else on the page. Something a little more substantial.

She thought about writing about her childhood memories or the things that had hurt her in the past. She wrote, and then scratched things out, and then wrote again. And then a new idea came to her, and her pen kept moving.

Bennie wasn't like the other chickens on the farm. She had softer feathers and a whole head of fluff. But boy, did she love to make friends.

Bee stopped herself. It was utterly silly and totally contrived. Where was she going with this? She didn't know, but she supposed the point was not knowing. The point was to keep going.

So, she did.

Janine came soon after with a cup of coffee, then another.

When her creative well stalled, Bee went ahead and started something else, some remnant of a story or start of a poem. She let her mind wander, and each time she felt that trickle of doubt creep in, she pushed it away and made herself stay right where she was, present and focused on the page.

When she finally felt like she'd made significant progress— none of it clean, hardly any of it linear—she packed up her things and made her way to the front of the restaurant to find Janine. She was standing behind the cash register, a corded black phone pressed to her ear. When she saw Bee, her eyes lit up. *One minute,* she mouthed.

Bee waited patiently until Janine hung up the phone. Then she handed her a twenty for the bill.

"Before you go, honey, do you have plans for Christmas Day?"

Bee blinked. "I hadn't thought about it. I was just planning to enjoy the house, actually."

"Well, we'd love to have you over at our place. We're hosting this year, since my sister-in-law passed on, and I think Jimmy would enjoy having you there."

Bee considered saying no, but her heart was too full. "I would love to," she said. "Thank you."

BACK AT THE Big House, Bee saw a familiar little chicken wandering around the grounds out front as Jimmy sat on the steps, watching her peck at the ground.

"She doesn't hang out much with the other chickens, I take it?" Bee asked as she closed the door of her rental car.

Jimmy laughed. "No, unfortunately not. They pick on her a little bit, the poor thing. But she's got a friend in one of the other animals around here, a horse we have named Tilda."

"Oh!" Bee couldn't hide the enthusiasm in her voice. "Knox mentioned that to me a few days ago. I haven't had a chance to meet her yet."

"You haven't?" Jimmy shook his head. "You ever ridden a horse before?"

"When I was younger," Bee admitted. "I used to love it when I was a kid, but it's been at least two decades."

"Well, then, it's about time you got back on one! Let me go and call Knox and see if he can help you out."

Bee rushed forward to dissuade Jimmy as he stood and brushed off his pants. "Oh, no no no. That's not necessary."

"I know I'm still young at heart, but to be honest with you, I wouldn't be able to take you around with Tilda for any decent sort of ride. Plus, Knox's family has horses of their own just around the way." Jimmy bent down and picked Bennie up, then set off toward the woods Bee had familiarized herself with just a few days ago. "He just passed by here about ten minutes ago, running errands."

"I really don't want to trouble him, Jimmy."

"It ain't no trouble, girl, the boy is strong as an ox and always asking to do this and that around the farm extra. He won't mind. Oh, there he is. Knox!"

Knox was leaning against an old shed, a clipboard in one hand and a pen in the other. He was wearing a thick parka and heavy snow boots but no hat this morning. Instead, his dark curls fell into his squinting blue eyes. Without noticing them yet, he raised the pen to his mouth in thought, and it was too late for Bee not to think about what it would be like if she were the pen.

She rolled her eyes to the sky. *So not the time, Bee,* she scolded herself.

"Knox!" Jimmy called again as they got closer.

Knox stood up straight when he saw them and tucked the pen behind his ear. "Yes, Jimmy?"

"I was just talking to Bee over here about Tilda. I know you got work and rehearsals and whatnot before the talent show on Christmas Eve, but do you think you could squeeze in giving Bee a quick ride?"

Knox looked over at her with an eyebrow raised, and she shrugged a little helplessly. "He told me you're the man for the job."

"I guess I am," he said. "What are you doing Sunday morning?"

Bee gave him a tight smile. "Nothing." Jimmy looked between the two of them a little longer than Bee would have liked. She cleared her throat and then clapped her hands together. "Anyway, that sounds great. I'll see you then, Knox."

She turned on her heel and began to walk away, but Knox caught up to her easily. "Hold on," he said, chuckling. "At least tell me when."

She sighed, but tried to keep a smile on for Jimmy. "Nine? Or so."

Knox looked back down at his clipboard and made a note. "I can do that. Oh, Fath—ah, Jimmy. Sir. I was about to drop off some more firewood at my mom's house and your sister's. Do you need any?"

Jimmy nodded. "I would appreciate that, son."

This time, Knox gave him a tight smile. Then he turned back to Bee. "Care to join me?"

She gave him a bewildered look. "Join you what?"

He shrugged. "You were getting pretty good at the axe before. Figured you might want to continue the lessons."

Bee squinted her eyes at him. He was just being polite or, at most, frustratingly charming. It was annoying, if she was honest, but also . . . hell. What did she have to lose?

"Five bucks says I can chop at least two pieces of wood without any help this time."

"You're on," he said.

"Y'all have fun," Jimmy called after them. She thought she saw him smile, but it could've just been her imagination. It had been running wild lately, after all.

"What are you working on?" Bee asked as they walked together. Knox was still looking at the clipboard.

"Oh," he said. "Just making sure everyone got their deliveries."

"For the wood?"

"In addition to that." Knox laughed. "Just planning a little something for the holidays."

She followed him into the forest, but no matter how many questions she launched at him, he refused to answer her, though he was just a little *too* amused by her admittedly highly piqued curiosity. Though she didn't get any answers out of him, she *did* actually manage to win that five bucks, and she gloated to him about it all the way back to the Big House.

"You are mighty proud of yourself for cutting two logs in half," he teased once the house was in sight.

"It starts with two," Bee said, "but then—the whole forest."

"Okay, slow down. We do need some of the trees to stay standing."

"Fine," Bee huffed. "I'll contain my wrath. For now."

Knox stared at her with an expression Bee couldn't quite place, and then he laughed with an expression so confused, she couldn't tell if *he* knew what he was laughing at.

"What?" she asked.

"You," he said. "I like you. You're a special kind of different."

Bee felt her cheeks grow hot. "I don't know if that's a compliment or not."

Knox gave her a genuine smile. "It is. We need different around here. At least every once in a while." He lifted the pile of wood he had in his arms higher. "I'll take this up for you and then drop off what Jimmy needs."

"Okay," she said.

"Thanks for accompanying me this afternoon, Bee," he said, and she smiled.

"Trust me. The pleasure was mine."

Chapter Nineteen

Clover

Saturday afternoon, December 16, 2023

Clover had never texted so much in her life. If she wasn't texting Hailey, she was texting Dee and Leilani, or Mo, or even Gillian, until eventually she was added to their group chat, the type of thing Clover had studiously managed to avoid her entire adult life. It was also the first time she'd ever wished she had a smartphone, since everyone seemed to be commenting with emojis that wouldn't load properly or GIFs that took ages for her to download. In what now seemed to be a past life, she would have never understood the need for that much interaction or attention, but it didn't feel like needless distraction anymore. Now it merely felt like connection. A togetherness with a world outside her head and outside her home that she didn't know she'd wanted.

She scrolled through the photos her friends had taken through the past week, taking in her own scrunched eyes and wide grin. She could guess how many drinks she'd had based off how big her smile was, and then one photo in particular caught her eye. It was her and Hailey, shoulder to shoulder, mouths open, eyes closed, arms crossed over each other as they pretended to hold mics and scream into them. Clover hit save. Then the phone vibrated again:

Gillian: Jupiter's tonight?

Mo: YES YES YES YES

Dee: I think that's a yes.

Mo: YES YES YES YES YES YES YES YES YES

Clover: What is Jupiter's?

Dee: Super gay. Much Christmas.

Gillian: Basically.

Lei: Jupiter's is a gay speakeasy, but they're having a burlesque Christmas show tonight.

What the hell is a burlesque Christmas show? Clover thought.

Hailey: You want to come, Clove?

Mo: COME COME COME COME COME

Gillian: Oh my god, please say yes.

Clover: . . . yes?

Clover closed her messages just as half a dozen WHOO messages from Mo came through. She was excited to hang out with her friends, but especially to see Hailey. She couldn't help thinking about the conversation she'd had with Dee and Leilani a few nights before, about Hailey being single "for now." It seemed like Clover had only a small window for fate to make its move, and she wanted to make it count. After all, apparently, burlesque indicated that there would be multiple barely dressed performers, and while she was sure they were talented, Clover wanted to be sure that the only person Hailey wanted to pay attention to was her.

Three YouTube videos later, Clover looked at her handiwork. Her normally unremarkable eyelashes looked thicker and longer, and her brown eyes popped against her black liner. Her eyelids sparkled, her cheeks glowed, and her lips were soft and shiny.

A few hours after that, Clover found her friends standing in a long line outside of the speakeasy, each of them well-dressed for the event. "Ho ho ho," Mo said as they pulled Clover into a tight hug that lifted her off the ground. They were essentially wearing a tailored velvet Santa suit and a red fedora that they wore cocked to the side. Leilani wore an off-the-shoulder white dress with striped candy cane stockings, while Dee wore a simple dark green suit jacket with a deep red tie over black jeans. Gillian completed the troupe, donning black leather pants with a black leather vest over brown pasties that covered her nipples.

She winked at Clover, and Clover hid her blush. They did all say this was a *burlesque* Christmas show. She supposed it was only a taste of what she was about to experience.

She looked around. Where was Hailey?

"Hailey said she's running late," Leilani whispered to her as if reading her mind. She gave Clover an apologetic smile, and Clover waved her off.

"Oh, of course. So, how long is the wait? For the speakeasy, I mean."

"No idea," Gillian said. "It's supposed to be, like, a whole experience. Some dapper dude is gonna keep coming out every few minutes, take everyone's phone and put them in one of those faraday bags, and then—"

"Shh, Gill, don't tell her!" Dee said exasperatedly. "Let her experience the fun herself!"

Gillian rolled her eyes and shrugged. "You'll see," she said to Clover.

A few minutes later, they finally made their way to the front of the line, and a Black woman with her locs tightly twisted into two braids on either side of her head greeted them. She wore reindeer antlers and a slick 1920s-esque suit. It was only if you looked hard enough that you could tell that the suit was also in the Christmas spirit, as it was a deep, deep green with a dark red bow tie, not unlike the outfit Dee was wearing, except the colors were so dark that they seemed black without the single bulb of light that cast a soft glow on the six of them. When Clover glanced down, she realized the woman's heels were six-inch stilettos.

The woman checked each of their IDs, then led them inside a small, cramped room with a bookshelf to one side. Just as Gillian had said, the woman took each of their phones and put them in their own faraday bag. "If you need to make a call, you can take the phone out in the hallway, where the bathrooms are. If you take it in the bar, you'll be asked to leave." She asked each of them for their verbal consent and understanding, and then pressed a button to her side. The bookshelf turned, and when the woman ushered them through, they walked into a dimly lit bar that was much bigger than it had looked from the outside.

People dressed in varying levels of dapper, glamorous, or risqué were spread out across the floor. Some people were huddled in groups or at their tables, talking over drinks, while others watched the stage, where an East Asian woman in an elf costume was currently doing the splits and then demonstrating shocking core strength as she shifted onto her forearms and kicked her legs up and over her head, essentially flipping onto the chair she'd placed nearby. Kelly Clarkson's rendition of "Merry Christmas Baby" played in the background.

"You're practically drooling," Clover heard a voice say from behind her. She knew that voice.

"Beth?"

"Yeah. Hi." Beth gave Clover one of her usual slow and appraising gazes, her lips quirking up slightly. "Wow. You look nice."

"Thanks," Clover said confidently, though she could feel that familiar vibration in her chest every time Beth was near. "You do too."

And of course she did. Beth always looked good—and not just good. *Precise.* Tonight she was wearing a simple wraparound dress with a thin gold chain that complemented her dark brown skin and gold wire earrings that looked like Santa's sleigh. It was a whimsical detail that Clover was surprised to see on Beth—but then again, she was surprised to see Beth at all.

"What are you doing here?"

Beth raised her eyebrow. "They do this every year. It's sort of *the* place to go if you're queer and even remotely interested in holiday cheer." She took a deep breath and cleared her throat. "Could I buy you a drink?"

Clover resisted the urge to point at herself. *Is she asking* me? The last time they'd seen each other, Beth had all but suggested Clover had terrible fashion sense. Now, amid the glow of yellow light and the slow, sultry beat of the performer's music, this frustratingly stunning woman was offering Clover a drink. *She did save me from falling that night,* she thought, *and she said I was cute. Which is funny, because she's gorgeous, but moody and extremely aggravating.*

For the barest of moments, Clover thought she might say yes—because Beth was giving her the same look she'd given Clover that night at the holiday market. Like she was a painting worth admiring. It made Clover's skin grow warm and her lips part. Suddenly, she was thinking about more than just one drink. But Clover was waiting for someone else—

someone, she thought, she might've been waiting on for half her life.

"No, thank you," Clover said, though she couldn't shake the feeling that her answer should've been *Hell yes.*

"Clover! Over here!"

She felt someone grab her hand, and before she could protest, Dee dragged her to the table they'd found. Clover looked back, but Beth was already lost in the crowd. She fought against disappointment, bringing herself to attention when she noticed Hailey finally approaching them.

Hailey, who had her arm wrapped around another woman's waist.

Clover felt the floor bottom out from beneath her.

"Hey, guys," Hailey said brightly. The woman beside her was Latina, and wearing a knitted cap and a belly-baring white tank top, with loose black sweats and beat-up sneakers. "Look who I found."

Clover hoped it was just a friend, but Gillian's sympathetic smile, paired with Leilani's subtle hand on her shoulder, suggested the exact opposite.

Hailey glanced at Clover and cleared her throat. "Clover, this is my, uh . . . Sherise. Sherise, this is Clover. The old high school friend I told you about."

Sherise took Clover's hand and they exchanged stale greetings before Hailey hastily pulled Sherise toward the bar. As soon as they were gone, Dee let out a long whistle and shook her head. "Not again."

"They've been on and off for, like, three years," Gillian muttered. "It is genuinely exhausting."

"Didn't Hailey just get back from Colorado, like, two days ago?" Mo said. "I thought she said Sherise told her it was done-done. For real this time."

"You know queers don't know how to break up," Dee said. She stared at Hailey and Sherise canoodling at the bar and let out a long, deep sigh. Then she turned her attention to Clover. "Okay, drink's on me. What'll you have? Or I can come up with a great concoction for you. Whatever you like. You said you like whiskey?"

God, was she *that* obvious? "I'll get my own drink," Clover offered brusquely. She didn't mean to be rude, but she needed to be alone. She needed to get away. Clover felt dizzy, and she knew whiskey wouldn't fix the problem. No. She'd have to drink ten shots to even begin to disappear, and she wanted to fall into a hole *right fucking now.*

Only when she approached the bar did she realize her mistake, as she'd now have to watch, up close and personal, as Sherise pulled Hailey into a deep kiss. She watched as Hailey's fingers trailed down Sherise's sides and then gripped the elastic of her sweatpants, pulling her thin frame closer as Sherise's arms wrapped around Hailey's neck.

Clover was going to be sick. She knew it. She'd never felt more nauseated in her entire life. Or was it jealousy? Or stupidity? She had no idea, but she was desperate for it to disappear, and fast.

"What are you having, sweetheart?" the bartender asked.

"Two shots of tequila. Please." Clover slapped two twenty-dollar bills on the bar, and when she downed the first two, she downed two more.

She wandered back to her group but couldn't stay still. Even as her friends whooped and hollered at the performances onstage, she found herself unable to focus. She'd thought the past few days had been building up to something special, that she'd gotten the second chance she'd always hoped for, or that she thought she'd hoped for. But this wasn't a love story, an adorable meet-cute of past lovers finding their way to each other again.

It was just Clover, all dressed up with no one to go home to.

"Clover, you want to take it easy?" Gillian asked. Clover wondered why. How many shots had she had at this point? She could still stand, so clearly not enough. She started back to the bar, but Mo caught the back of her shirt.

"Hey, friend," they said gently. "Why don't we get you a cab home?"

They were right, of course. Of course, they were right. Clover was getting too drunk, too messy, and she barely knew any of these people. They shouldn't have to take care of her. No one should. She turned back, looking for a bathroom or some place to collect her thoughts, but there it was again: a perfect view of Hailey and Sherise, this time pressed against each other in the corner by the bathroom, hands beneath each other's shirts, lips on every available piece of skin.

Sifting through her drunken thoughts, Clover mumbled that she was going to the bathroom, but really, she didn't want to be followed. Instead, she waited until she was out of sight of her friends, and then she stumbled through the hallway, only vaguely noticing someone calling her name as she went through the back exit.

The second she felt the chill of the air on her skin, the dam she'd been holding back broke through, and she collapsed against the wall, tears ruining the makeup she'd worked so damn hard to put on.

"Hey," she heard someone say. Her watery memory formed a name: *Beth.* "Let's get you home."

"I'm okay." Clover's voice wavered, and Beth scoffed.

"You're not. Clearly. I know the way. We'll take my car. I'll get your phone." Clover tried to protest, but Beth was already holding her wrist, gently guiding her away from the wall and toward a car parked on the side of the street.

"Why are you being so nice to me?" Clover asked, just as another sob hit her.

Beth frowned as she opened the passenger seat and then, once Clover was settled, pulled the seat belt across her lap. "Why wouldn't I be?"

That was an acceptable enough response for her very drunk brain. Clover closed her eyes as the car started and the world spun. The last thing she remembered was being led to Bee's bed and then the front door of the condo clicking shut.

"Don't leave," she whispered, but Beth had already gone.

Chapter Twenty

Bee

Sunday morning, December 17, 2023

The black boots with the fur on the outside had *seemed* cute to Bee when she'd bought them, but as she stared at her outfit, she felt caught between a T-Pain song and an ad for Justice girls' clothing at Macy's. The boots, paired with a fuzzy white sweater and big earmuffs, now seemed a bit . . . much.

I have other clothes, she thought, *right?* Bee turned to the haphazard pile of fabric now strewn across the floor like modern art: *Portrait of a Woman Undone.* Nothing was worthy of the occasion. Sure, some of them were functional; others were even cute. But when she thought of wearing any of it, they all seemed like itchy, ugly monstrosities yearning for the trash bin.

She closed her eyes and focused. Then she looked back at the mirror and gave herself a final once-over. This was fine for a simple winter outing. Just fine.

"You ready?" Knox asked when she finally emerged from the safety of the house.

"As I'll ever be!" she said brightly. Together, they crunched through the freshly fallen snow toward the back of the house, past the chicken coop and Knox's cabin, to a small white wooden stable. The whole time, she tried not to watch him, to pay attention to the sureness of his gait, or the curls in his hair, or even how his shoulders hunched, like he was maybe a little underdressed for the weather—a little cold and in need of warming up. Only when they stopped at the stable did he stand up straight, the posture of a man about to stand before a queen.

"Okay," he said quietly. "So, this is Tilda's home. She's an older girl, so she needs a lot of care, and she can't see or hear too well these days, so she can spook easily. Just don't make any sudden movements, and you'll be all right."

For a moment, Bee felt unsure. "Is she safe to ride?"

He nodded. "She never runs; even when she was younger, she'd deign to gallop. And besides"—he winked—"I've got you."

Bee felt her cheeks warm. This was a terrible idea. Even so, she watched as he knocked gently on the outside of the stable. Then he disappeared inside. A moment later, he reappeared with a brown-and-black-speckled horse with a white muzzle and a wavy black mane.

"Whoa," she said. "She's gorgeous."

"Sure is," he said. "Now I'm gonna show you how to pet her. Then we'll see if she lets you ride."

Bee nodded, but on the inside, she felt her stomach flip

over. Tilda might've been old and beautiful, but *God,* was she huge. Bee didn't think horses usually bit people, but what if *this one did*? Her muzzle was as big as Bee's entire face!

"You okay there?" Knox asked, his head tilted boyishly to the side.

Bee tried to give a convincing *mm-hmm,* but it must've sounded as strangled as it felt, because Knox chuckled a little and came over to her side. "Tilda's a big girl, but she's not gonna hurt you. I promise."

"Mm-hmm," Bee said, this time confident that the sound had at least come out clearly.

"You've . . . never ridden a horse before, have you?"

"Once," Bee said, "or twice. As a child, at the local fair."

"Okay. Good. Well, this is just like that. We're gonna put a helmet on you, I'm gonna lift you up, and then I'm just gonna hold the reins and walk with you both down that path there." He pointed to a gravel road that disappeared into another part of the forest. "It'll take ten minutes, tops. You okay with that?"

Bee took a deep breath, then squared her shoulders and dug her feet in. "Yes. Totally. I can do it. What?" She looked at Knox as he started to laugh. "What's so funny?"

"Do you always do that?"

"Do what?"

"The . . . the thing with your shoulders and your feet. You did the same thing when you were chopping wood."

"Oh." She blinked. "I . . . don't know."

She would've felt sheepish if he hadn't followed up with "Well, it's pretty cute, I have to say." But when she looked at him, he looked away. Again. Then he disappeared back into the stable, muttering something about Tilda's harness and how Clover's helmet would probably fit her.

It was only at the sound of Clover's name that Bee's blush started to fade. "Leave that man alone," Bee whispered to herself. When he returned, she gave him a respectable distance as he prepared Tilda to ride, rattling off safety instructions Bee tried diligently to remember.

The touch of his hand on her waist as he helped her up and the smell of his aftershave meant absolutely nothing to Bee. Nothing at all, she told herself.

As it turned out, Tilda didn't seem to care one way or another if Bee sat on her back. She barely paid Bee any mind at all, seeming alert only when Knox offered her a treat or a scratch behind the ear. The three of them walked in silence, and Bee made herself focus—on the skeletal trees whose branches hung heavy with snow, the occasional gray or brown rabbit that popped out from one bush and dashed into another, the faint smell of pine, and the gentle *swish-crunch-swish* of Tilda's hooves on the path. She settled into the rhythm of Tilda's back beneath her and the side-to-side sway of her own body in response. In this moment, Bee let whatever thoughts she'd had of Knox fade, because *this* was something precious—something rare. She was in constant motion, yes, and yet not a hint of stress had touched her. *Relaxed* wasn't quite the word—*calm*, perhaps.

She felt *calm*. And that—well, that nearly made her feel giddy. Her fingers tightened on Tilda's reins with a soft sense of surety as Knox led them farther down the road.

Soon the snowy path gave way to gravel, and the trees began to sprout decorative lights and artificial boughs of holly. "My family's house is just up the way," Knox said finally, his voice jolting Bee back to reality. She sat up straight and blinked as if coming out of a daze. When they finally approached Knox's home, Bee's fingers itched for her phone. Clover's house was gorgeous, but *this* . . . well, this seemed downright historic, with its deep red panels and dark wood beams, and two black lampposts wrapped in spiraled garland.

"Wow," she murmured, and she saw Knox try to hide a smile.

"We'll go around back to the stables there. Usually Tilda would already be tugging me, but we don't usually go past the front of the house," he said.

"Then why'd you take me this way?"

He shrugged. "I thought you'd like it."

Outside the stable, Knox let Tilda graze as he led Bee inside, and she balanced her sense of awe with the shockingly strong smell of manure and hay. The horses here were lovely and huge, and they stank to high heaven. And she'd thought the streets in San Francisco were bad.

"Everything all right?" he asked, as he began to brush one of the mares—a brown one with pale yellow hair named Doodle. "Short for Snickerdoodle," he'd said.

"Yup," she said, trying not to seem too suspicious between gulps of fresh air. "I'm totally fine, it's just . . . Wow, you know. Wow."

Knox wasn't fooled. He just gave a low rumble of laughter,

which Bee was starting to find far too enchanting, and began to lead Doodle out of her stable. "The smell of nature can be awe-inspiring, can't it?"

She glared at him playfully as he led them both back to Tilda's side. Suddenly, quiet old Tilda reared up and Doodle followed, both of them greeting each other with infectious enthusiasm as they bumped heads and rubbed their necks against each other.

"They all get along just fine," Knox said, grinning, "but these two are best friends. Ever since Jimmy brought Tilda home, she and Doodle have just been thick as thieves together."

"Are they the same age?"

"Nah. Doodle's basically a toddler compared with Tilda."

"And Tilda is Clover's horse, right?" Bee asked, surprised to see Knox's steady grin snap into a frown.

"Uh, no. She was her mom's."

Bee cleared her throat and gestured to Doodle. "So," she said. "We did the pony ride. Are you going to show me how to really ride a horse?"

Knox jumped over one hurdle, then another, each time with increasingly more flourish. If Bee didn't know any better, she'd think he was actually having fun. Not that Bee knew anything about riding skill, but as she watched him, he seemed confident, completely trusting that Doodle would follow his every move and never once faltering or slowing. Occasionally, Tilda would stop her grazing in the field they were in to gallop in Doodle's steps, but after a minute she'd return to her usual slow gait and wander merrily about the field.

Bee watched safely from just outside the gate, whooping and cheering Knox on, welcoming the show with spirited glee. He'd told her she'd be safe in the field with him, but Bee wasn't so sure—he'd said he'd been riding since he was a child, and that was obvious from the show he was putting on, but that didn't mean she was ready just yet to put her life in the man's hands.

Still, she loved to watch him—she could admit that in her own head. For the first time since she'd met him, he seemed entirely at ease. Sure, they'd known each other for less than a week, but she wanted him to feel as comfortable around her as she seemed to be around him. She wanted them to be on the same footing, at least.

She didn't want to think about why.

After a few more minutes, Knox slowed down, and Doodle trotted over to Bee's part of the fence. "Woohoo!" she shouted as they approached. "Encore, encore!"

He laughed. "I think you want me to die of exertion."

"Oh," she said, reaching up to pet Doodle as the horse pushed her muzzle through the gate. "I didn't know you and Jimmy were the same age."

"Har-har." He gestured toward the field. "You ready to do all that?"

"No," she said lightly. "I'm pretty tired."

"Uh-huh." He shot her a playful look and then jogged after Tilda, who was now on the other side of the field, munching on whatever she'd found there on the ground. He reattached her bridle and led her back over to Bee and Doodle. When he asked if she'd like to guide Doodle back to the stables, she acquiesced, and together they walked with the horses on either side of them, chatting about Bee's nonexistent riding skills.

"I'm just saying," she said, "I bet I would've been an award-winning equestrian if my parents had let me learn."

"An equestrian, huh? That's your secret dream?"

"Nope. Not a secret. I'm saying it right here, right now: if I could go back in time, I would've been a competitive horse-riding person. In the Olympics."

"I'd bet on you."

"Thank you," Bee said smugly. "Wait . . . Do people make bets on the Olympics?"

"Hell if I know," Knox said. "I'm pretty sure people will bet on anything."

Suddenly, a high-pitched screech pelted them both from the side, along with a sudden flurry of white aimed squarely at Knox's chest. The snowballs themselves were harmless, but Tilda reared up, pulling Knox backward just as he turned in the direction of the laughter and, soon, alarm. He let go of the reins just in time, but Bee watched as he slipped on the snow beneath them, landing hard on his back.

He bit back a swear as two Black kids no older than ten or eleven ran up to them, apologies tumbling from their mouths. "We're so sorry, Knox! We didn't mean to scare you! Are you okay? Sorry, miss! We're sorry!" One of them, a girl with short cropped hair, stumbled after Tilda, who had taken a few strides down the path and was now back to kicking at snow.

"Are you okay?" Bee asked, heart beating hard against her rib cage. She was hesitant to bend down or make any sudden movements, lest Doodle spook too.

"It's okay," Knox mumbled, sitting up slowly with gritted teeth. "Don't worry, I'm fine." He turned to the other kid, a boy with shoulder-length dreads, who was now standing in front of them looking lost. "Can you grab Doodle from Miss Bee here, Kendrick?"

The boy nodded numbly and took the reins from Bee, who hurried to Knox's side.

"Let me see your leg," she said as he tried to stand.

"I'm okay—ah!"

"You're not," she said sternly. She ran her fingers quickly over both his legs, and when he jerked away, she sighed and lifted his left pant leg. His skin looked sore and bloated, and while she wasn't a doctor, she *had* gotten certified as a first responder when she was in the eleventh grade.

"And how long ago was that?" he asked when she told him.

"Recently enough to know you've got a sprain. A bad one." He groaned, and she patted his shoulder empathetically.

"We can take the horses back to the stables, Knox," the girl who had grabbed Tilda said. "Can't we, Kendrick?"

Kendrick had big eyes that looked as if they might burst into tears at any moment. Bee's heart broke for him. She knew that look—that feeling. She'd grown up with it every day of her life. "Hey, it's okay," she said softly. "No one's mad, and you're not in trouble. Okay, honey?"

Kendrick nodded and wiped his eyes.

"Yeah, Kenny," Knox said, still trying to mask the pain.

"Everything's just fine. Go on now with your sister. I'll come by and get Tilda later."

Kendrick's sister bumped her brother's shoulder, and together they scurried toward the stables.

"Siblings of yours?" Bee asked, as she mustered as much strength as possible to help Knox stand.

"Cousins," he said once he finally got his footing. "Sort of. They're, uh, they're Clover's cousins. Known them their whole life."

"Ah," she said. She thought she recognized them from the tree lighting.

"Yeah." He shook his head. "They're good kids, when they're not trying to kill me."

She could tell immediately that he was trying not to lean on her, but that was a stupid idea, and she told him so. Begrudgingly, his body sank into hers, and Bee pretended not to think about how good it felt, to smell his aftershave and feel the brush of his hair against her cheek as he tried to keep his balance. For a moment, they locked eyes, and Bee swore she saw his eyes flick to her mouth. He cleared his throat and looked away. Slowly, they began to hobble together.

"To your family's house, I assume?"

"No way in hell," he grunted. "They'll never let me hear the end of it."

She stopped hobbling and looked at him. "You are not staying in that tiny shack in the middle of the forest on your own."

"It's not like I live miles from civilization," he muttered. "And where else am I supposed to go?"

"To my house," she said as if it were the most obvious thing in the world, until he gave her a look that quickly reminded her that it had once been *his* house.

"My place is closer than the Big House anyway," he said, and she couldn't deny that he was technically right.

"Fine," she said, and they began walking again. "Hey," she said after a moment. "You're kind of heavy."

He guffawed. "I apologize. I'll lay off the meat and potatoes."

"I'm just saying," she said cheerfully, "it's not easy being a walking stick. It's really working my legs. If we keep this up, I bet they'll be super toned by the time I leave."

"Your legs look great as they are."

She looked at him, but he looked away. Again. She tried not to show her annoyance—or disappointment. It was hard to tell what she felt with him. She tried another route of conversation. "Do you have any plans for Christmas?"

"I'll probably spend it with my family," he said. "We've shared the holidays with Clover and them for nearly a decade, and I think that's the plan again now." His laugh had an undertone of bitterness. "I tried to skip it. Truly, I did. But Aunt Janine is a bit more persuasive than my mother."

"Oh, so I guess we'll be spending the holidays together then."

Knox looked at her quizzically. "Why?"

"Janine invited me," she said. "And Jimmy said I had no business breaking an old man's heart if I said no."

"I see," he said quietly. "I guess we will then."

"I didn't realize your family still celebrated with Jimmy's," she said after an unbearable moment of silence, "or I would've said something to you earlier."

"It's fine," Knox said. "But I'm curious about something else."

"What's that?"

"How much do you think a professional walking stick could get paid? I'm saving up for a new place, and I could use a side gig."

She should've let him fall right then and there. "You are truly the worst, you know that?"

"Why, Bee," he said with a cheeky grin. "I think that's about the kindest thing anyone has ever said to me."

Somehow, as she took in the curve of his lips and felt the heat of his body against hers, she doubted that was true.

Chapter Twenty-One

Clover

Sunday afternoon, December 17, 2023

Okay, so I bought two large pizzas, one cheese and one with pepperoni, and a liter of ginger ale," Beth said as she came through the door again. "I didn't know if you ate meat or not, so I figured I'd get both. I eat either, so . . . And I got ice cream too, in case you're in the mood for that instead."

Clover frowned as she opened her eyes and then promptly shut them again. "Ow," she moaned. God, her head hurt. "What time is it?"

"Late," Beth said. "But you should go back to sleep."

"You came back."

"I said I'd be back," Beth said, setting food down on the kitchen table and pulling off her coat. "You said something along the lines of 'mrk.'"

"That sounds right," Clover mumbled, although she didn't

remember. How many hours had it been since she'd passed out? "I feel like hell."

"Yeah, and that sounds about right too," Beth said. "Here's some Tylenol." She came over and set it next to Clover, waiting until she'd lifted her head up long enough to take a swig of the ginger ale and down the painkiller. As Beth stood, Clover watched her, realizing that her clothes had changed since the night before. Beth must've gone home at some point. She looked, as always, perfectly put-together, only this time she wasn't wearing any makeup—at least, not that Clover could tell. She was in a loose black tee and fitted dark-wash jeans, and God, how did she look so hot all the time? It was like she wasn't even trying. Clover's eyes lazily wandered over Beth's flawless figure, noting with hazy curiosity how toned Beth's arms were. She wondered how her legs would look too, without all that fabric.

Clover groaned again. Even with Hailey and Sherise dancing in the back of her mind, Beth's very presence did something to her that was baffling and frustrating all at once. She closed her eyes to stop from thinking more and lay back down, one arm covering her face.

Beth, however, was busy pulling out paper plates from a shopping bag. "So," she said. "Pepperoni or not?"

"Why are you here?" Clover mumbled into her arm.

"Do you want me to leave?"

"No," she said. "No, I'm just . . . You're being *so* nice."

Beth rolled her eyes. "Yes, I've been known to express humanity on occasion."

"You're just very dry," Clover said. "And kind of rude some-times." She wished she could hold her tongue, but while her head had stopped spinning, her sense of propriety hadn't quite caught up to her mouth.

"Except when I'm nice?" Beth asked.

"Yes, it's very confusing."

At this, Beth actually laughed. "I've been told I'm not great with people. In my company, my sister does all the talking. Apparently, I'm too direct."

"Well, I think that is an accurate assessment." By now Clover had moved so that she was facing the foot of the bed, her arms pillowing her head as she watched Beth take a bite of pepperoni pizza. "Can I have a slice of cheese pizza?"

Beth put a slice on a paper plate and brought it over to Clover. Then she took a seat on the floor beneath Clover's head. "How are you feeling, aside from hungover?"

"What do you mean?"

Beth chewed her pizza without breaking eye contact. "I mean, you were sobbing last night. I assume you got wasted like a college freshman for a reason."

Clover collapsed dramatically, letting her arms drop out from beneath her so that she was facedown on the bed. "Ugh, God, please don't remind me."

"We don't have to talk about it."

"I just . . . thought this girl I knew liked me. And she doesn't."

"Bummer," Beth said. She took another bite of her pizza. "She clearly has bad taste."

Clover's head shot up. "What?"

"What?" Beth responded. "I did ask to buy you a drink last night. This can't be a surprise."

Clover laid her head back down and watched Beth skeptically. "You told me I had bad taste."

Beth wrinkled her nose. "I did not."

"You laid out three different outfits for me."

"I was trying to be nice."

"And you were pretty rude to me the first time we met."

Beth sighed and took a bite of her pizza. "I'm sorry, I was having a bad day. When I came to the condo the other day, Bee wasn't answering the phone—which is typical of her, mind you—and then I discovered that she had skipped town. It's always fun when your business partner disappears right before the holidays."

Clover's eyes widened. "You two work together?"

"Unfortunately," Beth muttered. Then she took a deep breath. "I don't mind it, most of the time. I mean, I actually kind of like it, when things are running smoothly. Bee is smart, creative. She keeps the business fresh. She's just flaky."

Clover considered this. "It's good to have opposites sometimes," she said. "I can get laser focused and to the point myself, and our farm manager keeps things light and in perspective. It helps."

Beth raised an eyebrow. "You run a farm?"

"It's the family business." Clover chuckled. "Technically passed down to me when my mom died and my dad had his heart attack."

Beth frowned. "I'm sorry to hear that." She wiped her hand on a napkin and then pointed to the uneaten pizza to

Clover's right. "By the way, you really should eat, or you'll just feel worse later on."

"Do you always take care of sad drunk girls at holiday parties?"

"Only the ones who are staying at my sister's condo unsupervised."

"Ah, I see," Clover said. She finally sat up and grabbed the ice cream instead of the pizza. "So, you're just doing damage control."

Beth paused and cocked her head, studying Clover for a moment before seeming to decide on a response. "I often do damage control for my sister, so it feels like second nature to me. But, also, I don't know. I have a good feeling about you, I guess." Beth shifted uncomfortably as she looked at her pizza. "I felt it the moment I saw you."

"It seemed like you didn't like me very much when we met."

"I don't like anyone the first time I meet them, especially when I'm preoccupied. Doesn't mean I don't have eyes. What's so funny?" Beth asked.

"I don't know," Clover said, still giggling. "I've always thought you were gorgeous, but also kind of scary? But in a *really* sexy way. It's very stressful to experience."

"Sorry I stress you out," Beth said. Her laugh was warm and low and infuriatingly inviting.

But Clover answered honestly. "I don't really think I mind."

There was a lull as Beth's dark brown eyes took her in again, and in that moment, Clover felt the cold little butterflies in her stomach start to dance again. *Oh no,* she told them. *Don't you dare. You have caused me far too much trouble the last few days.*

She forced herself to focus and took a bite of her ice cream. This was not the time to start thinking lasciviously about a new woman. Certainly not after last night, and *definitely* not when she was the twin sister of the woman she had swapped houses with. But as she licked her spoon, she couldn't help but notice Beth's eyes drop down to her lips. The *hell yes* from the night before screamed at her again.

"Look on the bright side," Beth said. "You've experienced a lifetime's worth of lesbian drama in the course of a week. Congratulations! It might be a new record."

Clover glared at her, but she was too hungover to disagree. "It seems like a very messy lifestyle."

"I mean, half of my friends now live in the suburbs with two kids and a rescue pit bull. Being single is always a little messy, I think. We just happen to have a smaller pool to work with."

Clover considered this. "Hm," she responded. Then: "Are you and your sister close?"

"That's a non sequitur."

"She didn't tell you she was skipping town for three weeks."

"Ah." Beth stretched. "No, she didn't. But it's not that much of a surprise."

"But you still take care of her?"

"She wouldn't say so." Beth looked around, her lips pulled to the side in a way Clover found adorable. "Our parents are strict. They care a lot about appearances. My dad's an investment banker and my mom's a corporate lawyer, and they're both way too proud of being Black people with money and assets. They consider us part of their assets. The problem with Bee is that she's a free spirit; it's hard for her to play by their rules. But she's also straight. All she'll ever have to do is marry a man and have a couple kids, and my parents will eventually forgive any missteps she's ever made. Me, though . . . I'm gonna have to keep working the rest of my life to make sure I don't fall out of their good graces."

"How do you know?"

"They told me." Beth laughed. "When I was thirteen, I asked this girl out, secretly, but you know, my parents found out. And then . . . they said that if I expected to uphold their family name, I needed to make up for the indecency. Well, they called it 'indecency,' and then Obama became president, and they just started calling it a 'blemish' instead. I guess it sounded less like a moral judgment. So, you know, I build our business, watch out for my sister, and keep my love life to myself."

"Beth, that's awful," Clover said. She reached for her hand just as Beth grabbed another slice of pizza.

"Yeah, well. It's just one of those things. We've got an industry party coming up the day before Christmas Eve, and I'll represent the company there—alone—while Bee is in Ohio, at your place. And then I'll . . . ha, represent the company at my parents' the day after. Alone." Beth exhaled through her nose and shook her head. "It's fine."

Clover thought about her family and her friends back home. From their perspective, they probably thought she was being a bit callous and flighty herself, leaving her father alone on his first holiday without her mother. Though Clover felt for Beth, she imagined Bee probably had her reasons, just like Clover did. She bit her lip.

"My mom was an amazing woman," she said softly, "and one of my best friends. But when I told her that I had ended my engagement with the guy I'd been with since we were kids . . . when I told her *why* . . . oh, wow, she . . . she did not take it well."

Beth watched her keenly, and Clover forced herself to continue: "She told me that I was misguided and that I was just scared of being with one person forever. She said that, um, she didn't raise me to be *that* way. She said a lot of things." Clover laughed bitterly. "And then she died. I mean, obviously that's not my fault, right? She'd been sick for months before I said anything to her about it. But to have that conversation and then to lose her . . ." She could feel the tears springing into her eyes, and she fought them back. "Anyway, my point is that family is complicated, I guess."

She let out a slow breath and was surprised when she felt Beth's hand against her cheek.

"Thank you for telling me that," Beth said softly. "And I'm sorry."

"Well, like you said, it's fine. Which is to say not fine at all." She laughed at her own joke and was satisfied when Beth joined in. Then she straightened her shoulders and looked at Beth head-on. "I have an idea."

"What's that?"

"What if I came with you to this party next week?"

Beth raised an eyebrow. "That is an idea."

"It's the least I could do, given that you had to rescue me from myself last night. And it's one less night where you have to be alone." Clover waited as Beth considered it. A few seconds passed, and Clover began to feel self-conscious about her bold proposal, until Beth stuck out her hand.

"I'll take that offer," she said.

Clover grasped her hand and shook it. "Then it's a date." They looked at each other, and Clover fought back the instinct to correct herself.

"I guess it is then," Beth replied, and smiled.

A knock on the door interrupted them, but before either one of them could react, it gently clicked open. Dee peeked her head through. "How is she feeling?" she asked Beth. Then she noticed that Clover was sitting upright. "She lives!" She stepped through the door fully this time, a CVS bag in her hand, and took a look at the hangover meal Beth had brought. "You did well, Beth, damn." She walked over and gave Beth a hug that Clover knew Beth had not been expecting, but she accepted it nonetheless.

"You two know each other?" Clover asked. At this point, she wouldn't be surprised.

"We do now," Dee said. "Formally, anyway."

"She and her wife came to check on you last night," Beth said.

"After we realized you weren't going to answer any of our eight thousand messages," Dee said pointedly.

Clover blushed. "I'm sorry."

"It's okay. Hailey has that effect on people, especially after a breakup. She means well, but . . ." Dee sighed but didn't continue.

Clover waved her comment away. "I made *a lot* of assumptions. And you technically tried to warn me."

Dee nodded and then looked between Beth and Clover. She seemed to decide something, because she lifted the CVS bag up and placed it on the kitchen counter before beginning to retreat. "Well, hey," she said, "you two enjoy yourselves. I've got, you know, things to do. Clover, there's a couple bottles of water in the bag and some microwavable noodles. You seriously have to do some grocery shopping, dude. Beth"—here she put her hand on her heart—"it was a pleasure." Then she turned back to Clover and mouthed, *Have fun,* before hurrying out the door.

Beth clearly didn't miss Dee's antics. "What was that about?"

Clover tried and failed to hide her smile. "No idea. Do you want another slice of pizza?"

Beth inched closer so that the skin of her arm brushed against Clover's bare legs. "Don't mind if I do," she said as she leaned forward, her breasts pushing against the fabric of her shirt.

Clover could feel her head buzzing, and this time it wasn't from the alcohol.

"Someone's calling you," Beth said helpfully.

"Oh." Clover looked around and then found her phone in the heap of her jacket and shoes beside the bed. "Oh," Clover said again. "It's your sister."

Chapter Twenty-Two

Bee

Sunday night, December 17, 2023

. . . and Bob and his wife. Am I missing anyone else?" Bee sat perched on the edge of the living room couch, a notebook balanced on her knees as she examined her list of names. Knox sighed, his body angled awkwardly so that his leg was elevated on a pile of pillows.

"Bee," he said for the ninetieth time that day, "I can have someone else do all of that." She ignored him.

"It's a good way for me to see the town and figure out what else this place has to offer," she said brightly. "I like feeling like a local."

Knox narrowed his eyes and let out an exasperated huff. The slight movement knocked strands of brown hair into his face, and Bee resisted the urge to tuck them away. Instead, she winked and double-checked her list.

"What are you going to do about it, anyway? Hobble after me?"

She hopped away with a surprised squeak when she saw Knox reach vengefully for a nearby pillow, and he was stopped only by Jimmy's arrival. He had a steaming cup of coffee in his hand, and when he saw the two of them in action, he only shook his head. Still, Bee didn't miss the ghost of a smile on his lips.

When Jimmy had first seen Knox leaning on Bee, he had howled with laughter. "You take the city girl out riding, and you're the one who comes back a mess?" He'd hee-heed and haw-hawed for what seemed like hours as Knox's pale cheeks grew red and he crossed his arms like a schoolboy getting teased on the playground. Then he insisted, like Bee had, that Knox stop being so stubborn and get himself up to the Big House.

"The kids told your mother, and your mother called me," Jimmy explained as he and Bee helped Knox up the steps. "Your mother is going to have a field day when she's done with you."

As predicted, Knox received half a dozen calls from both his mother and Janine while Bee prepared the couch and made sure he was as comfortable as possible. His mother would come and pick him up later that evening, but for now Knox was under her care. Despite his protestations, she didn't mind.

"It's technically my fault you're in this predicament," she'd said.

"Technically, it's Tilda's fault," he countered, "and you don't see me lying up with her and Bennie in the hay." Once his stubbornness finally subsided, though, he groaned with sudden realization. "Damn. I don't know how I'm going to get all those deliveries done now."

"Oh, right, you mentioned those. Is that the side gig you actually have? Since being a walking stick is out of reach now, I mean."

"Nah," he said with surprising seriousness. "Just something I had planned for the holidays, that's all."

She'd poked and prodded him for what seemed like ages, until he gave in, and now here she was, making her list and checking it twice, while Jimmy sat on his beloved love seat and sipped his coffee. She didn't know anyone who drank coffee so late at night, but Jimmy attributed it to his Cuban grandmother. "Helps me sleep," he'd said, and it was clearly true, because it didn't take long until she could hear his snore warm the house.

Bee and Knox exchanged amused glances, and the familiarity of it took Bee by surprise. Knox must have felt the same, because she saw his gaze darken and his eyes cloud over.

"I should go," he said. "I appreciate the hospitality, but I don't want Clover to feel some kind of way about me stomping through her house."

"She doesn't mind," Bee said, and then immediately regretted it. She'd meant to be a little more tactful. "I mean, I called her, while you were on the phone with your family. I told her the situation, and she basically insisted that you stay at the house too."

Knox stared at her. "You called Clover?"

Bee nodded slowly. "Yeah. I mean, we're swap-mates. I have her number."

"But you talked about me." Knox rubbed his face. "That's—that's crossing a line, Bee. Clover is my ex-fiancée."

"I know that," Bee said. "But I knew her before I met you—"

"No, you don't know her. You're staying in our house. Her house, I mean. You're a guest, a visitor, that's all. You don't get to come here and try to replace her. You're buddying up with her dad, you're spending Christmas at her aunt's house, and now you're trying to get me to—"

"To what?" Bee snapped. "I'm not trying to get you to do a damn thing except heal. I'm not one of your town groupies, Knox. I'm not following you around like a lost puppy. I have my own life. Contrary to what you might believe, not everyone's life revolves around whatever you and Clover had going on."

"Whoa, hey, hey." Jimmy sat up sleepily, rubbing his eyes. "What's going on here? What are you two yelling about?"

The muscles in Knox's jaw clenched. "Nothing, Jimmy. Sorry for disturbing you." With effort, he stood, and though Bee let her anger dissolve enough to try to help him, he waved her off. "I'm going to wait outside, if that's all right. I'm feeling a bit suffocated in here."

He limped around the couch, and Jimmy looked at him, bewildered. Then he scrambled up and tried to catch Knox's weight with his own. "Okay, son, now listen—"

"I'm not your son, Jimmy." Knox looked ashamed the moment he spoke. "Sorry. I'm sorry, Jimmy. I just gotta go." He made his way to the door and let it slam shut behind him.

Jimmy looked at Bee and sighed. "It's not your fault," he said.

Bee believed him, but it didn't stop the tears that had sprung into her eyes from falling.

Chapter Twenty-Three

Clover

Wednesday afternoon, December 20, 2023

Beth: Anything yet?

Clover: No. :(

Beth: I can call Bee and ask what's up.

Clover: I couldn't ask you to do that.

Beth: You didn't.

Can't argue with that logic, Clover thought. She sighed and slipped her phone back into her pocket. It had been three days, and still no word from Knox. She supposed she shouldn't have expected an update from him—after all, it's not like he was dying. Still, it pained her to know that he had gotten hurt, and while helping out a guest of hers no less, and yet he hadn't felt the need to tell her.

Just like the fact that he didn't tell her he was moving.

New things kept happening to Knox Haywood, and good or bad, they didn't involve her. Isn't that what she asked for?

"Not exactly," she muttered. Still, she figured it was best not to drown in her sorrows, and instead she focused her attention on Leilani and Dee's dog, who was currently panting in distress as she filled the bathtub. Though her friends were more than understanding of her mini breakdown last Saturday, she still felt the need to offer some sort of penance for getting wasted and disappearing in the middle of their night out together. She was leaving in a little over a week, after all, and she was hoping—praying—that these could be the sort of friends she could still take with her.

Of course, that started with her being a good friend herself. So, here she was, bathing Miss Cleo, the escape dog, while Leilani was out running errands and Dee was out picking up their lunch. Hailey hadn't reached out to her yet, but she *had* texted Dee, who relayed that "Hailey feels awful and doesn't know what to say. I know she wants to talk to you soon, though."

As awful as that night had been, Clover realized she wasn't waiting to hear from Hailey. Whatever happened between them, she took it as a simple case of teenage nostalgia, and she couldn't fault Hailey for that or for whatever feelings she'd invoked. Like Clover, she had her own life and relationships to contend with. It hurt, but it would heal. Besides, the trade-off was getting to know Beth better and . . . well, Clover would be lying if that wasn't what she'd been desperate to do since she'd seen her that first day getting off the elevator.

She blushed at how quickly that thought turned to heavier desires, and she refocused on the task at hand. She turned the bathtub faucet off. "Okay, Miss Thing," she said. "Time to hop in."

She double-checked that the bathroom door was shut tight, as instructed, and then leaned over and heaved Missy into the tub. With eyes as big as saucers, Missy sunk down into the water, ears back and head bowed.

"Don't look at me like that," she chastised. "It's for your own good!" She reached for the shampoo and gently began to work the lather into Missy's fur. Naturally, once her hands were fully soapy, her phone began to ring. She groaned. "Okay, one second," she said to Missy, whose eyes seemed to droop. Clover pouted back at her and then grabbed a handful of treats from the counter. "Peace offering." Then she rinsed off her hands and swiped at her phone. It was Knox.

"Hello?" she asked, cringing at the eagerness in her own voice.

"Hey," he said.

"Don't you 'hey' me, Knox Michael Haywood. I've been calling you for days."

"I know, I'm sorry."

"Are you okay? Is your leg okay?"

"It's fine. I'm fine."

"Good," Clover said. She relaxed on the closed toilet seat and leaned forward on her arms. "Good," she said again.

"It's just a sprain," he said, as if sensing the relief in her voice. "I'm sorry you were worried."

"It's fine," she said. "I mean . . ." She searched for the words she'd been thinking of this whole trip. "I know I'm not your fiancée, Knox, but I had hoped that we could still . . . that you'd talk to me. Eventually. And I understand you needing space, but then you got hurt, and I didn't hear from you, and I just . . ." She sighed. "What do you need me to do, Knox?"

She could hear him shift on the phone. "What do you mean?"

"I mean, do you need me to back off completely? To just leave your life and call it a clean break? Daddy told me you were moving."

"Oh." He cleared his throat. "Yeah. I mean, I was going to tell you."

"When?"

"I don't know." He sounded annoyed. "You went clear across the country for the holidays and sent me, like, a three-sentence email as a heads-up. Our families have spent every Christmas together for almost twenty years, so an actual in-person conversation would've been nice."

Clover was speechless for a moment. "Okay," she said finally. "That's fair."

"Yeah," he said.

"Yeah," she said.

There was silence on the line. Then: "Is it okay if I say I miss you?"

She closed her eyes and let out a deep breath. "Of course it is. I miss you too, Knox."

Another beat of silence ensued, and she wondered if he was waiting for her to say more.

When she didn't, he cleared his throat. "Listen, I don't know if your dad told you but, um, Bee, your Vacate guest, is apparently spending Christmas with us."

She frowned. "I know that."

"No, I mean . . . your aunt Janine invited her to have Christmas at the house, with the whole family."

"That sounds like something Aunt Janine would do." She wondered why Knox was telling her, or if there was something else he was trying to say. "Is that okay with you?" She asked.

Another pause. "I guess so."

"Do you not like her?"

"Who?"

Clover laughed. "Bee. The Vacate guest who has apparently been taking care of that sprained ankle of yours."

"She hasn't been . . . I mean." She heard the phone shift on his end. "I like her just fine."

Clover sat back in her seat. She wasn't sure what he was trying to say, or what he wanted her to say, but she knew Knox. She knew him very well. "If you like her," she said softly, slowly, "then . . . it's okay with me."

"Okay," he said.

"Okay."

"I hope San Francisco is treating you well," he said. "Really."

She smiled. "It is. Really." It was good to talk to him like this, even if neither of them were saying much. It was good to talk to him like it might mean they'd keep talking. Some day. From beside her, Missy whined, soap suds still covering her wet fur. "Oh," she said. "I've got to go. I'm on dog duty."

"Okay. Wait. What?"

"Long story," she said. "I'll tell you later?"

She heard him hesitate, and then: "Yeah. I want to hear about the dog."

"Seriously?"

"Genuinely."

Clover was almost too afraid to sound too eager, for fear that it would spook him, and whatever olive branch they'd just extended to each other would snap in two. Instead, she promised to call him soon, with one more "Make sure you stay off that foot!" before she returned to Missy's side, feeling for the first time since she'd arrived that she was looking forward to going home.

Once Missy was squeaky clean, Clover dried her off and let her scamper into the living room, where she was surprised to see Beth on the couch, perched on the edge of her seat with her brow furrowed in concentration. A Joy-Con was gripped between her fingers. Dee sat next to her, looking considerably more relaxed but no less focused.

"What is happening?" Clover asked.

"Back," Dee said. "Food's in the kitchen. I found this one skulking outside your apartment."

"I wasn't skulking," Beth said, her attention on the screen in front of them unwavering. It was *Mario Kart,* Clover realized incredulously. *She's playing* Mario Kart. "I was just stopping by. Your texts indicated distress—hey!"

"Don't hate the player," Dee cackled as a ghost-type character squirted ink on Beth's side of the screen.

"Oh," Clover said, taking in the scene in front of her. "I'm . . . less distressed now. But thank you."

"Did he call you back?" Beth asked, still glaring at the screen.

"Who?" Dee cut in, a maniacal expression on her face.

"The ex-fiancé," Beth answered.

"Ah."

"He's fine," Clover said. "And so is Missy, by the way. Although you could probably tell from how eagerly she's rolling around on her back."

Both Beth and Dee grunted in response, before Beth suddenly shouted in disbelief, while Dee shot up in victory. "Boom!" she shouted. "In your face!"

"I want a rematch," Beth said. Then she seemed to remember herself and sat up straighter, gently placing the controller on the coffee table in front of them. "Later." She finally turned to look at Clover fully, and when she did, Clover felt her breath catch. It was like someone had turned on a spotlight and beamed it directly at her.

"Hey," Beth said, her voice suddenly raspier than it had been a moment before.

"Hi," Clover whispered shyly.

"Okay," Dee said. "I'll grab the sandwiches. You two, uh, do that." She hopped over the back of the couch, and Beth rose and took her spot, making space for Clover to sit. When she did, the two looked at each other with a hint of apprehension. They'd been texting for days, ever since Beth had brought Clover home that night from the bar, but it felt so different for them to be next to each other now. The long messages they sent to each other, the details Clover had shared about herself, and Hailey, and Knox, and her family . . . all of that intimacy was now bottled between them, quiet and heavy. It's not that they didn't know what to say, but rather that they didn't know where to begin. Like kerosene, waiting for a match. One word, and who knows what could happen, and how fast.

In a moment, Dee would interrupt them, because hunger waits for no one. Then Leilani would return, and Missy would pounce, and laughter and warmth would fill this room of new friends and new feelings. In a moment, *this* moment was going to end. So they sat there and smiled and waited like two teenagers, awkward and hopeful, and knowing that something special, something *new,* was waiting to begin.

Chapter Twenty-Four

Bee

Thursday evening, December 21, 2023

Bee couldn't begin to imagine why Beth of all people would text her about Knox.

How's he doing? Beth had asked her the night before. Clover is worried.

She thought about screenshotting the messages and sending them to Ayana to decipher but thought better of it. Knowing Ayana, she'd probably send back a picture of a tarot card and wax philosophical about life's changes and the colors of the wind or whatever. Worse, Bee would then have to explain to Ayana why *she* had called Clover about Knox.

She felt a headache coming on. *Surely* her sister had not managed to become friends with the woman she had swapped houses with. *Surely* they had not become *such* close friends that Beth would be texting on her behalf. *Surely*. Bee said the word to herself so much it began to lose meaning. There was absolutely nothing sure about anything, as far as she was concerned.

And speaking of Knox, she hadn't heard a peep from him since he stormed out of the house, all red-faced and upset, because she had the gall to exist. She couldn't help that Clover's house was the house she had chosen. Nor could she help that she and Jimmy got along or that Clover's aunt liked her. She'd made absolutely none of these decisions in relation to Knox, and absolutely not so she could "take over" someone else's life. All she'd done was be herself—something that seemed to piss off all the people she cared about.

A knock on the door wrenched her from her thoughts, but Bee was thankful for the distraction. She was sure her next poem was going to be about murder. She disentangled herself from the blanket she'd shoved her feet under and walked to the door, surprised to find Knox on the other side.

"What are you doing here?" she asked.

"I wanted to apologize," he started, but Bee cut him off.

"Did you get a ride here?"

"From the cabin? No, why would I—"

"Why are you so interested in hobbling on your foot alone? Do you want a broken ankle? Is that what strokes your boat?"

He blinked at her. "Strokes . . . my boat?"

"You know what I mean!" She crossed her arms in an attempt to look menacing, but he only laughed harder.

"I don't. I have no idea what that means! What is stroking the boat? Is it an oar? I don't think you're supposed to use one that way. Although I do have a crutch now"—he looked thoughtfully at it for a moment—"which is kind of like an oar, I guess."

"Ugh." She threw her hands up. "Will you come in here out of the cold then?" She led him to the couch, though of course he didn't need any directions. Once he'd settled down, she stomped over to the kitchen. She poured herself and him each a glass of water and then stomped back to him. "Drink this."

"Why?"

"Because I needed something to do with my hands instead of throttle you, because you're injured. Now drink before I pour it on your head."

"Yes, ma'am," he said, still grinning. Bee watched the bob of his Adam's apple as he downed the glass, and it only made her want to throttle him more.

"Thank you," she said daintily. Then she took a deep breath and took a seat on Jimmy's love seat, crossing her legs and putting her hands on her lap primly. "Now then. What did you want?"

Knox's look turned serious. "I wanted to apologize for the other night. I was out of line."

Bee took a deep breath and let the anger that had been building up for the past few days seep out of her. "Thank you," she said. Then: "I understand why you'd be upset. But I'm not trying to Jordan Peele your ex-fiancée's life. I have my own shit to figure out. I'm just passing through."

Knox nodded. "No, I get that. Totally. I just got caught up in my own feelings about Clover, and the holidays, and how entwined both of our families still are. And then you come along and . . ."

She waited for him to finish. His eyes flicked down to her lips, and she felt her breath catch. Then he grunted and adjusted, moving his hand to the back of his neck.

"Anyway," he said, though she noticed his voice was just a *tad* deeper. "Anyway," he said again, but he didn't say anything else.

Bee rooted around for something to offer, but found herself grasping at nothing. She let the silence hang. If he wasn't going to talk about the elephant in the room, far be it from her to bring it up.

After another moment of silence, Knox cleared his throat and gestured toward the TV. "You want to watch something?"

Bee blinked. "Oh. Sure. What did you have in mind?"

"Something about boats. I figured you might need a primer on how they work."

Bee grabbed a pillow and threw it at him. He let it hit him, but it didn't erase the dimples in his cheeks or the way his eyes shined with humor. Whatever tension had been in the room dissipated almost instantly, and Bee suddenly felt that sitting on Jimmy's love seat created too great a distance. She wanted to be closer to him, to feel the warmth of his skin against hers.

But the words of Taylor's friends flashed through her brain like lightning through a storm: *Maybe he's playing the field.* The words echoed against her skull. He might like her, sure. That much was obvious. But Taylor had thought he liked her too, and how many other girls? How many other girls did he measure up against the one woman he'd been set to marry, and how quickly did he decide they failed? With Roger, she always wondered what it was she was measuring up against, what it was that he was looking for, since he never seemed to stop looking, even when she was standing right next to him. His eyes always wandered, and then eventually his actions followed.

Bee might've been Knox's current choice, but she had no way of knowing how many others he had lined up. *You're leaving soon,* another voice whispered in her ear. *What does it matter?* She supposed it didn't, except that this wasn't what she came here for. That much she knew.

"My sister and Clover seem to have hit it off," she said suddenly. Knox furrowed his brow.

"Your sister?"

"My twin," Bee elaborated. "I have a hard time imagining anyone finding my sister suitable as someone to 'hang out' with, but I guess they've gotten acquainted."

"Well, if she's anything like you, I can see the appeal."

Bee bit her tongue. She was trying so hard to avoid his charms, and he just kept shooting them at her like arrows. "Besides looks, we're nothing alike. My sister is . . ." Bee racked her brain. "She's amazing. I mean, if I'm one hundred percent honest—and I can be, because she's not here—she's just sharp, on top of her game, and utterly accomplished. I mean, when you talk about someone who rolled out of bed brimming with perfection, that's Beth in a nutshell."

Knox nodded thoughtfully. "It sounds like you like her."

"I love her. I just don't think she likes *me* very much. She and my parents, they're not my biggest fans."

At this Knox frowned and sat forward. "I can't imagine why. You're hilarious, and witty, and fun to be around. You light up at the smallest things, and it makes everyone around you light up too. You're always looking for ways to help people—you even helped Bob with his damn slogan for the grocery store. I know I made a big deal about it, but it's not hard to figure out why Janine asked you to spend the holidays with us or why Jimmy's always talking about you. You're incredible, Bee. Anyone who doesn't see that needs to get their headlights checked."

Bee stared at him, her lips parted with complete and utter surprise. "I . . . I don't know what to say to that."

Knox cleared his throat and sat back on the couch. "Yeah, well, I just think you should know, is all."

"Thank you," she said breathlessly. That was completely unexpected, and if she thought harder about it, she was sure she wouldn't be able to stop the tears that would start to flow. "So, um . . . what about you? Any sad family stories or big dreams you want to tell me about?"

He blew a puff of air from his chest. Even from her seat, she could feel his anger on her behalf still radiating, though he was trying hard to let it go. He thought for a moment and then seemed to find an answer she'd find most amusing. "I used to want to be a fighter pilot."

Her eyes couldn't help but light up. "Really?"

"Yeah," he said. "My dad was in the military and would tell me all about it. But then he and my mom divorced when I was sixteen, and it messed my mom up real bad. After that, I didn't think about the military too much."

"Oh my god, Knox," she whispered, suddenly feeling silly for her previous spark of interest. She leaned forward and touched his hand. "That's horrible. I'm so sorry."

"It's not a problem," he said. "I mean, I got a little sad, of course. Stayed with my uncle one summer just because, you know, after a couple months, I started to think I was a tough guy, or whatever. Tried to sneak stolen goods from Bob's store and all that. My mom sent me to stay with my uncle, and it straightened me out."

"What'd he do?" she asked.

"He made me clean out his horse stables for three months straight." Knox laughed. "I mean, I was used to the work, but my mom usually went easy on me, and anyway, we don't have that many horses. But my uncle is a racing man. His horses are no joke, and he made sure their stables were spotless. Or I did, anyway. Ooh, my back and legs ached for weeks. But it got my head on straight."

Bee tried to imagine him as a scrawny teenager with a bad attitude, mucking horse crap for hours on end. It was a pretty funny image, she had to admit. "It looks like it worked out," she said. "You seem like a perfect gentleman to me."

He gave her a shy grin and squeezed her hand, making her finally realize she hadn't yet let go. "I've heard that a few times, I guess."

His eyes searched hers as his thumb ran across her knuckle. She knew that if he moved forward, she would meet him halfway. She would let herself give in. And for the briefest moment, she thought she might.

But then she pulled back. Resettled into her seat. His eyes

stayed on hers, but she pretended not to notice. Instead she reached for the remote and handed it to him.

He sighed but kept a smile on his face. "What do you recommend?"

After three episodes of *The Real Housewives of Atlanta,* Knox nodded off, succumbing to the two pain pills Bee insisted he take. She tucked him in with a heavy blanket and allowed herself only the briefest moment to brush his hair from his eyes. She resisted the urge to kiss his cheek, no matter how sweet he looked.

Her gaze swept over his sleeping form, and she resolved to give herself at least that moment. What she was going to do with it, if anything at all, was a problem for another day. Then she turned and made her way up the stairs.

Chapter Twenty-Five

Clover

Saturday night, December 23, 2023

Beth was already waiting outside when Clover emerged from the building. She was leaning against her black BMW with arms and ankles crossed, looking like nothing short of a bored supermodel. But when she saw Clover, the smile she gave was radiant. Clover had to wrestle herself to stop from grinning ear to ear. Beth nodded to Clover, then walked over to the other side of her car to open the passenger seat. Once Clover settled in, Beth returned to the driver's seat, slipping in one long leg after another. Clover loved watching her move, all finesse and certainty.

"Are there going to be a lot of people at the party?" Clover asked as the car started. Even when they pulled out onto the street, Beth was precise, tracking the cars around her as she followed every street sign.

"Maybe a hundred or so," Beth said, "give or take."

Clover sucked in a breath. It's not like she wasn't used to big crowds, but one hundred was a lot. When her parents threw their Christmas party, it was more like fifty people, max, and even then they were hosting people they'd known for years. Clover was having trouble imagining what it would be like to be a guest at an "industry" event full of people she could've read about in a magazine.

"You nervous?" Beth asked. The fog had turned to heavy rain, but Beth didn't seem the slightest bit anxious or rigid. Everything about her was certain and without distraction. Her right hand rested on the console between them. Clover wondered if it was an invitation.

"A little bit," Clover said. "I don't want to embarrass you."

Beth snorted and shook her head. "The thought didn't even cross my mind."

"But your sister is just as much a part of this world, and it seems like she embarrasses you all the time."

At that Beth went silent. Then she sighed. "I'm not embarrassed of Bee," she said softly. "If anything, I'm envious of her. Sometimes it feels like she couldn't give a damn what people think of her." She took a quiet breath. "I can't imagine how freeing that must feel." Then she looked over at Clover more closely. "What, you think because I judge my sister, I'm going to judge you too?"

Clover shrugged and looked at the hand that wasn't clasped in Beth's gentle grasp. "All I know is farming, and I don't own a smartphone or use any fancy apps. I even check Vacate on the computer or through my email notifications. I won't be able to speak any of these people's language."

"I don't care what they think," Beth said. "Just focus on having fun. I've got your back."

Clover appreciated her vote of confidence, but she couldn't help feeling woefully inadequate. How she'd found her way from a farm in Ohio to a BMW in San Francisco seemed awfully like a fairy tale, and she was sure tonight would be the night that clock struck midnight.

Until "Can You Stand the Rain," by New Edition, started blasting through the speakers.

Clover looked at Beth, aghast, but Beth was only just getting started. As the song continued, Beth mouthed the words to her with increasing gusto, just like the men in *The Best Man Holiday,* only stopping long enough to make sure she didn't crash her very expensive car. Clover covered her mouth, but the laughter escaped through her fingers, and by the time the song ended, she barely remembered where they were headed or why. All she knew was that she really, *really* liked the woman sitting next to her, and the surprises she always seemed to have in store.

When they arrived at the party, Clover was taken aback at just how casual it was. Sure, everyone looked nice and were no doubt wearing designer clothes from brands she'd never heard of, but she was satisfied that she didn't stick out like a sore thumb in her black cocktail dress and diamond earrings, both of which she'd borrowed from Leilani the night before. She took a deep breath and settled in, her arm comfortably nestled in Beth's as she led her through the crowd and introduced her to that founder, and this investor, and that CEO.

Beth left her for a moment to grab them both a drink from the open bar, and as Clover considered the food at a nearby buffet table, a white man sidled up to her, red hair slicked back and a gold watch strapped to his wrist. "Hi," the man said smoothly. "I haven't seen you before."

"I'm here with a friend," Clover said politely.

"Which one?" he asked. "Maybe I know them."

She smiled politely. He wasn't being rude, but she didn't like the way his eyes hovered on her cleavage either. "Maybe you do," she said.

"I'm Roger," he said, sticking his hand out.

"Clover," she said.

"That's an unusual name." He smiled. "Like the leaf, right? Were your parents gardeners?" He chuckled at his own joke.

"Farmers, actually."

"Roger, hi!" Ayana appeared beside him, with her long locs swept to the side and wearing a formfitting red dress. "How are you enjoying the evening?"

"Good," he said. "Just talking to my new friend here—"

"That's nice," Ayana interjected, cutting him off. "Listen, a few investors were looking for you. Said they wanted to talk shop." She waved at two men of color who did not seem to be paying either of them any attention. "You should head over there soon. I hear they're leaving in a few minutes to try to beat the rain."

Roger straightened his tie and speed-walked to the men without so much as a goodbye. The second he was out of earshot, the grin on Ayana's face fell and she took a long sip of the cocktail in her hand. "God, he's the worst," she muttered. She turned her attention to Clover. "I hope he wasn't bothering you," she said.

"You came just in time, I think," Clover replied, laughing.

"Thank God," Ayana said. "And I'm so glad you got my invitation!"

Clover blinked at her. "What invitation?"

"The one I sent on the app . . . Isn't that why you're here?"

Clover blushed. She didn't have the app, and hadn't checked the website since she and Bee started texting. "Um, I'm actually here with Beth. She invited me."

Ayana looked like she was going to spit out her drink.

"Hey, Ayana," Beth said from behind Clover. She handed Clover her whiskey and soda and took a quick sip of her own seltzer and lime. "Sorry I took so long," she said to Clover. "I saw Roger over here trying to talk to you. Are you okay?"

"I sent him on his way," Ayana responded.

"Thank God," Beth huffed. "He really is the worst."

"I know," Ayana said. "You know he tried to get back together with Bee *three times* after he cheated on her?"

"Four, actually," Beth said. Her eyes searched for him in the crowd. He was facing the men whom Ayana had pointed out, and they both looked like they wanted to be anywhere else. "I should say something to him," she said. Clover tried to stifle her smile. Beth really was protective of her sister. "But"—she turned back to Ayana and Clover—"now's not the time."

"Agreed. However, what we do have time for is a little catch-up. So, you two are here as . . . friends?"

Beth looked at Clover, and Clover looked at Beth, and Ayana's grin looked like it would break her face in half.

"Say no more. I don't mean to put you on the spot. Please, have fun. Enjoy. Free drinks, all that jazz. Clover, please, if you need anything, you know where to find me." She squeezed Beth's shoulder and touched Clover's arm, then scurried away as quickly as she had arrived.

"She is definitely going to tell Bee about this," Beth dead-panned.

Clover bit her lip. "Do you think she'll be upset?"

Beth sighed, and this time she took two heavy sips from her glass. "No. But I will never, ever hear the end of it."

Clover slipped her arm back through Beth's as they walked to a more private corner of the room, in front of a large window that let in the light of the moon in the clear night sky. "What do you think you'll tell her?"

Beth's eyes searched hers. "Honestly? I think I'll have to tell her thank you."

"For what?"

"For giving me the chance to meet you."

Clover was smiling so hard her lips hurt. "I guess I have to thank her too, then."

Beth's eyes dropped to her lips, and Clover thought for a moment that she might kiss her. She wanted her too. Badly. Even if the thought scared her.

She'd kissed two people her whole life, and both of them were still embedded in her life, though she'd barely heard from Hailey, aside from a quick I'm sorry if things seemed unclear. And while she could choose to be safe and sensible and always wonder what-if, she could also take the leap and find out.

Before she could lose her nerve, she pressed her lips tentatively to Beth's, then all at once. Beth's lips met hers fiercely, and she felt her arms encircle her back, pull her closer. Clover reached up and pressed the back of her fingers to Beth's chest, her thumb pressing against Beth's bare collarbone, and she felt a sharp thrill course through her when she heard a groan slip past Beth's lips.

"Ahem," someone muttered as they walked past, and Beth and Clover pulled apart. Beth's eyes sparkled, and the two of them broke out into giggles like a couple of teenage girls caught out on a school night.

Once they'd both grown tired of shaking hands and hobnobbing with people whose names neither of them could remember anymore, they made their way back to Beth's car. Twenty minutes later, they passed the sign welcoming them to Berkeley, as the clouds darkened and it began to rain, Clover could see that Beth's neighborhood was gorgeous. It was filled with bungalows and shingled homes packed closely together, covered in bright white fairy lights and elaborate holiday decor. The streets curved along brick sidewalks and stairways, and it was only then that Clover remembered that Beth ran a tech business.

They pulled up a short driveway to a small cottage-style home. Large windows loomed beneath a steeply slanted roof, like the entryway to a storybook. A figurine of a sleigh in white lights sat tastefully in front beside a proud maple tree.

"This is your house?" Clover said, not bothering to mask her awe.

"It's a one-bedroom," Beth said, as if that somehow diminished its impressiveness.

"Oh, well, in that case," Clover muttered, but she enjoyed the smirk it put on Beth's face.

"I'll grab an umbrella from the trunk," Beth said, but Clover had already opened the door. In a stroke of bad luck that seemed to never let her down, her foot sunk deep in a muddy puddle in the grass by the driveway's pavement. It reached high enough to encircle her ankle, nearly swallowing her shoe whole.

"I'll just . . . go inside with you," Clover said.

She hobbled quickly to the door with Beth, who was trying valiantly not to laugh with each squelch beneath Clover's foot. Mercifully, they were inside within seconds, and although Clover could leave her shoe outside, there was still the problem of her mud-splattered dress.

"I have sweatpants you can wear," Beth offered.

"You keep trying to get me out of my clothes," Clover said, sighing playfully.

"Can't blame me for trying," Beth said. She winked and then disappeared into her bedroom, bringing out gray sweatpants and a towel. "Do you want to rinse off?"

Clover didn't really think she had much of a choice at this point, unless she wanted to spend the evening caked in dirt. She watched as Beth peeled off her own jacket, which had kept her dress mostly dry. *Shame,* she thought.

While Beth started on dinner, Clover showered quickly, wincing only slightly when she brushed her hands unthinkingly over her new piercing. Then she threw on Beth's sweatpants and a tee-shirt Beth had laid out for her.

When she emerged, she found Beth in her kitchen, pouring tea into two porcelain Stanford mugs. The look she gave her made her shiver. "Hi," Clover said.

"Hey," Beth murmured. "You look nice."

"I'm not even wearing anything remotely next to nice."

"I don't care about what you're wearing," Beth said.

Clover nearly tripped. Heat spread down her stomach, and she realized, quickly, that she'd need to either sit down or start walking, fast. She swallowed her surprise and hastily pulled her damp hair back into a haphazard bun. "So," she said. "Tea?"

Beth's lips pulled into a sly smile that made it difficult for Clover to resist pressing Beth against the counter and discovering how flawless she imagined Beth looked beneath her perfectly precise clothes.

Beth handed Clover her cup of tea, and Clover blew at the steam, willing her brain to think about literally anything else but Beth's lips as she tested the heat of her drink or Beth's fingers as they cradled her mug.

"Dinner is on the table," Beth said eventually, turning to a small wooden table struggling under the weight of four potted plants. Clover caught her wrist. *What the hell,* Clover thought, but it wasn't a question. She set her mug down and wrapped her arms around Beth's waist. She pulled her closer. Beth came willingly.

Their kiss was soft and slow, and when they pulled away, Clover realized she was shaking.

"I got you," Beth whispered.

Clover kissed her again.

Her hands found the back of Beth's head, and their lips

pressed and pulled. Beth's tongue slipped into Clover's mouth, and Clover wasn't sure if the sound that made her dizzy was Beth's moan or hers. She felt her back hit the edge of the counter.

Without stopping, Beth's hands found the backs of Clover's thighs and lifted her up.

"You're a lot stronger than you look," Clover said breathlessly, before Beth's lips crashed against hers again. Clover's legs wrapped around her waist, and Beth's mouth found Clover's neck, sucking gently on the skin beneath Clover's ear, then at the space just below, on the pulse of her throat.

Clover wasn't sure her heart had ever beat so fast in her life.

Beth adjusted, and her hips met the heat between Clover's legs, forcing out a delighted gasp that Clover couldn't think long enough to contain.

"Too much?" Beth asked.

"Not nearly," Clover whispered. With her hands on Beth's cheeks, she pulled her in for another kiss, harder, more insistent, and Beth responded, her hands grasping Clover's thighs and swearing low as Clover bucked against her. The husky, delicious sound nearly made Clover lose herself.

It was then that she realized they were both still fully clothed.

She pulled away slightly, amused at the hypnotized way Beth's mouth followed hers. Her eyes were hooded and dark with obvious desire.

"Beth," Clover said, "do you want to take me to bed?"

Beth let out a low chuckle, brushing her forehead against

Clover's as she captured her gaze. "Do you want me to?" she said.

Clover let her breathing slow to a manageable pace, but she didn't need to think about what she wanted. She knew.

"Yes," she said softly. "I do."

Chapter Twenty-Six

Bee

Saturday night, December 23, 2023

Bee couldn't bring herself to think clearly, the texts from Ayana searing into her brain.

Ayana: Clover was at the party tonight

Ayana: with Beth

Ayana: WITH BETH

Ayana: Did you know they were still talking to each other?

Ayana: They were cozied up too. Like, this was not a platonic get-together between gal pals.

> **Ayana:** I saw them kiss before they left.

> **Ayana:** Bee, they kissed

> **Ayana:** BEE ARE YOU THERE

> **Ayana:** okay my wife is telling me that I shouldn't hyperventilate when guests are around

> **Ayana:** CALL ME

Bee put her phone down and rubbed her eyes. Then she picked her phone up again. The texts were still there, clear as day. She had not, in fact, hallucinated them. Knox's ex, whose bed Bee was currently sleeping in, had been seen kissing her sister. She thought, perhaps, that her head might explode. She took a deep breath and put the phone back down. This had to be a problem for Morning Bee. Midnight Bee was going to lose her shit.

Her phone buzzed again, and Bee thought it might finally be time to go off grid, but when she looked to see what fresh horrors her best friend had wrought on her, a different name caught her attention.

> **Knox:** I think Kandi might be the only one who doesn't stress me out on this show.

She stifled a giggle and then a groan. What was happening right now? Still, as she read and then reread Knox's text, a thought she hadn't allowed herself to let blossom stuck in her mind. If Clover was spending time with her sister, would she mind if Bee spent time with her . . . well, her ex-fiancé? Thinking it out loud, Bee could admit the two situations were not exactly comparable.

Still, she hadn't crossed any lines yet, and she didn't intend to. But it was late, and now she knew it would be impossible to sleep. She checked her phone again. It was unlikely Knox would have fallen asleep in the three minutes it had been since he first sent his text. Before she could convince herself otherwise, she put on her warmest pajamas and a large over-coat, making sure her twists still looked cute in the bun atop her head. Then she turned on the flashlight on her phone and trudged into the night toward Knox's cabin.

Knox answered on the first knock, his eyes wide with be-wilderment. "Hi," he said.

"Hey." She lifted her phone for him to see, his text bright on the dark stoop of his cabin. "Want to explain this to me?"

He laughed and put his hands up defensively. "I needed the distraction! And I wanted to know what happened."

"Without me?" she asked, her voice rising with a joking shrill.

"I'm sorry!" he exclaimed. "I now see the error of my ways. Your rage was so powerful that you trudged through the snow in the middle of the night to chastise me?"

"Absolutely," Bee said. "I couldn't let you get away with your transgressions."

"You should come inside," Knox said, still laughing. "It's seriously cold out here." That was when she realized he wasn't wearing a shirt. She could see the smooth ripple of his muscles against taut pale skin, and she resisted the urge to run her fingers over his chest.

"Then why aren't you wearing a shirt?" she asked instead as he closed the door behind her.

"Oh." He cleared his throat, one hand gesturing toward the heater in the corner of the room. "I get night sweats," he said. "It makes sleeping in the cold a little complicated. I have to wear thin layers, and I take my shirt on and off throughout the night. One reason among many I'm getting a new place soon."

The thought came to her far too easily: *I could keep you warm.* Suddenly, Bee realized coming to his cabin in the middle of the night was not the best decision she'd ever made in her life.

"So," they said at the same time, and then Bee laughed awkwardly.

"I'm so sorry," she said. "I shouldn't have just come over without asking."

"It's fine," he said quickly. "I mean, I could use the company. Who else is going to explain the backstories of the *Housewives* cast to me. Without you, I wouldn't have been able to place Kim Fields for the life of me."

"I'm still bothered that *The Facts of Life* rung a bell before *Living Single*."

"Only for a split second," Knox said. "And don't tell Jimmy. He'd never forgive me."

"I'll consider it," Bee said with a practiced air of haughtiness. Knox took a seat at a small desk by the door, and she hesitantly sat on his bed. As she looked around, her eyes caught on a guitar leaning next to it. "How are rehearsals going?"

"Pretty good," he said. "I'm still working out a chord, though, for the solo I'm doing."

"You never said you were doing a solo!" Bee shrieked.

"I'm full of surprises," Knox said. She couldn't deny that.

"What are you planning to perform?" she asked.

"You'll find out," he said, his dimples starting to show. But then his look turned thoughtful. "I wanted to do something for Jimmy. It's been a hard year for him. He won't show it, but . . . I wanted to thank him for everything he's done for me over the years. Even after everything with . . ." He looked at Bee and paused for a second. "Everything with Clover," he said finally. "He still acts like my pop."

"Do you still miss her?" Bee wanted to know. She needed to.

"Yeah," he said with a breathless laugh. "She's my best friend. I think I'm always gonna miss her."

Bee thought about that for a moment. "She sounds like someone worth missing."

"Yeah," he repeated. "It's been over a year, though. I think it's about time I let the part of her I had go."

Bee didn't think she'd ever felt so hopeful in her life, but she tamped it down with all the force she could muster. She didn't say anything. She didn't trust herself to. Knox looked to the side, seemingly thinking about something for a little while longer, and then he reached for the laptop on the desk. He picked it up and brought it over to her. "Can I join you?" he asked.

She nodded, and he pressed play on his screen. They sat

next to each other stiffly for a few moments. Then, as *House-wives* rolled on, their bodies began to lean and shift, until, eventually, Bee found herself snuggled beneath Knox's left arm, both of them now horizontal, the computer on his stomach. Her fingers splayed out on his chest. They were both unusually quiet. As the credits for the episode rolled, Bee looked up at him, curiosity in her eyes. He matched her gaze.

In one swift motion, he moved the laptop to the floor and shifted Bee's body beneath him. His lips met hers, and she let him in without hesitation, his tongue probing, tasting her with an intensity she thought only she had felt. Her fingers wrapped around his neck and pulled him closer. He moved his arm beneath her waist and pulled her body up to meet his. She moaned, and the sound he made in response made her kiss him harder.

All at once, it became far too apparent that she was wearing too many layers. Embarrassingly, her sweater got caught on her thick twists, but Knox's fingers were deft. He gently lifted the sweater and she shimmied out, and when her bun came undone, he offered to fix it for her. Instead, she let her hair unravel. The way he looked at her made her ravenous.

His fingers hesitated on the skin of her stomach, beneath the hem of her thin pajama shirt. Bee searched his eyes and then arched her back, slipping her shirt off and sinking into the feel of his mouth on the swell of her breasts, now pushing against the fabric of her bra.

She moved her palms over his chest, letting her fingers graze his skin as his lips moved to her neck. Her nails dug into his back. He lifted one of her legs and wrapped it around him, and when his tongue found the tip of her nipple, she swore.

She could feel how hard he was as he pressed against her leg. She wanted him to feel her too. She reached for the band of his pajama pants, but a thought crashed into her mind with such sudden ferocity that her hand was pushing him away before she even realized what she was doing.

"Are you okay?" Knox asked. He was breathing heavy, blue eyes darkened, lips swollen, hair messier than ever. "Do you want me to stop?"

"I . . ." She paused, letting her thoughts collect. "I really like you," she said.

"I like you too, Bee," he said.

"No." She pushed gently against his chest, and he sat up this time, giving her space to sit up and adjust her bra. "I mean, I think I actually *like* you. And I don't want to be your rebound. I know I'm just a guest here, and I'm leaving soon, but I still don't want this to just be . . . for fun."

Knox swallowed and leaned the back of his head against the wall. "I understand," he said.

She waited for him to say something else, and when he didn't, she moved to grab her shirt and the many layers of clothing that now covered his still-open laptop.

"I'm catching my thoughts," he said. He grabbed her wrist gently and pulled her back onto the bed. "I like you," he said. "A lot. And we don't have to do anything you don't want to do."

Bee shuddered out a breath. It was nice to hear, but it wasn't *enough* of what she wanted to hear. She pulled away from him again. Knox watched her quietly from the bed as she finished dressing.

"I'm gonna go," she said finally.

He stood up quickly and followed her to the door. "I'll walk you back," he said, but she stepped away from him and grabbed the door handle.

"No," she said. "I think I'm okay on my own." She reached up and touched his face, and when her fingers brushed his lips, he turned his face to kiss them. "Good night, Knox."

"Good night, Bee," he said. He sounded so unsure, and Bee hated the way it made her heart hurt. But that was the frustrating thing, wasn't it? No matter how good they felt together, she *needed* him to be sure. She knew all too well what it felt like to fall for guys with one foot out the door.

When she closed his door behind her, Bee adjusted the scarf around her neck and steadied her breathing. Then she turned her phone's flashlight back on and let its light lead her home.

Chapter Twenty-Seven

Clover

Sunday morning, December 24, 2023

Clover lay still wrapped in Beth's sheets, her head resting on her folded arms. Kisses trailed along the column of her spine, starting from her waist to the back of her neck. They felt like heaven against her skin. She could feel the rise and fall of Beth's breath as her breasts followed the trail, and Clover delighted in their warmth, in the weight of Beth's body still pressed against her.

"You feel good," Clover said.

"Mm." Beth kept kissing her. "You do too."

"I'm leaving soon."

Beth stopped, but her breath remained hot against Clover's skin. "I know," she said finally. She let the silence press on for a few minutes more, then shifted, lying beside Clover so she could look into her eyes. "What do you want to do?"

Clover reached over and brushed away a strand of hair

that had gotten caught in Beth's eyelashes. "I want to stay with you," she said. "I mean, I miss my dad, and the farm, and . . . but I don't want to leave you."

"I can come visit," Beth said.

"Don't you run a fancy business?"

"Don't you run a fancy farm?" Beth touched Clover's cheek. "I can make the time. Can you?"

"I'm willing to try," Clover said. She shifted, framing Beth with her arms so that she lay on top of her, and covered her mouth with another slow and gentle kiss. In all her years, and in all her fantasies, she could never have imagined she would feel this way. So free, and whole, and . . . right. When they finally pulled away, Beth's eyes searched her with a lightness and clarity that took Clover's breath away.

"What?" Clover asked.

"Do you want to come home with me?"

Clover looked around playfully. "I think that is where we are right now."

Beth chuckled softly. "I mean to my parents' home. I want them to meet you."

"I thought you'd never brought a girl home before."

"I haven't. They've never wanted me to." She shifted so that Clover lay beside her, and she propped herself up on one arm. "But Bee left, and it brought you to me. It had me thinking—maybe I should try things her way sometimes. Be a little bit more selfish."

Clover brushed her fingers against Beth's lips. "I think you mean honest."

Beth kissed her fingers. "That too." She bit her lip. "So,

what do you think? Do you want to come over and meet the folks?"

Clover thought about it. It was one thing to meet Bee's friends and colleagues, another to meet her family, especially when she knew it was tonight.

"My dad doesn't know about me," Clover said. "And it wouldn't sit right for me to bring my authentic self to your parents' table when I haven't even been able to do that at my own."

Beth looked down, trying to hide her disappointment, but she nodded in understanding. "Makes sense." Then she reached forward and pressed a soft but firm kiss to Clover's mouth. "Honestly, it makes me like you even more."

"Well, if I can't celebrate Christmas Eve dinner with you, then the least I can do is make you Christmas Eve brunch. Are you hungry?"

"Yes," Beth said, a mischievous look on her face. She made no move to leave the bed. Clover grinned.

"Good," she said, and the two slipped back beneath the sheets, a feeling far too close to love thrumming rapidly through Clover's veins.

Chapter Twenty-Eight

Bee

Sunday evening, December 24, 2023

Bee couldn't stop pacing. She'd paced in her bedroom the night before, in the kitchen that morning, and outside the coffee shop that evening as she tried to make sense of what the hell she had gotten herself into. She and Knox had kissed. They'd done *more* than kiss. And she'd left him hot and bothered while she froze to death in her own bed.

Well, that wasn't true. The bedroom, as always, was perfectly comfortable, but that didn't mean Bee hadn't been wide awake the whole night, staring at the ceiling. What was she thinking? She *knew* what it was like to get involved with men with easy smiles and divided attention. Knox was sweet, and gorgeous, and kind, but he was also just getting over the love of his life. The woman whose bed Bee happened to be sleeping in. She had absolutely no business getting involved with him.

She had tried to write a poem about that too. Something about heartache and forbidden love, or whatever the hell intellectual sophists more talented than her waxed on about. But then she decided that she hated poetry, and she hated her hormones, and she hated her stupid, traitorous heart.

It was a whole thing.

"Bee," Jimmy said, clasping her on the shoulder. "Missed ya this morning."

Bee turned and gave the man a warm hug. "Just nervous about tonight," she said. "Still haven't decided if I'm going to perform. Thought I'd feel better if I came here early. Write through the cobwebs."

"Any luck?" he asked.

"No." Her voice was light with nonchalance.

Still, Jimmy grasped her hand with both of his. "Either way," he said, "I'm proud of you for giving it a shot."

Bee felt her skin warm. No one had ever told her that before. That they were proud, even if all she did was *try*. She gave Jimmy another tight hug. "Where's Knox?" she asked when she pulled away.

"He'll be here," Jimmy said. "Told me he's just finished a few things up."

They found a table close to the door, opposite the side of the stage. Soon more people streamed in and the lights began to dim. A barista took the stage and announced a brother-and-sister duo who would play a rendition of "Blue Christmas." Someone in the crowd whooped, and then the two appeared, white teenagers wearing matching brown vests and blue jeans.

"Those are Christine's kids, down the street," Jimmy whispered. "They've got the voices of angels."

When they were done, another white kid took the stage, blond hair parted neatly on the side, with big blue eyes. He looked little more than three or four years old, and he wore a reindeer costume, his nose painted to look like Rudolph's. Bee recognized him as the little boy who had fronted the chorus with his electric lantern the first night she'd come to town. In the audience in front of the stage, his mom helped him through "The Itsy Bitsy Spider." It didn't exactly match the theme of the night, but the child seemed delighted.

"Joe's son, from the hardware store," Jimmy said.

As each new performer took the stage, Jimmy shared some tidbit or another about them, and soon the show began to feel less like an impending nightmare and more like an evening shared among friends. Maybe she would read something, she thought. The sign-up sheet was on the counter, where the baristas were still serving hot cocoa and wine. But where was Knox?

She looked around and saw Bob from the grocery store standing nearby. He was clutching a candle in one of his hands. Then Clover's cousins, Kendrick and Simone, ran giggling up to Jimmy and attacked his torso with glee.

"Hi, you two!" Jimmy exclaimed, though he kept his voice low so as not to disturb the Black woman playing flute onstage. "Where's your mom?"

Janine waved at him from beside the door. She was chatting with a Latina woman Bee didn't recognize who also had a candle tucked under her arm. When Bee caught Janine's eye, she waved, and the kids ran off, possibly to tackle some other neighbor Bee hadn't yet met.

The flautist finished her song, and the little boy took the stage again, this time with the chorus. Taylor stood right behind him alongside her friends, and they sang a medley of Christmas classics. Then the barista came onstage with a barstool, and Knox hobbled onto the stage. The crowd whooped and hollered, and Bee didn't miss the long eye roll that Taylor responded with. Then they sang through a series of famous pop songs at a faster tempo, with Knox accompanying them on the guitar. By the time it was over, the whole crowd was on its feet, even Bee, who hadn't managed to take her eyes off Knox the whole performance.

Then the choir walked silently off the stage, not giving enough time for an extended round of applause.

Suddenly, the crowd hushed. The tension in the air was taut, and everyone around her buzzed with anticipation. They were waiting for something. Knox still hadn't left the stage. Bee took a deep breath, afraid that if she blinked, she might miss something huge.

"This is for a very special woman in all our lives," he said. "A woman who brought a lot of light and love to this community. And"—he looked up, finding Jimmy in the crowd—"it's for a man we're all very lucky to still have with us. It's been a hard year, folks, but we're still standing. Mae Mills, we love you and we miss you."

With those words, Bee watched as Bob, and Kendrick, and Simone, and two dozen other people seated in the audience, including those who had just performed, lit their candles and held them in the air. Someone handed a candle to her and then to Jimmy. Knox began to strum his guitar, and Bee recognized the chords to Jeff Buckley's version of "Hallelujah."

I've heard there was a secret chord . . .
But you don't really care for music, do you?

Knox's voice was low and powerful, and as he began to sing, she heard a quiet sob from beside her. Jimmy was crying. He covered his face as his body shook. The Latina woman from before came over quietly and wrapped her arms around his small frame. Bob came over too and put his hand on Jimmy's shoulder. Bee gently took the candle from his hand. She held it for him.

Around them, the crowd sang along to the chorus. *Hallelujah, hallelujah.* Knox's voice carried over them, and she could hear his voice break. *Hallelujah,* she sang with him. *Hallelujah.*

When Knox finished, the lights went on. The barista announced a short intermission, and the crowd surged toward Jimmy, who was still drying his eyes. Unnoticed, Bee left the table and stepped outside, breathing in the cool evening breeze. She heard the sober tone inside turn to laughter and chatter, and she watched the stars. How bright they burned in the night sky, so far away and still so powerful, so present. In the midst of all that, she was really quite small, wasn't she?

If it were another night, another city, surrounded by different people, the thought might make her feel insignificant.

Instead, she felt free.

The door behind her opened, releasing another rush of voices. In their midst, she heard her name, and then a hand was on the small of her back.

"Hey," Knox said, coming around to face her. "I was worried you left."

"Oh, no." Bee shook her head. "Just wanted to clear my head. That was beautiful, what you did in there."

Knox shrugged, a shy smile playing on his lips. "Thanks," he said. "You think you might perform something?"

"How am I supposed to follow that?" she asked teasingly.

"It's not a competition," he said, and Bee laughed.

"I'm not used to that," she said. "I'm not really used to any of this. All this love, and support, and community. You're all family out here."

"You deserve that," Knox said. He ducked his head when she looked at him, like he wasn't sure if he was ready to say what he was about to say. Then he stepped closer and grabbed her hands. "Bee, about last night—"

"We don't have to talk about that."

"I want to," Knox said, "if that's all right." She let him continue. "Bee, I've spent most of my life in love with one woman. And I thought I'd never feel the way she made me feel ever again. And you aren't the first woman to try. Not that you were trying." He cleared his throat. "What I mean to say is, a lot of women in town kind of tried to flirt with me over the last few months, when they learned I was single. And it didn't feel right. It didn't feel *natural* the way it does with you."

Bee listened to him, tears springing to her eyes, but he wasn't finished.

"Bee," he continued, "you might just be the strangest woman I've ever met, and definitely one of the most stubborn, which is saying something. You're smart, and sharp, and breathtaking, and you drive me a little bit crazy." He took a breath. "I don't want this to just be a fling. I'd like to see if we could, maybe, have this be something more."

She couldn't stop them. The tears flowed freely. She tried to rub them away, but they were fast. "But I didn't write you a poem," she said.

Knox laughed and pulled her to his chest. "Funnily enough," he said, "I think we'll survive."

The door behind them opened again, but this time someone was screaming.

"Knox!" Kendrick yelled. "Come quick! Uncle Jimmy fell!"

Chapter Twenty-Nine

Clover

Monday morning, December 25, 2023

If getting arrested by an air marshal wouldn't delay her even further, Clover probably would've tried to fly the plane herself. Everything took too long. The countless calls to her airline. The drive to the airport. The flight itself. Clover needed to see her dad, and she needed to see him now.

Knox met her at the airport. "It's not a heart attack," he told her again, as she buckled her seat belt. Hours earlier, he had said the same thing, but she needed to see for herself. It was early in the morning, but he drove her straight to the hospital anyway.

"Thank you for calling me," she said. "And for making sure he was okay."

"Of course," he said. He grabbed her hand and squeezed it. "You know I'm always gonna be here for you two."

Clover squeezed his hand back. "I know," she said.

An hour and a half later, Clover hurried through the corridors of the hospital, while Knox stayed at the nurses' station, asking questions. "Daddy," she gasped when she finally saw him, lying in the hospital bed looking so much older than his fifty-seven years. An IV stuck out from his right arm.

Jimmy opened his eyes and turned his head. "Baby girl," he said. He let out an *oof* as Clover ran to him, wrapping her arms around him. "I'm okay, sweetheart, I'm fine. Just old, like you tell me."

"The doctor said it was your blood pressure," she said.

"The Black man's disease," he muttered. "It got a little high last night, but nothing to worry yourself over. You didn't have to come all the way back from your trip."

Clover ignored him. He already knew how she'd respond, so no point in lecturing him about it. Instead, she kept her arms wrapped tightly around him. They stayed like that for a while, her head on her father's chest, with his hand on her back. She let herself feel comforted by the steady rhythm of his breathing, of the proof that she hadn't lost him yet. "Daddy," she said after what felt like hours.

"Yes, baby girl."

She took a shaky breath, already feeling the tears prick her eyes. "I miss Mom."

"I know," Jimmy said. "I miss her too." When she lifted her head to sniffle, he brushed the tears from her eyes, and then he squinted. "Did you pierce your nose?"

"Oh," Clover said. "Um, yes."

He paused to consider it. "It looks good," he said, finally. He nodded in approval. "Your mama would like it."

She laughed. "You think so?"

"Mm-hmm," Jimmy said. "Your mama would like everything about you, Clover. Brave, smart, fiery. You're everything she raised you to be."

Clover looked down. "I'm not sure about that," she said.

Jimmy looked at her for a long time, and then he shook his head. "Is this about why you and Knox broke up?"

Clover's head shot up. "Mom told you about—"

"Mama and I didn't keep secrets from each other. You know that."

"Daddy, I . . . I don't know what to say. Or how to explain everything."

Jimmy gripped Clover's hand and brought her closer. "You ain't gotta explain yourself to me. I'll tell you exactly what I told your mom, Clover. That you are the best of both of us, and the only thing we've ever raised you to be is happy."

Clover felt something in her chest break loose, and tears began to fall freely from her eyes. "Daddy," she whispered.

"We love you, Clover. You understand that? And you know what else?"

"What?"

"Your mama had a tattoo of a snowflake, and I ain't gonna tell you where. Point is, don't you worry about that nose ring."

Clover didn't know if she was laughing or crying, but she hugged her father anyway, feeling for the first time in too long like she was exactly who her parents wanted her to be.

Soon they lay on Jimmy's hospital bed together as he asked about her trip, and Clover responded as honestly as she could about her new friends, and about Hailey, and then about Beth. She wondered when her dad would stop her, ask for more details, ask if she was sure. But he didn't. He just listened and held her close. Clover leaned into him and, finally, allowed her heart to rest.

ONCE THE NURSE shooed her away, Clover made her way down to the waiting room. Knox was still there, which didn't surprise her. What did surprise her was another woman, the near spitting image of Beth except with long twists and winter clothes. *Bee,* Clover reminded herself.

Bee stood up and stuck out her hand. "Hi," she said. "It's nice to finally meet you in person." She grabbed two paper bags and lifted them for Clover to see. "I brought you guys sandwiches. I figured you must be hungry, since you just got off the plane."

"Oh," Clover said. "Thank you, that's sweet." She laughed a little. "That's something Beth would do."

Bee frowned. "Is it?"

"How has the Vacate been for you?" Clover hurried on, wishing she could bite off her reckless tongue.

"Oh, it's been—" Bee and Knox spoke at the same time. They looked at each other. They looked at Clover.

"It's been great," Bee said.

Clover looked at them both with a gnawing suspicion, but her phone distracted her. She looked at the caller ID. "Oh, it's . . ." She cleared her throat. "It's Beth."

"I heard that you two had gotten along well," Bee said, and Clover wondered if she'd talked to her sister.

She glanced at Knox guiltily. "We did."

Knox looked at her and then he looked at Bee. There was a mix of emotions on his face, and in that moment, it became clear that all three of them had had a very adventurous two weeks. Quietly, Bee excused herself, and Clover and Knox were left sitting beside each other in the waiting room, alone but for a middle-aged white woman, the telltale sounds of *Candy Crush* creeping from her phone.

After a few moments of silence, Knox cleared his throat, and for only an instant Clover saw the five-year-old boy who became her best friend, blue eyes peeking out from beneath messy brown hair. "So," a very adult Knox said now, his voice low and shy.

"So," she said. She reached out a hand, and he hesitated before grabbing it between both his palms.

"So," he said again. "Beth, huh?"

Clover felt her brown cheeks brighten. "Yeah." She took a deep breath. "And Bee?"

He nodded slowly. "I think so." He put his head back and looked up at the white ceiling above them. Another silence passed between them, this time gentler and more forgiving. He closed his eyes tight and then opened them again. "I can't believe we fell for a set of twins."

Clover let out a bark of laughter. "Oh my god, you're right."

"Right? Like, we won't get married, so instead let's find another way to get involved in the same gene pool."

"Wow," she said. She leaned her head back like his. "That's ridiculous."

"You know what your mom would say, after she got used to the idea?"

"What's that?"

"The Lord works in mysterious ways."

This time, Clover laughed so hard she felt tears come to her eyes. "Knox," she huffed out between "Oh my god, why?" He grinned at her, holding her hand with a flexed arm to keep her from tipping over completely. When she could finally collect herself, he wrapped his arm around her shoulders and leaned his head against hers.

"It's good to hear you laugh," he said softly.

She smiled. "It's good to hear you making jokes again." She moved her head so she could look at him. "It's not weird to you? The . . . me . . . being with a woman . . . thing?"

He took a sharp inhale of breath and then let it out slowly. "It's weird you being with someone else in general. But no, I'm not exactly surprised. I'm pretty sure I almost lost you to that girl in high school."

Clover almost knocked his head back as she shifted to look up at him. "You knew about Hailey?"

"Ah, right. Hailey. That was her name." He frowned as he remembered. "I mean, I knew the way she looked at you, the few times you tried to get us all to hang out with each other. And the way you looked at her. I didn't want to regret not saying anything, so I took my shot." He looked down at her. "And I'm glad I did, even if it didn't last." Then he cleared his throat and looked away. "Do you . . . do you regret it? Choosing me over her?"

Clover thought about it for a moment. Then she shook her head. "That's the thing, Knox. Even if we're not together *like that,* I'm always going to choose you. Every day." She closed her eyes when she felt his lips against her forehead and his arm tighten around her shoulders.

Then: "It was the trapper hat."

She frowned. "What was?"

"Bee falling for me. I wore the trapper hat one day, and she was smitten."

"I hate you so much, Knox."

"I know. I don't know how you can stand me."

He winked at her, and she laughed again, her heart feeling full, and light, and whole. "Lots of love and whiskey, Knox Haywood," she said. "Lots of love and whiskey."

Chapter Thirty

Bee

Monday morning, December 25, 2023

Bee pressed the phone to her ear so hard that she swore she felt a migraine coming on, or maybe that was just preparation for the conversation she was about to have with her twin as she paced the living room of the Big House. "Pick up," she muttered. "Pick up, pick up, pick up."

"Hello," Beth answered.

"Did you sleep with my Vacate guest?" Bee asked.

Beth took too long to answer, and Bee thought she'd die right then and there. *Oh my god,* she thought. "Oh my god," she said. "How? I mean, why? I mean. Tell me everything!"

"I don't think that's something I should talk about with you," Beth said.

Bee huffed. *Fine then.* "I made out with her ex-fiancé."

"You *what?*"

Bee collapsed on the sofa and told her sister everything,

with Beth stopping her periodically to ask how that happened, and why this happened, and what was Knox like? In a shocking turn of events, Beth responded with actual details when it was Bee's turn to ask rapid-fire questions about Beth's last two weeks with Clover.

That this would turn out to be how Beth and Bee would have their first non-work-related exchange since they were teenagers was not on Bee's bingo card for the year, but she was getting used to the unexpected. Her sister's laugh, for example. She didn't know when she'd heard it last. And almost better than that was the fact that Bee wasn't the only one getting chastised. "I can't believe you slept with her," Bee said again.

"You've said that three times now."

"So you have to admit it then."

"Admit what?"

"Admit that you're glad I went on a somewhat reckless, totally impromptu vacation."

Beth was silent.

Bee waited.

"Fine," she said, as if it physically pained her to do so. "I'm glad. Really glad." Bee could've laughed herself silly, but Beth kept talking. "I didn't go to dinner with Mom and Dad last night."

Bee felt her heart stop. "You didn't?"

"No," Beth said. "I decided to take a page out of your book and actually enjoy myself. I spent it with Clover."

"But Mom and Dad love you."

Beth rolled her eyes. "They love you too. You still went across the country to avoid spending a day with them."

Bee considered this. It hadn't occurred to her that Beth could feel the same way. After all, Beth was the golden child, the one with all the accolades. "Didn't you win some tech award this year?" she asked.

"They'll be more impressed if I meet a handsome man like you," Beth deadpanned.

"Oh," Bee said. *Oh.* The gears in her brain spun as she put together the pieces: all their histories, all their potential futures. "Bethy," she murmured, and Beth groaned over the phone.

"It's fine, Beatrice."

"It's not, Bethy!" The idea that her perfect, polished sister—so accomplished and brilliant that she was *literally* terrifying—was still not enough for their parents simply because she wasn't straight made her . . . enraged. "Do they not know how amazing you are? They're so . . . so . . . *ugh.*"

"I concur," Beth said.

"I'm coming home," Bee said.

"Sorry?"

"I'm coming home," she repeated. "You're not spending the last of the holidays alone. Clover has to be here with her dad, and our parents are literally the worst, so I'm coming home. We're spending New Year's together."

"I . . ." For once Beth seemed entirely speechless. There was a pause that seemed to stretch into eternity, and Bee steeled herself for a lecture or, worse, another familial rejection. "Okay," Beth said at last.

Bee resisted the urge to press the phone fully into her ear. "Really?" She heard Beth shifting on the other end, and thought she'd let her sister take her time and potentially give something longer than a two-word response.

"I like spending time with you," Beth said finally. "I mean, it's hard, when we're focused on business, and Mom and Dad are always breathing down my neck to 'take care of you.' I guess I've . . . let myself get resentful. Of you."

"I don't need you to take care of me, Bethy," Bee whispered.

"Yeah, you do." Beth laughed, and Bee remembered how much she loved her sister. "I mean, with our parents the way they are, it doesn't hurt to have someone else have your back. That's . . ." She coughed. "I've been trying to do that ever since we started working together. When Dad suggested it. I'm sorry if, um . . . I'm sorry that it's hurt more than it's helped."

Bee fought back the tears that burned at the corners of her eyes. "It's okay," she said. She took a deep breath and wiped her eyes. "Honestly, now that I know you were actually *trying* to help, it means a lot. But it's not a one-way street. You have to let me have your back too. Like, actually talking to me about stuff—stuff that isn't related to our bank accounts."

"Sure," Beth agreed. She sighed. "I guess that makes sense."

"New Year's resolution: next year, we'll actually work together. Like, as sisters, and not just business partners. Deal?"

"Gross," Beth said. Then she laughed again, and Bee made another resolution: to laugh more with her twin. "Yes," she said. "Deal." She cleared her throat, then: "But if you're spending New Year's with me, what are you going to do about Knox?"

That made Bee hesitate, but she shook her head resolutely. "He'll still be here," she said.

"If you go back," Beth said. "Have you guys talked about long distance?"

"No," Bee said. "Have you and Clover?"

"Sort of," Beth said.

They were both silent. Then Bee asked, "What if we did something completely ridiculous?"

Epilogue

Monday morning, January 1, 2024

A blanket of snow covered the streets of Salem. Families young and old had already begun to take down their fir trees, decorated with memory and tradition, in favor of yellow and gold streamers that promised new memories, and another year worth celebrating. Lights and music flooded the streets. Children ran to their front yards and declared themselves victors or underdogs as snowballs flew through the air.

Outside the Big House, Clover sat on the steps of her porch. The door opened, and Bee appeared. She handed Clover a mug of hot chocolate and sat beside her. "It's been a wild few weeks, hasn't it?" Bee asked.

Clover sipped her cocoa. "I think that's an understatement."

"Oh yeah. Definitely." Bee chuckled. "But I like it."

"I do too," Clover said. "Even if Beth and Knox can't decide what the post–New Year breakfast should entail."

"I'm just happy she's found someone else to boss around,"

Bee said. She shook her head incredulously. "I'm glad she's here, though. I never thought I'd say that."

"I'm glad you're here too," Clover said. "You and Knox . . . you're cute together."

Bee smiled into her mug. Then she laughed. "You and Beth are frighteningly adorable. I've never seen Beth blush as much as she does when she's with you."

Clover smiled too. From a distance, the chickens clucked. Another record spun inside, and through the open windows they could hear Jimmy crooning to a Stevie Wonder Christmas song. "I'm glad you two are staying in the Big House. I can't believe you thought about staying in *another* Vacate."

"We didn't want to impose!"

"I understand," Clover said, and laughed. "But honestly, it's the first time in a long time that this house has felt so full of life."

"Honestly," Bee said, "it's the first time *I've* felt this full of life. I have you to thank for that."

"I could say the same to you."

Behind them, a window opened and the sweet smell of freshly baked brownies found them before Knox did, his tousled brown hair poking out from the white frame. "Breakfast is ready," he called.

"And coffee!" Jimmy shouted.

"Is this chicken always inside?" Beth's voice sounded skeptical. Clover imagined her leaning against the doorframe of the kitchen, eyebrows raised and lips pulled into a smile. A moment later, she appeared beside Knox, and the two stood there together, welcoming Bee and Clover back into a house that finally felt like home.

Bee laughed as Beth gave her an expectant look, and Knox caught Clover's eye and winked.

"I guess we're being summoned." Bee put her hand out to Clover, who grasped it with her own. "Happy New Year, Clover," Bee said.

"Happy New Year, Bee."

Acknowledgments

There are a lot of people to thank, but I'll start with my two pups, who have stayed with me late this evening as I type these words. They must be exhausted after a full day of doing . . . not much of anything. Oh, the life of a dog, and I, their willing enabler.

My thanks next go out to my wonderful editors, Alli Dyer and Alessandra Roche, who stuck with me and provided so much encouragement and enthusiasm for this project. Nicole Fisher, of course, who believed in this book enough to first bring it to life at Avon, and Erika Tsang, who helped keep it on its tracks. Many thanks to the whole Avon team from production to design and man ed, of course, for your diligence, patience, and careful attention to detail and style, and to Yeon Kim for this gorgeous jacket design.

Thank you to Quressa Robinson, my agent, who helped keep me sane during the pandemic years and those after, and to Kwame Alexander and Margaret Raymo, my constant mentors.

Thank you to Gabby Abbate and Liz Agyemang, my first readers.

Thank you to Stevie, who read this book and assured me that my interpretation of the Bay Area was accurate. Thank you for all the dillydallying, my friend.

Thank you to Jaz Joyner, for keeping me on track and keeping me confident.

Thank you to Carrie, for showing me writing magic when my ADHD brain felt overwhelmed by details and deadlines. Thank you for taking care of me.

Thank you to Asha, for reminding me to look at things a different way. Thank you for always helping me grow.

Thank you to Alex, for loving me, and being the one who keeps me brave.

And as always, thank you to my family, friends, and community, for lifting me up and encouraging me to keep writing.

About the Author

Georgia K. Boone is a writer, a poet, and the daughter of storytellers. Sometimes she writes songs she may one day share. Once, in a Brooklyn community center, she read James Baldwin's quote "You can't tell the children there's no hope," and she carries those words from the city to the desert and beyond.